INJURED PRIDE SERIES - BOOK ONE

CROSSROADS OF
REVENGE

DANIELLE M HAAS

Cover created by Deranged Doctor Designs.
A Danielle M Haas Publishing Book
Crossroads of Revenge - Injured Pride Series

To anyone who has ever made a giant step toward a terrifying dream. Keep moving those mountains and taking those risks. Taking a chance on yourself is always worth it.

Erin,
    So nice to meet
    you.

    Darrell M
    run

L incoln Sawyer poured a shot of tequila down his throat then took a long pull of the bitter ale. The liquor burned a trail down his esophagus, and he winced. But the fire burrowing in his gut was nothing compared to the constant pain zapping the nerve endings in his right hand.

His shooting hand.

A growl seized his vocal cords, but he managed to keep it trapped in his mouth. He'd drawn enough stares in the hole-in-the-wall bar in the middle of Nowhere, USA. Huddling over his brown bottle, he tried to pretend like the curious glances from the patrons lining the weathered bar weren't chipping away at him.

He hated attention—being watched over. Learning to cope with sideways glances had come at an early age. Even in a city the size of Nashville, twins always brought on oohs and awes from passersby. But now, with the heightened awareness of being somewhere he didn't belong, each narrowed glance constricted his muscles just a little bit more. Biting the inside of his cheeks, he continued to avert his gaze and focused on the skipping beats of the music from the ancient jukebox in the corner.

He shoved a hand through his too-long hair, cringing at the slickness of grease coating the strands. Christ, how had his life come to this? Sitting alone in a poorly lit bar, looking like a homeless schmuck, with his career torn to shreds. He tightened his jaw. No, he would get his career back on track, no matter what. That's what had brought him to this back-woods mountain town in Tennessee to begin with. If he could prove to his superior his head was on straight after the car accident that had nearly cost him his life, he'd be reinstated.

As long as his damn hand healed.

He tightened his fist as much as possible on top of the table, fighting the urge to slam it hard against the oak bar top. Pain shot down his arm, and he gritted his teeth. No amount of pain or discomfort would keep him from getting back in a uniform. He just had to find a way to prove he had full range and control of his dominant hand.

And he had to get through two weeks of hell at some wilderness retreat. Irritation clawed at his chest. As kids, Cruz had always talked him into all sorts of shit, but this was the first time his twin brother had convinced him to do something so stupid. How the hell was time in a cabin with some granola-eating, Mother-Earth-loving woman and her gang of do-gooders going to improve his mental health? Just the idea of playing hippie made his blood pressure soar and his head spin.

Okay, so the head spinning might be more a product of three shots of tequila and multiple beers. If he didn't slow down, he'd need an Uber driver to act as a human crutch and walk his drunk ass to the door of whatever little shack he'd be forced to sleep in.

Shit. Do they even have Uber drivers up here?

Not wanting to chance being stuck in this hick dump boasting mounted deer heads and stuffed bears for the night, he grabbed his phone and sent off a text.

-Need a ride. Pick me up outside the Chill N' Grill.

Pocketing his phone, he downed the rest of his beer and approached the bar to pay his tab. A wave of dizziness rattled his brain, and he stepped outside to wait for Cruz. Warm air greeted him at the threshold, and he breathed in deep, filling his lungs. He might miss the city lights and bustling streets of Nashville, but damn, the air out here was good.

Muffled bickering reached his ears, and he stilled his muscles, straining to hear more. The low baritone of a male's voice boomed, followed by the distinct sound of a slap. A sharp, feminine cry split the night.

Lincoln took off in a sprint to the back of the parking lot, adrenaline erasing the effects of the alcohol. Gravel crunched beneath his boots. The dark silhouette of a man stood at the edge of the lot. "Hey! Stop! What the hell are you doing?" He squinted as he ran, trying to make out any distinguishing features of the asshole, but the lamplight didn't reach the back of the lot.

The man turned, then whirled around and pushed a woman to the ground before he fled toward the dense trees that surrounded the back of the building.

Lincoln hurried to the woman and dropped into a crouch in front of her. "Are you okay?"

Tears streaked her face and blood coated the side of a cracked lip. She wiped at it with the backs of trembling hands. "I'm fine. Thank you. I...I don't know what happened."

Lincoln cupped her elbow with his palm and helped her to her feet. "Is there anything I can do? Anyone I can call?"

Sniffing, she shook her head. "No. Really. I'm okay. I just want to get home now."

Headlights turned off the road toward them and gravel crunched under tires. Lincoln squinted, barely making out the large truck that was his brother's pride and joy. He waved an arm high above his head to get Cruz's attention. "My brother," he said to the woman with a tilt of his head toward the approaching vehicle.

The woman groaned.

Lincoln faced her with a raised brow, curiosity piqued. "Something wrong?"

"Cruz Sawyer is your brother?"

Her reaction almost curved his lips. The lack of lights in the parking lot and his facial hair must have hidden the features that were nearly identical to his brother. "You know him?"

Sighing, she pushed a strand of jet-black hair behind her ear. "You don't live in Pine Valley without knowing everyone. Especially one of the few police officers in town. I'm Julia, by the way."

He dipped his chin low. "Lincoln. Nice to meet you."

Cruz stopped the truck and jumped to the ground. "What's going on? Julia, is that you?" He crossed over to her then faced Lincoln with familiar blue eyes narrowed into slits and his square jaw clenched. "What the hell's going on?"

Lincoln tightened his own jaw, just as square as his brothers but covered with a week's worth of growth. "I came out to wait for you and heard a fight. The sonofabitch who hit her ran into the woods."

"And you didn't go after him? What the hell, Linc?"

Julia took a step forward, squeezing herself between the two men staring icy daggers at each other. "Really. It isn't a big deal. I just want to go home."

Lincoln heard the wobble of her voice. He might not want to be stuck in this one-horse town, but he couldn't leave this poor woman alone after what she'd dealt with. "Are you all right to drive, Ms.?"

"I might as well drive you both," Cruz cut in before Julia had a chance to respond. "You're both going to the same place. Meet the assistant cook at Crossroads Mountain Retreat. Julia, my brother, Lincoln, your newest recruit."

Lincoln suppressed a groan and rolled his eyes to the cascade of stars brightening the night sky. Damnit all, he hated small towns. Someone else's shit was always sitting around, waiting to be stepped in. And more times than not, the shit smell lingered with you, too. You couldn't get away from it.

But he wouldn't be here for long. He'd put his head down, do what was asked of him, and get on with his life.

Come hell or high water.

THE MOON SHONE high above The Smoky Mountains and cast shadows over the gentle dip of the valley Brooke Mather called home. She leaned against the deck railing, taking in the scattering of stars before dropping her gaze to the lake. Lights blazed in the cabins dotted along the lakeshore.

All except two.

Lincoln Sawyer had yet to check in to Crossroads Mountain Retreat. The cabin she'd readied for him the day before sat lonely and dark against the dense patch of woods that surrounded the little slice of heaven she'd carved out.

Well, the little slice she'd scrubbed, quite literally on hands and knees, and transformed with some wood and paint from an abandoned campground for the area's youth to a thriving retreat for wounded law enforcement and military veterans. As a child, she'd loved to come here to learn survival skills from her grandfather and bask in the wildness of the Smoky Mountains. Finding her purpose in the very place that had been the sole source of positivity in a broken childhood was fate.

She shifted her glance to the second darkened cabin, the one right next to where Lincoln Sawyer would hopefully be staying if he showed. Her aching feet yearned to take her from the main lodge back to her private retreat—cabin number seven. The same cabin she stayed in year after year until her grandfather passed away and the place had fallen into disrepair.

A door opened behind her, and soft paws padded across the wooden planks of the deck. Shifting, she smiled down at her giant mutt—a big ball of cream-colored fur and sappy brown eyes that had been her constant companion for the past two years. A stray who'd wandered into her life after she'd broken off her engagement, who had shown her it wouldn't kill her to start trusting again, to open her heart a bit. Even if only to a dog.

Her willowy best friend crossed the threshold behind her dog and slid the glass door shut. A gentle breeze blew a long piece of Brooke's brown hair across her face, but Zoe's deep auburn locks stayed secured into a tight bun on the top of her head.

Zoe settled into a wicker rocking chair and smiled. "Still waiting for Lincoln to get here?"

Brooke sighed and buried her hand into the soft fur of Wyatt's side. "If he wasn't the brother of a friend, I would have gone home by now. Left him to the elements for being so inconsiderate of my time."

Chuckling, Zoe rocked back and forth. "I spoke with Cruz, and it sounds like Lincoln needed a lot of convincing to sign up for a two-week stay here."

Brooke rolled her eyes. "I'm not surprised. Not many big city cops choose a cabin in the woods with a new-age woman hellbent on improving their mental health."

She used the term she'd heard more often than she cared to admit. She wasn't hellbent on anything other than keeping her own life on the right path. Falling into the same pattern she'd witnessed time and time again as a child, she'd chained herself to a man who used his fists instead of his words. It had taken a knife wound to the gut and a career-ending knee injury that forced her out of the local police department to give her the courage—and anger —she needed to walk away. Now she used her past personal experiences in healing to help others who found themselves forced onto a path they didn't know how to navigate.

The fact that she could use the same place her grandfather had spent so much of his life helping others as the backdrop to her new career made the success she'd found the last year even more fulfilling.

"I can stay and wait for Lincoln if you want to head home." Zoe crossed one long leg over the other and shimmied against the back of the chair.

Brooke bit back a grin. Cruz mentioned dragging his brother to the retreat kicking and screaming. No doubt Zoe took him at his word. Zoe might argue her and Cruz were nothing more than friends, but Brooke wasn't buying it.

She wouldn't push Zoe, though. Her friend had her own internal struggles waging after returning from war a few years ago. She didn't need pressure from anyone to discuss things she'd rather leave alone—even if it concerned a good-looking guy and some harmless flirting.

Glancing down at her watch, Brooke twisted her lips to the side. "I hate to leave you to check him in, but I am exhausted." A 5 a.m. group hike had her out of bed much earlier than usual, and her muscles begged for a hot shower.

Zoe waved away her concern. "I'll give him a key and lead him in the direction of his cabin. Cruz has been here enough times to be his tour guide and make sure he gets settled for the night. I planned to crash in the employee room here tonight anyway. I'm teaching a sunrise yoga class by the lake before I have to head into town. You joining us?" Amusement made her Julia Robertesque smile grow.

Shaking her head, Brooke cringed. Zoe knew she much preferred a run or session in the gym with a trainer than the awkward stretches that proved just how little flexibility she possessed. "I was up early this morning. Maybe I'll catch it next time."

"I've heard that before." Zoe laughed then patted the side of her thigh to gain Wyatt's attention. He hurried to her, and she bent over to squish his face between her hands. "Keep your mama safe on the way home. I'll see you in the morning." She plopped a kissed on the middle of his forehead.

Brooke snapped her fingers, the signal for Wyatt to follow, then offered a little wave. "Thanks for this. If Lincoln has any issues, or you have questions, just call."

She slid the door back open and stepped into the large,

open room of the main lodge of Crossroads Mountain Retreat. She'd brought the old cabins along the lake back to life, but the lodge was completely new. Thick logs formed a three-story structure that housed the reception area, training area for wilderness skills, a gym, and a pool.

She'd sunk her entire life-savings into making the space exactly what she wanted. She'd feared her dreams were too big—her hopes too high. But if she wanted to create a safe space where men and women who'd been through hell could build themselves back up, she had to provide everything they could possibly need. That meant providing well thought out spaces for both physical and mental well-being.

Crossing by the desk she used to check guests in, she surveyed the smooth lines and calming earth tones around her. Taxidermy and remnants of hunted down animals didn't adorn the walls, but the three-story stone hearth and beautiful wooden beams stretched across the high ceiling made it very clear that this was a lodge that was meant to be in the woods. That is if the floor-to-ceiling windows showcasing the scenery didn't make that clear enough.

She breathed in the air, pride mounting in her chest at what she'd created. As she exited through the main entrance, she found a fleet of golf carts sitting ready for use. She hopped on the closest one. Wyatt leapt onto the seat beside her, and she took off for her cabin. A soft breeze cooled the summer air and raised the hairs on her arms as she headed for the trail that wound around the back of the lodge and spilled onto the path circling the lake.

Wyatt glanced over his shoulder, a low whine coming from his mouth.

"Sorry, boy. Not tonight." With one hand on the wheel, she scratched him behind his ear. Most nights she took Wyatt over to the kennel where the therapy dogs were housed, nearly all of them retired or injured dogs from various K-9 Units in the area. Wyatt loved to play with the pups, running the grounds and chasing balls. But not tonight. Tonight she was way too tired, and the handler for the dogs was long gone. "I promise we can stop by tomorrow."

She laughed at Wyatt's sad brown eyes then continued on to her home. She parked the cart on a patch of gravel beside the porch then took the porch steps two at a time, the wood creaking just a little under her weight, and hesitated. The screen door was closed, but the thick barrier behind it was slightly ajar. The hair on her arms stiffened even further, but this time it wasn't from the cool wind off the water. She was certain she'd turned the little golden lock on the door handle before she'd left.

Wyatt stood beside her and hunched low, baring his teeth. A growl crept up from his throat.

Something shifted in the air, the energy changing. The fact that the fur on Wyatt's neck stood on end told her that her instincts weren't crazy. She tightened her resolve and pushed through the door. She flicked on the light switch and scanned the home. Nothing was out of place in the studio-style cabin—the bed still made, the butcherblock counter free of clutter, and the striped pillows anchored the sides of the couch. But something didn't feel right.

Wyatt shuffled in alongside her as she flipped on every light and searched the bathroom then circled back to stand in the middle of the living room. A piece of paper leaned against a framed picture of her and her grandfather that sat on the mantle above the fireplace. She stepped closer, squinting to figure out what was scrawled along the thick card stock that wasn't there before she'd left this morning.

Keeping her hands to her sides, she skirted around the

coffee table and stopped in front of the fireplace. The thick black letters came together and turned her blood to ice.

A save-the-date card stared back at her, the date she'd never forget, with a big red X slashed across the message.

June 3rd, 2018.

The day she was supposed to get married.

2

———————

Bright moonbeams highlighted the steep drop offs and rugged terrain on the winding road up the mountain. Lincoln fought the urge to squeeze his eyes shut on the hairpin turns and held his breath until Cruz rolled to a stop in front of a sprawling lodge straight from a damn movie set. Rounded logs stacked together to build a three-story structure that pitched up to form a giant triangle of a roof. A porch wrapped around the front, bending out of sight at the sides. White lights were strung across the top of the covered porch, making the space impossibly inviting.

Maybe a brief stay here wouldn't be so bad after all. He could hole up in a room for a few weeks, hit some trails, and pretend like he hadn't been ripped away from the life he'd worked so damn hard to carve out for himself. Then he'd return to the job and find the asshole who'd nearly cost him his life—the man responsible for selling drugs to a child who died of an overdose.

Ian Samuels.

He tightened his jaw, pushing the immediate and

pulsing red need for revenge from his mind. The sono-fabitch who'd crashed into his life might still be at large, but Lincoln had found his supplier and locked him safely behind bars. A dealer couldn't do much damage on the streets if he didn't have any drugs to sell.

"Let's get inside," Cruz said, cutting into his thoughts. He shut off the engine and twisted toward the back of the cab. "Julia, do you need help to your room?"

"I'm fine. My room is in the main lodge, right down the hall. No chance of getting lost." A forced laugh lifted her sentence.

Lincoln unhooked his seatbelt and jumped down from the truck, thankful to land on solid ground that didn't threaten to spill him down a jagged cliff. He took in the expansive building in front of him and let out a shrill whistle. He tilted his head back to take it all in. Huge windows lined almost the entire top third of the structure, no doubt providing spectacular views.

The sound of the driver's side door shutting echoed around him. A hard hand slapped down on his shoulder, Cruz's grip clamping tight against his shirt. "Don't get too excited. This is just where I let Brooke know your stubborn ass finally made it. You'll be staying in a cabin behind this place."

Lincoln groaned. He should have known better. No way he'd be put up in the lap of luxury when a tattered pile of wood, probably infested with rodents, waited for him somewhere out of view. Grumbling, he rounded the back of the truck and grabbed his bag then headed for the front door. Might as well get settled for the night and get this god-forsaken stay behind him.

He opened the door and held it for Julia to walk through first. She'd given her statement of what had transpired behind the bar to Cruz on their way up the mountain. Exhaustion hung heavy under bloodshot eyes. She gave a nod of gratitude then scurried toward a dark corridor that jutted to the right of the building.

Cruz glided through before Lincoln released his grip. "I should have called ahead, but Brooke knew we were coming. Though I'm sure she's pissed you kept her here waiting for you. Don't be an ass when you meet her. Pine Valley's a small town. I don't need people talking about how the local cop's brother is a dick."

Lincoln grunted and set his bag at his feet. The interior of the lodge was as stunning as the outside. Warm wood lined the walls and windows dominated the far end of the wide-open room. Dark beams jutted across the high ceilings, and gray stone towered above a fireplace on the center wall, brown and deep red furniture scattered around it.

Spinning, he searched for the woman who could tell him where he needed to go. "Where's this woman, anyway? No one's here." Irritation tightened his throat. All he wanted was to collapse into a warm bed and sleep.

A door off the back of the space slid open and a tall beauty with a wide smile and kind eyes offered a wave. "Hey, Cruz. I'm here to get your brother checked in and let him know where he's staying." She aimed her bright white teeth his way. "You must be Lincoln. So nice to meet you."

With his hands shoved in the front pockets of his jeans, he offered her a nod. "You must be Brooke."

She laughed. "I'm Zoe. The yoga instructor here at Crossroads Mountain Retreat. Brooke had a long day. I offered to stay so she could head home for the night."

It took all the self-control he possessed not to roll his eyes. "Yoga?"

Amusement lit her hazel irises. "Don't worry. I won't

force you to try the class. But it is a good way to heal. Physically and mentally."

"Zoe also owns a yoga studio in downtown Pine Valley," Cruz said, rocking back on his heels. "I've taken a few classes. Those fancy poses are a lot harder than they look."

Lincoln couldn't hold back a bark of laughter. "Well, Zoe, I'll promise to come to one of your classes if my brother joins me. That's something I have to see for myself."

Cruz grumbled something beside him.

Zoe smirked. "I'll hold you to that, Mr. Sawyer. Now let's get you settled so Cruz can take you back to the cabin you'll be staying at. Brooke will help set you up tomorrow morning with whatever classes you plan to take while you're here."

He cringed and followed her to a desk set up in the corner of the room. A sleek laptop sat open on top of the desk, but nothing else cluttered the area. A dark brown file cabinet matching the wood beams that crisscrossed the high ceiling stood against the wall behind the desk, along with an antique armoire displaying candid photographs of smiling men and women sitting around a campfire and laughing around the lake.

Dear God, what had he signed up for?

Zoe reached into a drawer at the top of the desk and produced a skeleton key and a notecard-sized piece of paper. She handed them over, her smile never faltering. "You're in cabin number 8, which is on the side of the lake behind the lodge. Cruz can't get his truck back there, but feel free to take one of the golf carts."

"Golf carts?" Better than traipsing around some dusty path in the middle of the night to get where he needed to go, but damn, he hadn't driven one of those in years. He slid the paper into his back pocket then palmed the key. "Last time I rode in a golf cart with Cruz, we ended up in the pond by the seventh hole of Little Creek Golf Club. I'll drive. He can point out the way."

A phone rang from the side pocket in Zoe's black yoga pants, and she held up a finger as she fished it out and answered. "Hey, Brooke. Just checking in Lincoln Sawyer."

A sharp intake of breath had Lincoln taking a step closer to the desk that separated him from the woman. A paleness washed over her warm complexion, and she widened her eyes. He glanced at Cruz, who'd taken notice as well and stood with a clenched jaw and rigid set to his shoulders.

"Cruz is here, so you don't need to call the police. We'll be right there." Zoe disconnected and locked her gaze with Cruz. "Someone was inside Brooke's cabin. Do you mind checking it out?"

"Not at all. Let's go."

Lincoln pushed out a sigh and followed the frantic Zoe and his brother outside. He had been in this town no longer than a few hours and already he'd crossed paths with two troubling situations. Trouble was what he was supposed to be avoiding right now.

Instead, he climbed into the back of a golf cart and hung on for dear life as Cruz sped across the uneven yard. He just hoped this time, he wouldn't end up in the water.

BROOKE STOOD on the front porch with her arms wrapped over her stomach, tapping her foot on the wide wooden planks. She hated this feeling of being violated. A feeling all too familiar that she worked so hard to leave behind in her old life—with her old lover.

Shay Lawrence.

The name sat like a boulder in her gut. It had taken years to harden her heart to the man she'd once loved. To move past the self-loathing and meekness he'd instilled in her. And now, all it took was one brazen act to bring back the vulnerability and weakness she vowed she'd never show to anyone ever again.

The anger this helplessness made her feel had her dropping her hands to her sides, tightening her fists over and over. What happened tonight wasn't a brazen act—it was a violation of her privacy. It was an act of cowardice meant to rattle her. She may be rattled, but she wasn't the woman Shay had left bleeding on the ground. She was stronger and more determined than ever to never let him take a damn thing from her. Even her peace of mind.

The motor of a speeding golf cart wound through the trees and reached her ears, and a bit of the tension she held in her neck unwound. Wyatt stood on alert at her side, and she ran a hand over the top of his head to calm him. "It's okay, boy."

Headlights bounced around the lake until the cart skidded to a stop. Zoe leapt out as soon as Cruz hit the brakes. "Are you all right? What in the world happened?" She bounded up the stairs and threw her arms around Brooke before releasing her and running a palm over the tail-wagging dog.

Cruz rounded the front of the cart with a deep frown etched on his mouth and another man—presumably Lincoln—hopped off the back and shuffled forward. The same frown pulling down the same full lips as Cruz's, only Lincoln's scruffy beard could distinguish the two men.

Brooke blinked twice, adjusting to the handsome stranger who looked so much like one of her close friends. Even with just the porch light the similarities between the two men were remarkable. "I'm fine. Just upset someone came into my personal space."

"Is anything missing? Property damaged?" Cruz might be dressed in jeans, a faded red flannel, and a cowboy hat, but there was no denying the cop in his voice.

"Nothing's missing or damaged, except the front door. The wood is splintered where someone forced it open." A condescending snort drew her attention to the man beside Cruz, putting her on the defensive. "Is there a problem?"

The man scuffed his booted foot across the ground, keeping his gaze downcast. "Whoever forced their way into your home must have some muscle to break through a lock. You did have the deadbolt engaged, didn't you?"

She smoothed down her dirt-smeared shirt and fixed a sickeningly sweet smile on her face. "Lincoln Sawyer, is it? I don't believe we've met. I'm Brooke Mather, the owner of this retreat. Glad you finally found the place."

Tilting his head to the side, he studied her with narrowed eyes, obviously not expecting this cheerful greeting. "Wasn't too hard."

Keeping her eyes wide, she thinned her lips into a tight smile. "I assumed you were lost and that's why it took you so long to show up. But to answer your question, no. The deadbolt was not engaged. We aren't in the city, Mr. Sawyer. Locking up tight isn't the way things are done around here."

"Maybe it should be," he said with a shrug.

Cruz shoved his brother with his shoulder. "Mind if I step inside and check everything out?"

"Not at all. Whoever was inside left something on my mantle. I bagged it up and have it waiting for you. I was careful not to get my prints on it." Her police career might have ended years before, but everything she'd learned was still trapped in her mind. She led the way back inside the house.

Zoe stayed glued to her side. "Where's the paper?"

Being one of the only people Brooke had confided in about her past, she'd told Zoe exactly what she'd found. Scooping the plastic bag from the table, she held it away from her body as if it might burst into flames.

Zoe took the bag and studied the cardstock. "Is this the actual save-the-date card from your wedding?"

Brooke shook her head and fought back the tears threatening to fill her eyes. As hard as she tried, she couldn't stop the slight tremor shaking her body. "No, but it's so damn close." Not like the plain save-the-date card she'd sent out on her shoestring budget had been anything special. Anyone could have replicated the information after only a cursory glance, but why would any of the small number of family or friends she'd invited to her wedding want to?

"Can I see it?" Cruz asked.

Brooke nodded, and Zoe handed over the evidence.

Lincoln stood by the door with his feet planted hip-width apart. "Do you mind if I have a look around?"

"Not at all." Having trained professionals sweep through her home didn't bother her. Especially ones with records like Lincoln Sawyer. Her initial impression of the guy might scream asshole, but she carefully vetted every guest who stayed at her retreat. Lincoln had worked his way up to Detective with dedication and amazing busts. If he could find something she'd overlooked in her frazzled state, so be it.

"I assume the date on the paper means something?" Cruz asked, regaining her attention.

She breathed in deeply, hating that this part of her life

was being ripped back open. "I was engaged a few years ago. This is the day we planned to get married."

"Are you still in contact with your ex-fiancé?" Cruz flipped the plastic bag over in his hands then set it back on the table.

"Never."

"Does he know where you live? Is there anyone else who knows about your past and would want to upset you?"

A shudder tore through her as her mind raced. "I honestly don't know. I didn't go to extremes to keep my whereabouts hidden. Hell, Google my name and the retreat pops up. Anyone who wanted to find me could."

Zoe ran a palm up and down Brooke's arm. "Why don't you sit down, and I'll get you some water?"

She nodded and lowered herself onto the hard chair at the head of the kitchen table. The wide-open space kept Lincoln and his prowling in her line of vision until he disappeared into the bathroom. Reemerging, he glanced toward her bed and heat burned her cheeks. She'd never had a man in her cabin—outside the few friends she trusted with her life—and his perusal of such an intimate space was just another invasion of her privacy.

He turned the narrow corner to the back of the house then clomped back into the open space. "You have a back door."

Brooke shifted her gaze to Zoe, who shrugged while filling a glass with water from the sink, then set her gaze on Lincoln. "You're one hell of a detective, aren't you?"

A slight smirk ticked up the corner of his mouth. "Why would someone break in the front when the back door is surrounded by a dark forest? Forced entry is bound to draw attention if anyone was around. Especially a place full of law enforcement. Doesn't make sense for the perpetrator to break into your home in the most conspicuous way."

Frowning, she considered his words. "You're right. That doesn't make any sense. But what does that mean?"

The smirk faded and Lincoln met her stare head on. "Whoever left you a little note didn't care if they were caught."

"There's another option." She took the cup Zoe offered and gulped down the cool liquid.

Lincoln arched a brow. "What's that?"

Her heart raced and her knees threatened to buckle. She thought she was finally free, but Shay had shattered that illusion in an instant. "That my ex has come back to finish what he started."

3

The state-of-the-art gym housed inside the main lodge was one of Brooke's favorite places on the entire property. Shiny equipment and free weights stood waiting to be used, as well as a boxing ring for anyone wanting to spar. Giant windows looked out into the mountains, providing the perfect backdrop to focus on instead of her aching muscles and burning lungs as she finished another mile on the bike. Her knee throbbed, but the pain was worth it. A much-needed outlet to let her mind slip away and prepare for the day ahead.

She wiped beads of sweat from her forehead with a towel and heaved a sigh. She longed to beat out all her frustrations on the punching bag, but she didn't have time. Not like it would help soothe her nerves the way it usually did. No matter what she tried this morning, nothing would take her mind away from the constant questions that had plagued her all night. She'd laid in bed for hours after everyone left her cabin. Every sound setting her on high alert. Every shifting shadow spiking her anxiety. She should have taken Zoe up on her offer to crash at her place, but she had to prove a point to herself that she was not easily rattled anymore.

Jumping off the bike, she threw the dirty towel in a laundry bin and chugged water from the bottle she'd filled at home. A quick glance at the clock told her she could make Zoe's sunrise yoga class. Even if it felt like torture, it could provide the outlet she searched for.

As she burst through the lodge doors, crisp air greeted her and she inhaled the sweet scent of morning dew. She cut across the yard and moisture wicked against her ankles from the blades of grass that would need cut soon. Periwinkle blue pushed against the black sky, creating space for the sun to spill over the giant peaks and bring on a new day.

She trudged down a slight hill. The clear blue lake came into view, and she couldn't help but smile. No matter what drama was happening in her life, this was her happy place. A place filled with memories from her childhood and hope for her future. A place so damn beautiful, it made her soul soar higher than the birds that flew overhead, chirping out their morning song.

A few people dotted the darkened landscape, standing on colorful mats placed along a flat patch of grass as they waited for class to start. They faced the lake, oblivious to her approaching from behind. Zoe stood tall, fingers entwined and palms faced toward the sky. She leaned to the right, then the left, stretching her sides.

Brooke waved. "Good morning. Have an extra mat for me?" She should have thought to bring one from the gym, but she didn't mind standing in the cool, green grass if she had to.

The approaching daybreak created swirls of blue and

bursts of deep orange that couldn't hide Zoe's concern. "I always bring a few spares. I'm happy you're joining us, even if I am a bit surprised."

She didn't have to ask the question in order for Brooke to hear it—Zoe wanted to know if she was all right. Not that she could blame her friend for being worried. If the shoe was on the other foot, she'd be a mother hen, fluttering around Zoe to make sure she was fine.

A few guests turned her way and smiled.

Brooke nodded at each of the guests who'd gathered. She didn't want them to be aware of what had happened last night. If things escalated, then she'd alert others staying at the retreat, but not until then.

Infusing as much enthusiasm in her movements as she could, she swiped a mat from a pile beside Zoe and found a spot at the back of the class. "I woke up earlier than expected. Might as well get in a good workout, right?" She kicked off her tennis shoes and socks and curled her toes over the spongey mat.

Zoe brought her hands to prayer and started the class.

Brooke lost herself in the gentle timbre of Zoe's voice as she called out move after move. She might not have the best balance, or technique, but the challenge to her muscles dictated her mind stay present—stay focused on keeping her upright. By the time she was back in prayer pose, she'd found a calmness she'd searched for all night.

The men and women around her cast smiles and offered waves as they rolled up their mats. The faces were familiar, but most of the guests currently residing at the retreat had only been there a handful of days. Not long enough to really know them.

Wanting to enjoy the tranquility of the moment, she sat on her mat and crossed her feet beneath her. The sun peered above the lake, sending sparkles of pink shimmering over the surface. As it continued to rise, the dark of the night vanished, taking with it the vulnerability of the unknown.

But the questions lingered.

"Penny for your thoughts?" Zoe settled on the ground beside her and stretched out her legs.

"I didn't sleep well last night. I came in early to check the security cameras again then biked, hoping it'd blow off some steam. When that wouldn't work, I remembered your sunrise class." She shrugged, keeping her gaze on the calm water. "Figured what the hell?"

"Did you see anything that was missed last night?"

She sighed then let out a deep breath, releasing her disappointment and frustration on a gust of air. "No. Maybe I need to set up more cameras to face the cabins around the lake. I never thought I would need them anywhere but the lodge."

"I hate this is happening to you." Zoe squeezed her arm.

Her gut twisted. "Me, too. But I don't want to freak out. I need to treat it like anything else. Attack the problem head on. Follow the facts. Figure out what the hell happened. I can't fall apart."

"You won't. You're too strong to come unhinged."

Appreciation squeezed her chest, and she bumped her shoulder against her friend. "Thanks for that, but do you know what I really need right now?"

"Huh?"

"A giant cup of coffee. Breakfast won't be ready yet, but Julia and Chet should be in the kitchen. Which means a hot pot is ready to go." She hopped up then pulled Zoe to her feet before rolling up her mat.

Zoe moaned. "Coffee sounds like heaven. I'll grab a cup

to go. I have another class in the studio in about an hour. A little zip of caffeine will keep my ass moving."

Brooke followed the trail back up to the lodge and dropped her dirty mat into the laundry pile she'd deal with later before dragging herself to the kitchen. She'd need more than coffee to get her through this day, but at least it would be a start. Then she could check her schedule before returning her focus to where Shay could be and why he'd returned.

The bitter smell of French Roast greeted her as she pushed through the door to the kitchen. Julia stood at the gas stove with a whisk in her hand, stirring something in a large pot.

"Morning, Julia. Where's Chet?" Julia had started helping Chet in the kitchen a few months prior when she'd graduated from college and struggled to find a job. Brooke hadn't known her, but Chet had vouched for his cousin, pushing Brooke to hire one of the only people at the retreat who didn't have a military or law enforcement background. But the girl had proven herself a good worker in the short time she'd been around.

Julia's dark hair trailed down her back, and she wiped an arm over her forehead before turning around. "I told him I'd handle the prep this morning."

Brooke stopped with her hand halfway to the orange handle of the coffee pot. "What happened to your lip?" Shifting gears, she hurried to Julia and studied the cracked lip and bruised skin.

Julia's chin quivered, and she dropped her gaze to the tile floor.

Zoe took a step forward. "Did someone hit you?"

"It's no big deal. Just some guy I met at the Chill N' Grill last night."

Brooke's stomach turned. How many times had she claimed the same thing—that the physical and emotional blows heaped upon her didn't matter? That they weren't a big deal. "Someone putting their hands on you is a very big deal, honey. Who was it?"

She shrugged. "Some guy I thought I knew from college, but I was wrong. Cruz's brother ran over and scared the guy off before things got out of control. Then Cruz gave me a ride here when he dropped his brother off. Really, I'm fine. Please don't make a big deal of this or Chet will lose it."

Brooke braced her hands on Julia's shoulders, forcing Julia to meet her gaze. "Did you tell Cruz?"

Julia nodded. "On the way here. I told him the same thing. It was no big deal. I drank too much and was stupid. I shouldn't have followed the guy outside. When I finally figured out I made a mistake and tried to walk away, he got mad. I should have known better."

"Honey, some man hitting you is not your fault. No matter what kind of decision you made or how much you drank." From the time she'd fallen for Shay as a young teenager, he'd ingrained in her that his temper was always her fault. Something she'd never take credit for again.

A tiny tingle tickled the back of her neck. "Would you be able to point this guy out if you saw him again? Or even a picture?"

Red stained Julia's cheeks, and she turned away. "Probably not. The bar was dark and like I said, I drank a lot. Too much."

Brooke blew out a long breath. "Hopefully the ass is far from here and you never have to worry about him again." She hoped what she said was true. Julia was a nice girl who didn't need to get caught up with a bad guy. But what were the odds Shay had stormed back into her life the same night Julia was hit by some angry man at the bar?

Her every instinct screamed that the odds were too high to ignore.

CRADLING A STEAMING cup of instant coffee in his hand, Lincoln rocked back and forth in a rocking chair on the porch of his temporary cabin and took in his surroundings. The reflection of the mountains bounced off the soft, lapping waves of the lake. Vibrant green covered the hillsides, the trees lush and plentiful. Multiple cabins curved along the rounded boundary of the lake. Since the interior of his cabin matched that of Brooke Mather's, the rest probably followed suit.

Brooke Mather. A sprite of a woman and not at all what he'd expected. He'd imagined the owner of a wilderness retreat catering to injured law enforcement and military would be a little sturdier. Not a pixie with thick chestnut hair and bright red lips. Her brown eyes had flashed fire last night when talking about the break-in, but he had to hand it to her, she hadn't cowered over such an invasion of privacy.

Hell, the break-in rattled him more than it appeared to upset her. She'd been calm and to-the-point when relaying parts of her story. Fury had flooded his system as he'd searched her house. No one should have to worry about his or her safety, especially in their own home and at the hands of someone they'd once loved.

Even if the person she loved had put that hint of fear in her eyes. Fear she'd tried hard as hell to cover. But he'd seen the way survivors responded in tough situations too many times not to understand that Brooke's ex was more than a burglar. He was an abuser.

Pushing to his feet, he took a long sip of the bitter liquid and cringed. As nice as it was to have certain provisions available, he wouldn't last long if he had to cook for himself. He'd been told meals were provided. Hopefully that meant more than the deli meat and carton of eggs he'd found in the fridge. Might as well make his way to the lodge and get a better understanding of what he was in for.

Leaving his mug of mud-like sludge behind, loose stone crunched under his boots as he walked along the gravel path. Cruz had left the golf cart for his use, but Lincoln wasn't in a rush. A nice walk to stretch his limbs sounded downright luxurious. He took the bend toward the lodge and stopped to stare at the tire tracks imbedded on the path from the night before. His wheels spun. Did the person who'd broken into Brooke's cabin come back in a golf cart or foot? Maybe they'd missed foot prints the night before.

Moving on instinct, he walked toward Brooke's cabin and rounded to the back. The exterior of the cabin had been dark last night, even with flashlights, and the morning light might provide some new clues. Maybe tracks—either from a vehicle or a person—could point him in the direction of where someone either approached the cabin or left.

Overgrown weeds and dense woods met him on the opposite side of the structure. A small stoop surrounded the door with two steps leading up, but no sidewalk connected the back of the house to the front. Not many reasons came to mind to be back here, especially since the buzz of mosquitoes already tickled his ears. He swept his gaze over the ground, but nothing stood out—nothing prodded him to step further into the woods.

A deep growl in the pit of his stomach had him changing

directions back toward the lake. He turned the corner and stopped short. Ms. Mather stood with her hands fisted on her ridiculously small waist, the same fire from the night before shooting from her eyes. He doubted her upturned nose and pouty lips had the ability to look anything other than pissed off.

"What the hell do you think you're doing?" She asked.

"No pleasantries this morning?" Last night she'd made sure to at least say hello before jumping all over him.

Her eyes narrowed into slits. "I don't take kindly to people snooping around my cabin. Especially after it was broken into last night."

He scratched the top of his head, cringing at the strange texture of his hair. A shower should have been the first thing he'd considered this morning, but it'd have to wait. "Sorry. Just wanted to search for any tracks we might have missed last night."

His explanation didn't soften her tough-as-nails exterior. "That was already done last night. I don't need guests of the retreat traipsing around, scaring me to death when they pop out of the woods."

Annoyance flared in his gut. She was well aware of his position on the Nashville Police Force. She should count her lucky stars he was around to assist the small-town force his brother had settled for. "You didn't mind having me around last night."

"That was different. Don't try to act like this is even remotely acceptable. This is my home, and I'm already terrified about who was in here when I was gone yesterday." Her voice cracked, and she took a second to compose herself. "I don't want to be nervous every time I come home."

Shaking his head, he threw his palms in front of him to show his surrender. "Fine. I'll stay out of your hair."

"Wait. I heard about what happened last night with Julia."

"Julia?"

"The young woman who was hit at the bar. She said you stopped the man who attacked her." She wrinkled her nose. "Thanks for stepping in. No telling what would have happened if you weren't there. I wish you or Cruz would have mentioned something last night."

"Unbelievable," he said on a snort. "Which is it? You want me interfering in other people's business or you don't?"

She reared back her head. "Excuse me? I didn't ask for interference, just a heads-up would have been nice."

"If that girl didn't want to tell you what happened to her, it wasn't my place to spread word about it." He charged forward to go past her, but a hand on his arm stopped him. He glared down at her, but the worry contorting her fragile features extinguished his irritation.

"Look, we got off on the wrong foot, and I'll take partial blame for that. But when some asshole hits one of my employees, I want to know about it. Not to be nosy, but to help make sure it doesn't happen again."

He glanced down at her small hand that still clung to his bare skin.

Her gaze followed, and she quickly released her grip and took a step back.

He cleared his throat, choosing to ignore the jolt of electricity that had shot up his arm at her touch. "I get that, but there's not much to tell. I ran over when I heard them argue. The guy took off into the woods. She didn't know his name, and I didn't ask too many questions. She said she was fine. Now, if you'll excuse me Ms. Mather, I was on my way to grab some breakfast."

She dipped her chin, her top teeth sinking into her bottom lip. "Of course. And please, call me Brooke."

He nodded and forced his feet to move away from the fiery woman with the magic touch. He had enough to worry about without letting her get under his skin.

4

A twinge of guilt pinched Brooke's chest at the sight of Wade McKenzie's disheveled sandy brown hair and the dark circles ringing his blood-shot eyes. Either he'd had way too much to drink the night before, which didn't often happen when he worked the bar, or he'd had a long night filled with activities she'd rather not dwell on.

Offering one of Chet's fresh blueberry muffins in an attempt to garner peace, she settled onto a stool at the bar of the Chill N' Grill and smiled. "Thanks for meeting me here. I really appreciate it."

She glanced over her shoulder and took in the darkened space. The neon lights hadn't been plugged in yet, and chairs still sat upside down on the tables. The wooden bar gleamed from last night's polish, but the smell of breakfast being prepped wafted to her from the kitchen.

Wade accepted the muffin and winked. "I wouldn't have dragged myself in here so damn early for anyone but you, darling."

She laughed, unmoved by the charm he oozed even

when he looked like shit. "Save the sweet talk for someone it'll work on."

He crossed his hands over his heart and winced, squishing the muffin against his red and black flannel shirt. "You take pleasure in wounding me, don't you?"

She rolled her eyes but couldn't help her wide grin. Wade might be the biggest playboy in town, but she was nevertheless endlessly amused by his antics. "Anyway. Did you get a chance to look at the surveillance video before I got here?"

Lincoln hadn't provided much information about the man who'd attacked Julia, and the girl's unwarranted embarrassment over what happened kept her from confiding many details. But Brooke couldn't get over the fact that the very night an unknown man fled into the woods after being confronted for hitting a woman, someone had broken into her cabin and left a little piece of her past.

Someone who very well could have a history of intimidation and abuse. If she could catch a glimpse of the man with Julia last night, she'd know for sure if Shay was lingering around town, waiting for his moment to pounce.

A frown pulled down Wade's narrow mouth. "I did, and there isn't a good shot of the bastard talking with Julia. I can see her back when they're inside, but he's mostly out of the shot. The few times he slips into the frame, his cowboy hat's pulled too low to see his face."

She swished her lips to the side. Shay was more of a suit and tie kind of guy, not a cowboy hat type who'd blend into a small-town bar. But time might have changed him, and he'd always been good at blending in—hiding the monster he kept on a tight leash until all witnesses were out of sight. "What about in the parking lot?"

Wade shook his head. "Sorry. It was like the guy knew

where to stand, where to park, in order to stay under the radar."

Her phone rang in her pocket.

Wade raised his light eyebrows. "Want to get that?"

"Nah. Whoever it is will leave a message if they need to talk to me. Do you mind if I take a look at the footage you pulled? Even if I can't get a good look at the guy's face, his build or the way he carries himself might be familiar."

"Why not?" Wade wiped crumbs from his shirt, finished off the muffin, then led the way to a small room tucked behind the bar.

A monitor sat on an old desk like the one her childhood teachers used in their run-down classrooms. Black and white images were frozen in four different quadrants, each depicting a different area of the Chill N' Grill.

Wade pulled out the chair and motioned for her to take a seat. "In each of these frames, he's just out of the shot. Press play to watch more of the feed, but I'd be surprised if you catch anything more than I did."

Sitting, she clicked play and scrutinized one section of the video at a time. Wade was right. A tip of the man's hat or a shot of his shoulder were the only pieces of him caught on screen. While inside, he was seated so she couldn't even gauge an accurate height. On the outside cameras, he was too far away to guess anything. Though the way he carried himself, as if his inflated ego angled his chin in the air and puffed his chest, struck a chord with her. "Where's his car?"

"What do you mean?" Bracing his forearm on the back of the chair, Wade leaned forward.

She pointed to the top left of the screen. "He took her back here by this truck. But when Lincoln runs over, the guy takes off into the woods. Is the vehicle still there?"

Wade scratched the whiskers on his pointed chin. "Only

two vehicles were in the parking lot when I got here this morning. One was Julia's, the other Cruz's brother's. He called to let me know he'd given them a ride and would be leaving their cars behind for the night. This guy must have waited until the coast was clear to come back and grab his truck."

"Can you fast forward the footage to see when that was? Maybe we can get a clear shot of him or his license plate when he drives away." She watched Wade skip through the footage. People spilled out of the bar and cars drove away. The frantic pace would have been comical if anticipation wasn't squeezing her chest.

A woman approached the truck, jumped in the driver's side, and pulled away.

Defeat slumped her against the chair. "That wasn't his truck. Sonofabitch."

Wade rubbed the back of his neck. "I can scan the rest of the parking lot and see if a guy in a cowboy hat emerges from the woods and gets in one of the vehicles. Might get lucky."

"Sure. Let me know if you find anything. But chances are that whoever he is, he's way too smart to just stroll out from the woods and climb into a car we can identify with a camera. He knew how to stay out of sight, and he probably had a plan for how to get the hell out of here." Which didn't bode well. Regardless of if the man at the Chill N' Grill last night was connected with her break-in, Pine Valley didn't need an abusive asshole scouring the local bars for women. "Thanks for trying. I'll get out of your hair."

Wade clapped his hands together, the sound deafening in the small space. "Time to crack open some eggs. Folks will be stopping by before church to fill their bellies. Will I see you later?"

"I wish, but probably not tonight. I have a lot of new guests and haven't had a chance to get to know many of them yet. I should probably stay around all day—dinner included. But maybe you could make that Sunday night special for me tomorrow instead." She aimed her best smile his way and even batted her lashes for an added effect. Most of the town showed up Sunday evenings for the Chill N' Grill's famous fried chicken and collard greens.

"What would I get out of this little favor? I mean, cooking Sunday's chicken on Monday is almost blasphemy." Wade's dimples tucked deep into his cheeks, and he wiggled his eyebrows.

"I offer you my undying devotion and gratitude."

He tipped his head back and a roar of laughter belted from his mouth. "Nice try, sweetheart. Come back when you have something a little more tempting to bargain with. Now get on out of here so I can get the dining room ready. People will be showing up any second."

Raising on her toes, she squeezed his shoulder and placed a quick peck on his cheek. "Thanks for everything. See you later."

As she swept through the empty bar and grill, she swiped her phone from her pocket to check the missed call from earlier. A voicemail waited from an unknown number. She pressed the call button to connect to her voicemail and burst out of the dark restaurant into the bright morning. A few vehicles parked with their motors running, waiting to be let inside. Another truck pulled in, the woman behind the wheel lifting a hand in greeting.

Brooke smiled and returned the gesture. A familiar voice floated from the phone speaker, and she stopped dead in her tracks.

"Hi Brooke, it's me. Shay. It's been a while...but...I really

want to talk. If you could call me back and just listen. Just
for a couple minutes. I have some things I need to tell you.
Please, Brooke. For old time's sake."

She dropped her hand, letting the phone dangle to her
side as her heart pounded against her ribcage. Shay had
stormed back into her life and once again turned it upside
down, and she hadn't even laid eyes on the bastard. Now she
had to figure out how to handle it. Face him head on, chal-
lenging him in a way she'd never done before, or sit back
and hope he'd leave as soon as he realized she wouldn't fall
under his spell again?

Determination surged through her heating her face.
Who was she kidding? She couldn't sit back and let him try
and destroy her again. She didn't want to see him, but also
couldn't be afraid to stand up for herself. She just prayed he
didn't try to finish what he started years ago before she
could finally speak her peace.

THE WINDING ROAD along the mountain leading into town
wasn't nearly as nerve-wracking in the light of day. Lincoln
actually kept his eyes open and appreciated the lush
greenery jutting from the earth and the brilliant, clear sky. A
sense of awe washed over him as his brother drove him back
to the hole-in-the-wall bar where he'd left his truck.

"You ever gonna cut that damn hair?" Cruz asked. "Mom
would shit if she saw what a hobo you look like."

Cruz kept his voice light, but Lincoln could sense the
worry behind the question. The same worry his entire
family had expressed since he'd been told to take time from
work. Hell, the same worry that gnawed away at him every
time his hand refused to cooperate. He ran his fingers

through the brown strands that curled around the nape of his neck. "Maybe that fancy ass retreat has a place I can get a makeover. As long as I can keep the beard."

Cruz snorted. "Don't think Brooke's too concerned with prettying up the riff raff who walk through her doors."

Lincoln's mind wandered to the woman he'd bumped heads with already this morning. For someone who chose a career centered around bringing peace into the lives of others, she was wound awfully damn tight. "I don't think she's too fond of me."

"I told you not to be an ass last night. I get the whole cop-mode thing, but you were a little gruff with your delivery. A woman like Brooke doesn't take kindly to some man stepping on her toes." Cruz turned off the country road and the tree-line thinned. He motored through a scene right out of a classic television show. Manicured grass with colorful flowers accented the lawns. People strolled down the sidewalks with wide smiles, children skipping along beside them.

"Where are we? Mayberry?" Lincoln took in the square that made up the bulk of the town of Pine Valley. Four streets, connected at the corners, with a white gazebo bearing an American flag smack dab in the center. Mom and pop shops boasted colorful awnings and splashy white letters across their windows, declaring the homemade goods and services for sale. No box stores or chains in sight. "Where do you people get your groceries?"

Cruz chuckled. "People around here shop local as much as possible. If there's something we can't find, it's about a thirty-minute drive to get what we want. But that doesn't happen as often as you'd think."

Sidewalks cut through the crisp green grass in the middle of the square. Benches littered the paths, providing plenty of seating, and lampposts waited to be lit. More flags dotted the landscape, and he could only imagine the spectacle the townsfolk made of the area at Christmas. A sight he'd be long gone to see for himself.

Taking a left toward the opposite end of town, Cruz headed away from the quaint city center. Houses lined the road with plenty of space between them, and side streets jutted off to what Lincoln could only assume were neighborhoods. A couple miles outside of town, the bar where he'd spent a little too much time last night came into view.

"People are already at a bar on a Sunday morning? Maybe this place isn't so bad after all." The gravel parking lot was nearly filled with an interesting mix of people headed toward the front door—some in their finest clothes, others in what looked like pajamas, a few in rumpled outfits possibly from the night before. "Interesting crowd."

"The Chill N' Grill serves the best breakfast around. It's not just a place for out-of-town dimwits to overindulge on a Saturday night." Cruz found a spot near the front of the building and parked. "Is that Brooke?"

Lincoln squinted in the direction Cruz extended his finger. Sure enough, the spitfire he'd already had two run-ins with sat on one of the picnic tables in a covered pavilion. "Is she all right? She looks a little lost."

"Not sure. Let's go find out." Cruz hopped out of the truck and slammed the door.

Following suit, Lincoln bit back a groan. The last thing he needed was more tongue lashings from Ms. Mather. After their latest round of verbal sparring, he planned to put his nose to the ground and avoid her as much as possible. Inquiring over why she appeared as though she'd seen a ghost wasn't high on his bucket list.

Cruz stopped in front of her and cleared his throat. "Brooke? What are you doing here?"

Her head snapped up at the sound of Cruz's voice. Her tanned skin had paled. She darted her gaze around the busy parking lot before locking eyes on Cruz. "I swung by to look at the security footage from last night. I wanted to see if I recognized the man who hit Julia."

"Did you?" Cruz asked.

She shook her head.

Lincoln studied the tight lines between her brows and her grip on the phone. As much as he wanted to avoid this woman, he couldn't keep his questions to himself. "Is that why you look like a cat who's just lost his eighth life?"

She blinked up at him, as if his words wouldn't compute.

He dipped his chin toward her hand. "Rough phone call?"

Standing, she shoved her phone in her pocket. "Call from my ex."

A million questions formed in his head. He might be on a leave of absence, but that didn't just shut off the cop in him. "Same ex who you were supposed to marry? Who would know the date of your wedding and could have left the note in your cabin?"

She nodded.

A pang of sympathy twisted his gut. He didn't know this woman's story, but it couldn't be good. If nothing else, he understood being screwed and dumped at a place in life he didn't want or deserve. He wanted to help, to roll up his sleeves, and clean up this mess for her.

But it wasn't his job, and she'd made it clear his help wasn't wanted.

"Let's head back to the retreat and talk. Does that sound good?" Cruz asked.

She blew out a long breath. "Yeah. That's a good idea."

Lincoln retrieved his keys from the front pocket of his jeans. "I'll follow you guys. Thanks for the ride, Cruz."

Cruz nodded and headed back toward his truck.

Lincoln fell into step beside Brooke. He didn't speak, waiting for her to peel off in the direction of her car. His rusted old pickup was wedged between two full-sized trucks. He gave a little wave. "Good luck. See you around."

She offered a tight smile and veered toward the opposite side of the parking lot, across from the front door.

Habit had him watching her get into her SUV before he turned toward his worn-down hunk of junk and took two long strides to the driver's door. The glass from the driver's side window was smashed onto the cloth bench seat of the truck. "What the hell?"

He yanked open the door and anger flared in his veins. Sunlight filtered through the fractured window; jagged shards scattered along the dashboard. He gritted his teeth. Whoever smashed his windows had messed with the wrong guy, and he couldn't ignore the nagging feeling telling him whoever had crossed this line was connected with Brooke Mather.

5

The small brick building that occupied the Pine Valley Police Department sent a wave of nostalgia crashing over Brooke. The space might not house as many desks as the precinct she'd worked at in Gatlinburg, but a familiarity had her yearning for her days in uniform. The coffee station with burnt sludge coating the bottom of the pot, the officers hunched over computers as they worked, and the chatter of the scanner blaring out directives.

No matter the size, something crackled in the air that set her muscles to attention.

Cruz pecked away at the keyboard attached to his computer monitor and continued studying the security footage Wade sent over.

Brooke leaned back against her chair and rubbed at the tension building in her head. "Find anything?" She asked the question even though the answer was obvious. Not only had she, Cruz, and Lincoln all watched the footage twice, Cruz would have alerted her if she'd missed something.

Cruz grunted what she thought was a no, his eyes still fixed on the screen.

Lincoln stopped pacing and gripped the edge of the chair beside her. He leaned forward then backward, a constant motion, as though he needed to move to keep the energy from exploding from his body. "You're wasting your time. The guy made sure we wouldn't get one useful thing on that camera."

She winced at the sharp bite of his words, but Cruz didn't seem to notice. "We can always hope for a slip-up." Although she agreed with Lincoln, every officer had his or her own process. Cruz was thorough, something that served him well more times than not.

Sighing, Cruz ran a palm over his mouth and frowned. "Nothing on the footage. Damnit."

Lincoln rounded the chair and dropped down into it. "Do you think this could be your ex? Would he have had time to be at the bar last night then make it to your place to leave a note?"

"Probably not, but he could have been at my cabin before heading to the Chill N' Grill. I hadn't been home for hours." A shiver had her clamping her teeth together. If Shay made sure to sneak into her cabin while she'd been at the lodge preparing for new guests, that meant he had an eye on her and she'd been completely unaware.

"Does your ex have a history of violence? Do you think he'd be capable of hitting Julia and busting out the windows of Lincoln's truck?" Cruz wiped any hint of emotion from his face as he asked the questions, cop-mode fully engaged.

Brooke squeezed her eyes closed for a brief second to collect her resolve. Moving away from the town and the people who witnessed her unhealthy relationship with Shay —hell who'd witnessed her unhealthy relationship with her own mother—had been like shedding shackles that had weighed her down her entire life. Reopening these old wounds for all to see wasn't something she wanted to do. Damn Shay for forcing her hand.

A light touch on her arm shifted her gaze beside her. Lincoln's cool blue eyes dipped down in the corners, spilling concern. Her breath caught. This man had received the sharp end of her tongue twice in less than twenty-four hours. Although it hadn't been completely undeserved, the empathy emanating from him now stole her guard.

"You don't have to tell us anything you don't want. Just the basics. Just what could help us figure out if he's the one we need to find." His beard hid his jawline but couldn't keep the small smile he offered from view.

She nodded, sucking in her bottom lip. She understood what needed to be done, and she'd do it to make sure that if Shay was the one leaving chaos around town, he'd be stopped before hurting anyone else like he'd hurt her. "Yes, Shay is more than capable. Added to that, if he's decided he wants revenge on me, he'd go to any lengths get do it."

Lincoln tightened his fists on his lap, wincing then relaxing his right hand. "How long have you been apart?"

"Close to two years."

"And is there a reason why he would choose to come after you now? Have you two communicated? Has something or someone clued him into where you are?" Lincoln swiveled his head toward Cruz. "Sorry, man. Don't mean to step on your toes. I can back off and let you ask the questions."

Cruz shrugged. "You've got way more experience with this kind of thing. As long as Brooke's good with it, so am I."

Lincoln swung his gaze back her way, the question clear in his raised brows.

She blew out a long breath. She had planned on answering these questions today, needing to give Cruz more information in order to find who'd broken into her cabin. Who asked the questions didn't matter. They'd both hear her statement, and both could help put an end to a nightmare she didn't want to live through again. "It's fine. I haven't had any communication with Shay since I left him, and the call from him earlier was the first time he's attempted to contact me since he got out of jail a year and a half ago."

Lincoln tilted his head to the side and pressed his mouth into a hard line. "Jail?"

She forced herself to keep eye contact—forced herself not to drop her gaze to her lap. She had nothing to be ashamed of. No reason to hide. "Shay was abusive. Had been from the start. For me, it was just how a relationship looked. He told me he loved me and if I was good, he wouldn't hit me. I craved that love and believed him. I didn't know anything else. A slap on the face, a cigarette burn on my thigh, all things I thought were my fault. When I finally realized I didn't deserve to be someone's punching bag, I left. He'd always been possessive, always had to have his way, and didn't handle my leaving well. He found me, shoved a knife in my side and did as much damage as he could until the police came and dragged him away."

"Shit." Grit coated Cruz's voice.

She kept her eyes on Lincoln. Kept herself grounded in the tiny speck of green in what was otherwise a sea of blue.

Lincoln swallowed hard. "I'm sorry you went through that and am happy as hell you got away. Not everyone's as lucky, or as strong."

She nodded and fought against the pressure building in her sinuses. Crying now wasn't an option. She'd wait until she was tucked safely at home with Wyatt and could let all her walls crash at her feet. "As for 'why now'?" She shrugged. "I don't know."

But she might know someone who did. Lincoln posed an interesting question earlier. Could someone from her past have talked to Shay? Disclosed information that ignited a need to reclaim what he thought was his?

Only one person from her former life would talk to Shay. Only one person could lead him right to her doorstep.

As soon as she left the police station, she needed to make a phone call she always dreaded.

INTERVIEWING countless women and men who'd been abused and mistreated hadn't prepared Lincoln for sitting down with Brooke and learning about the abuse her asshole ex had subjected her to. His coiled muscles ached as he fought not to react to her words. He might not know this woman well, but one thing was certain—she'd never want his pity.

Not like that was the emotion erupting inside him. Hell, she didn't need his pity. She'd picked herself up and built a damn good life.

No. Hot, hard fury fueled the blood pumping through his veins. Anyone who'd treat someone the way this Shay asshole treated Brooke deserved a lot more than a few months in jail.

He brought back an image of the paper left at her cabin the night before. The date was crossed off. "What about the date from the card on your mantle?"

Brooke hooked her long hair over her slender shoulder then combed her fingers through the silky strands. "I told you last night. The card had our wedding date on it. Or what would have been our wedding date."

"June 3rd. That's at the end of the week. That can't be a coincidence." He turned to his brother. "Have there been any other similar crimes happening recently? Anything to indicate multiple people could be responsible for what happened at the bar and at the cabin?"

"Nothing like this." Cruz shifted in his seat and leaned his forearms on his desk. "Brooke, I need to speak to Shay. Can I get his number from you?"

"Sure." She fiddled on her phone then read off a number.

"Did you plan to call him back?" The answer wasn't any of his business, but Lincoln couldn't help himself.

"Yes. I wanted to tell him to leave me alone. But that was before he smashed your windows. I...I don't know if I can face him."

Instinct moved his hand on top of hers. "Then you don't have to."

She widened her eyes, and he pulled away, wiping his palm on his thigh and ignoring the heat spreading from his core.

"I need to get back." She stood and lifted the thin strap of her purse onto her shoulder. "Do you want a ride?"

Shit. He didn't plan to leave the retreat much, but not having a vehicle of his own would be a pain in the ass. He needed to get his windows replaced as soon as possible. Cruz had enough on his plate without chauffeuring him around. But that was an issue he'd figure out once he was back at the cabin. "That'd be great, actually."

"Do you mind driving? I'm a little shaken up." The words came out as if spoken around a mouthful of molasses, and she cleared her throat.

"Sure." He took her keys then dipped his head at his brother. "I'll be in touch."

"Lucky me," Cruz said on a snort. "Brooke, I'll let you know when I speak with Shay. Call if anything else comes up, no matter how small you think it is."

She smiled. "I know the drill."

Her statement piqued his curiosity, but he didn't have time to question her before following her out to her SUV. He climbed inside, and his legs scrunched up to his chest. "Shit, woman. How the hell do you fit in here?"

She strapped on her seatbelt. "My legs are a little shorter than yours."

He adjusted the seat then turned over the engine. He cast her a quick glance before pulling onto the road. "I'm gonna need you to tell me where I'm going, by the way."

She extended a finger out her window. "Right here. At the first stoplight, take a left. That takes you back up the mountain."

"Easy enough." He slid to a stop at the red light and waited for it to change to green then made the turn. He couldn't help but smile at the sight of kids running around the lawn in the middle of the square, and couples sitting on the benches in their sundresses and suits. Small town life might never be for him, but it didn't mean he couldn't appreciate the simplicity of it as he passed through. "What am I supposed to do when we get back?"

"What do you mean? You can do whatever you want."

"Any chance I can get a tour of the lodge? I'd like to know what my options are for spending my time. No way I can just sit on the porch of my cabin and admire the view the entire time I'm here."

She slapped the palm of her hand to her forehead. "Oh my god, I forgot to give you the tour. I'm so sorry."

He chuckled at her dramatics, happy to give her something else to focus on. "No problem. You've had a lot going on."

"Not to mention you were late." She bumped him with her elbow. "The other two guests who arrived yesterday were given the proper information in a timely manner."

His chuckle grew into a laugh at her haughty tone, the sound coming from his mouth foreign to his own ears. "Sorry. Took some liquid courage to get myself to your doorstep."

"You're not the only one who's said that. I understand coming to Crossroads Mountain Retreat isn't always a choice for people. But I hope you find whatever you're looking for while you're with us." Leaning forward, she indicated out his window with a flick of the wrist. "You'll turn here."

He did as she said and began the climb back up the mountain as he thought on her words. He tightened his grip on the wheel, cringing at his inability to close his fist all the way. The fracture in his carpal bones might have healed, but he still didn't have full range of motion in his tendons. "I don't think you can give me what I'm looking for. No matter what all that place of yours has to offer."

She lifted a shoulder. "You might be surprised." Swiveling around, she let out a disgruntled huff. "That van's coming up on us pretty fast. Reckless drivers irritate the hell out of me."

He flicked his gaze to the rearview mirror. "He'll slow soon. I'm not used to these narrow roads. I won't speed up just to make some jerk happy."

She settled back in her seat.

Sweat coated his palms, and he kept his focus ahead. The steep drop-off on the right side of the road made his stomach pitch. Heights weren't his thing. But he couldn't let Brooke see how nervous the change in altitude made him.

"This guy's a maniac." Brooke glanced over her shoulder. "He's almost caught up to us."

Swallowing hard, Lincoln licked his suddenly dry lips. "He'll slow." The driver had to ease up on the gas. Unless he was an idiot who planned to pass as the road curved around the side of a mountain.

The white utility van drove up to his bumper then followed close behind. Lincoln pressed down a little harder on the gas, putting distance between them.

He unlatched his gaze from the rearview mirror and focused on the road ahead. "How much longer before we turn off for the retreat?"

"Just a couple more minutes. We're almost there." One hand gripped her seatbelt while the other stayed glued to the handle on the door.

Brooke glanced over her shoulder. "I can't get a good look at the driver."

A hard bump hit the back of the SUV, and he jolted forward. "What the hell?" Flashes of another accident invaded his mind. His limbs trembled. His breath hitched in his throat.

The van rammed the bumper again, whipping him against the steering wheel. The seatbelt tightened its death hold across his chest. He pressed the gas pedal to the floor. "Hold on!"

The roar of a revving engine blasted behind him. The van motored to the side of the SUV.

"Oh my God." Brooke shrieked.

"Come on. Go!" He urged the SUV forward. The sign for the retreat was ahead on the left. Just a little bit further.

Whack!

The van slammed against the driver's door. Lincoln turned the wheel to keep the vehicle from bouncing off the short guard rail that lie between him and plunging off the mountain.

The van pressed against the vehicle, forcing the SUV to the side of the road.

Lincoln gritted his teeth and steered the wheel toward the center line. Sweat dotted his hairline. His heart hammered in his ears.

The van braked and stopped in the middle of the road.

Lincoln yanked the wheel to the side as the missing pressure from the hunk of metal made the SUV swerve. Panic surged in his chest. The vehicle flipped and landed upside down, the edge of the cliff coming closer and closer. Lincoln's head snapped forward, hitting the top of the steering wheel. Pain erupted in his skull.

Brooke's screams were the last thing he heard before his eyes slid shut and a weightlessness lifted his body.

6

Terror clasped Brooke's vocal cords, making her screams come out tight and shrill. She squeezed her eyes shut, her muscles tight. The airbag deployed and smashed against her chest. The death grip she had on the door handle wouldn't help her when they smashed into the ground, but she couldn't let go. Couldn't bring herself to loosen her hold even if the firm grip didn't stop her body from banging around in her seat.

The car flipped and landed upside down with a thud so hard it rattled her teeth, but the car continued to slide down the slope of the mountain. A sea of evergreens rushed past in a blur. Outstretched branches beat against the car and a flurry of leaves flew by. The SUV's forward momentum down the side of the mountain could not even be slowed by the boulders and trees as she continued to be hurled toward her death. All her blood rushed to her head, causing a spike of dizziness to leak through the fear coating her body.

A jolt stopped the movement and slammed her against her seatbelt. The sound of shattering glass rang in her ears.

Sudden pain seared her abdomen. She held her breath, waiting for the car to move again—for her life to end.

Nothing happened.

Filling her lungs with air, she dared a peek through one eye. Pellets of glass littered the car and the thick green needles of an evergreen tree protruded through the busted windshield, nearly brushing the tip of her nose. The sweet scent of sap and pine overwhelmed her senses.

Blinking, she tried to gain her bearing's. The spider-webbed window beside her made it impossible to see what lay outside her door. She had no way of knowing how far the car had gone down the mountain or how precarious her current situation was.

She let out a shaking breath and took mental stock of her body. Aches and pains called for attention, but nothing life-threatening. Hell, not even anything that needed medical assistance.

Brooke turned toward Lincoln and a different kind of fear had her relaxing her shaking fingers from the door. He hung beside her, eyes closed, blood trickling from an open wound on the side of his head. The branches of the toppled tree that had stopped them from tumbling the rest of the way down the mountain rubbed against his forehead. She needed to get them both out of the vehicle before the smashed tree gave way.

With one hand braced against the ceiling now beneath her, she unhooked her seatbelt and tumbled from the seat. A slight tremble rocked the car, and she held her breath, stilling every fiber of her being. When the rocking stopped, she shifted onto her knees and pressed her fingers against the side of Lincoln's neck. An even, strong pulse. Good. But now she needed to get him safely out of his seat, while making sure his weight didn't shift the balance of the car too much.

"Lincoln? Can you wake up?" His closed eyelids fluttered. "Come on. Open your eyes. This will be so much easier if you're awake."

A soft groan emanated from his throat, but his eyes remained closed.

Damnit. She couldn't waste time trying to rouse him. She needed to get them both out of the car. With slow, deliberate movements she pushed against the passenger side door, but it wouldn't budge. Panic threatened to consume her, but she took one deep, calming breath.

The window. It was already cracked. She could crawl through. Loading her leg, she kicked her foot through the fractured glass. She knocked away as much of the window as she could before slipping through the narrow space. Rocks scraped against her knees and palms. Adrenaline pumped through her veins, and she hurried to her feet. The towering evergreens clustered together blocked out the sun and cast long shadows on the ground. She cringed at the sight of her car laying on its roof, smashed against a pine tree. But she didn't have time to dwell on the destruction.

Finding her footing on the inclined land and upturned roots on the ground, she raced between the tall tree trunks, rounded the front of the car, and busted out the driver's side window. She winced as the pellets of glass rained down on Lincoln. "Lincoln. It's Brooke. If you can hear me, I'm going to release your seatbelt and try to help cushion your landing."

Leaning through the window, she brushed aside the pointy needles on the tree limb and hooked one arm around his waist, using her other hand to release the seatbelt from the clip. The vinyl strap sprung across his chest, and all his weight fell forward.

Her body lurched under the pressure. Lincoln crumbled against the roof, trapping her arm under him. The car rocked back and forth. Terror rose with the bile from her stomach. She had to get him out of the car. Now.

"Lincoln. Please. Wake up." The frantic plea flew from her mouth while she yanked her arm free. The prickly needles thrusting through the window scratched at her skin.

Lincoln moaned. His body twisted. The protruding branch through the windshield brushed against the top of his head. His body curled into a ball. The SUV tilted with the added weight on the driver's side. The sound of a branch snapping set her on high alert, alarm pounding with every rapid thud of her heart.

"Brooke?"

Her name on his lips was the sweetest sound she'd ever heard. "I'm here. Are you able to move? Can you get out of the car?"

He carefully touched his fingertips to the bleeding spot on his head and winced. "Sonofabitch."

"Lincoln. Look at me." Her knees were just on the outside of the broken window, her palms pressed against the scraggly mountainside grass. She leaned forward, wanting to provide as much comfort and reassurance as possible, but not wanting to disturb the delicate balance of the vehicle. When Lincoln's glassy eyes locked on hers, she pressed on. "You need to get out of the car as carefully as possible, but quickly. The SUV flipped. It's upside down, with only a tree keeping it in place. The tree could give way any second. Do you understand?"

His eyes widened, but alertness rippled across the plains of his face. "Okay."

"Do you need me to help?" The man was double her size —his tall, broad form the complete opposite of her petite stature. She wasn't sure what exactly she'd be able to do to move him, but she'd figure it out. No way would she let him fall down the mountain with the car.

He shifted and winced.

"What? What hurts?" Her emergency medical training was top notch, but his position inside the car rendered her skills useless.

"My head." He moved to his side and a pasty pallor took over his face. His eyes glazed over as tremors shook his limbs.

"Lincoln," she snapped, afraid he was going into shock. "Focus on me. On my face. You need to move."

Another snap of wood vibrated underneath the still sky. The car slipped forward, pushing the branches further into the vehicle. She winced as the sharp needles pricked at his exposed skin and the branches pinned him to the roof.

He swallowed hard.

"Take my hand." She extended her palm like a lifeline. His fingers brushed against hers. She clamped on tight and pulled, unable to budge him. "Move your ass. Now."

He blinked, seeming to snap back to the present. He lunged forward, sliding his way through the smashed-out window.

A bit of relief released its nasty hold on her heart. Brooke kept her grip locked on his, scurrying backwards as he stretched forward. The effort was comical, she couldn't move him, but she could at least show him she was here. That she would use all the strength she possessed to motivate him to get out of the damn car.

Lincoln's booted feet kicked out of the SUV. More snapping echoed in the air. The car inched forward. Letting go of her hand and clamping his arms around her waist, Lincoln pressed her against him and leapt from the car. Air swept between her and the ground until Lincoln landed on top of her.

Hinges creaked as the driver's door swung, the car charging past the crumpled evergreen. Brooke buried her head in Lincoln's neck and fisted his T-shirt in her trembling hands. His chest rose and fell against hers.

Strong fingers brushed against her cheek, and she opened her eyes. His face lingered above her and a strange urge to feel the coarse hairs on his chin had her biting her lip.

His gaze dropped to her mouth then back to her eyes. "Are you okay?"

Unable to speak, partly from shock and partly from him crushing her with his muscular chest, she nodded.

He rolled to her side, and her body yearned for his heat to cover her again. A reaction as unexpected as unwanted. Sharp rocks dug into the small of her back. She swiped dirt and debris from her wrinkled shirt and rose. "What about you? Anything else injured beside the spot on your head?"

"I don't think so." He roamed a hand over his arms and legs before climbing to his feet beside her. "Did you get a look at the bastard who just tried to kill us?"

His words chilled her to the bone, the truth hitting her square between the eyes. If Shay was the driver, he didn't just want to take back what he thought was his, he wanted her dead and didn't care who else he took down along the way. "His cowboy hat hid his features, just like in the videos from the Chill N' Grill, but I did see the name on the side of the van. As soon as we call the police, we need to make an inquiry about a psychopath driving a van from CJ's Plumbing."

THE CRACKLING fire in the giant hearth at the lodge wasn't necessary on such a warm June evening, but something about the dancing flames calmed Lincoln as he sat on the soft leather couch and tried for one damn second to forget about the horrors of the day.

Sharp jabs of pain beat against his skull. He'd popped a few aspirin as soon as he'd gotten back to the lodge, but they hadn't helped. The sofa might be comfortable, but it's the last place he wanted to be. He understood the location being ideal for him, Brooke, and Cruz to discuss everything that transpired, but the curious glances of people passing by made his skin crawl.

Just like the night before, all he wanted was to get to his cabin and burrow into bed. It didn't matter that the evening was young. The day had been long and way too eventful for his liking. After waiting at the scene of the accident for Cruz and giving their statements, he'd let Cruz push him into a quick trip to the hospital. Now, all he wanted to do was pull a blanket over his head and sleep.

Too bad the fury brewing in his veins demanded he find answers before he rested. He might have ample faith that his brother could do his job and get to the bottom of what happened, but damnit, he wouldn't let his life be hijacked by some jackass again. Not when he was capable of digging around and getting answers himself.

Not when doing his job—whether he was on the clock or not—could wipe away the furrowed brow and worried eyes that had taken over Brooke's delicate face.

Cruz turned from where he stood by the fireplace, lines creasing his tanned forehead. He pocketed the phone he'd had pressed to his ear moments before. "Bad news. A van was stolen from the plumbing company close to a week ago. The company's out of Knoxville."

Lincoln squeezed the bridge of his nose. "Linking the guy back to the plumbing company would have made things easy, but it still gives us another line to pull."

"Agreed." Brooke sat on the loveseat next to him with her legs tucked under her and her giant dog nestled beside her.

The front door burst open. The man who'd handed them the security footage from the bar rushed in with his thin lips pulled in a deep frown and a bag of food dangling from his side. A quick survey of the room had him heading straight to Brooke. "I just heard. Are you okay? Damn, woman. You sure know how to give a guy a heart attack." He let the plastic bag drop on a coffee table and landed a quick kiss on her forehead.

The dog's tail thumped wildly against the armrest of the leather couch, and the bar owner ruffled the top of his head.

A quick jolt of jealously had Lincoln gritting his teeth. Was this guy involved with Brooke? He hadn't been aware she was dating anyone, not like it was any of his business. Hell, it didn't matter what the woman did with her free time. All that mattered was he helped find the asshole who'd tried to kill her.

Brooke offered a quick smile that looked more like a wince. "I'm fine. Just a little banged up. Could have been so much worse."

"I'll ring the neck of whoever the hell was responsible for this little escapade."

Lincoln snorted at the word used to describe his tumble over the side of a mountain.

Brooke nodded his way. "Wade, meet Lincoln Sawyer. Cruz's brother. He was driving the SUV. I'm sure if he hadn't remained calm behind the wheel, things would have ended up a whole lot worse."

Her words puffed his chest, even if he didn't believe them. He hadn't done jack shit except slip into a panic as his past and present collided. When he'd needed to keep his head on straight and focus, the night of the car accident that had led him here invaded his mind and wouldn't leave—the crushing memory of being trapped under steel and glass leaving him paralyzed. If he'd thought faster, reacted better, he might have kept them from almost dying.

Pivoting, Wade extended a hand. "Nice to meet ya. Everyone in town's buzzing about what happened. I had to see for myself Brooke was all right, so I brought over some food for you folks. Not sure if you're in the mood to eat or not, but I know Brooke can't say no to my fried chicken."

He took the offered hand and inhaled deeply. "That was awfully nice of you. Food was the last thing on my mind until I smelled that. I don't think I could refuse even if I wanted. Much appreciated."

Cruz leaned over and dipped his finger into the white plastic, peeking inside. "Did you happen to bring enough for three? It's been a long-ass day. Don't want to have to stop by for my usual order on the way home."

A deep chuckle belted from Wade's scruffy face. "I figured you wouldn't want to be left out. There's enough food for a few of ya."

"Will you stay and eat with us?" Brooke asked.

"Not tonight, darling. The place is packed, and I need to get back. Call if there's anything else I can do for you." He shot her a wink and turned back to him. "Nice to meet you, Lincoln. Enjoy the grub."

"I'll grab some plates and silverware and we can just eat

in the lobby if that's okay with you guys." Brooke bounced her gaze between them.

"I can grab what we need," Cruz said. "No need for you to get up." He retreated toward a darkened hallway before she could respond.

Lincoln stared into the firepit, not wanting to meet the curious gazes of the few people who lingered in seating areas tucked around the large room. An uneasiness settled over him like an itchy sweater. He'd almost died beside this woman, had just experienced a caveman reaction to seeing her with another man, and he had no idea what to say to her. Didn't know a damn thing about her.

"How's your head?" Shifting, she leaned forward and pulled white Styrofoam containers from the bag and set them on top of the coffee table.

"Been better." The quick stop to the hospital had resulted in a few stitches above his temple. "I'll take some aspirin again before I go to bed. Hopefully it won't be too bad in the morning. How are you feeling?"

She rolled back her shoulders and circled her neck. "Achy. I'm torn between hopping in the hot tub to loosen my muscles before I go home or just heading for bed."

The thought of her in a hot tub had him squirming in his seat. Better to steer clear of any topic centered around her wet and half-naked. "Umm, I didn't say this earlier, but I wanted to thank you. You got me out of that car. Without you, I wouldn't be here." The confession wedged in his throat, but he needed to get it out.

She dropped her gaze to her slender hands resting in her lap. "I'm the reason you're caught up in this whole mess to begin with. I don't deserve your gratitude."

"Are you kidding me?" He rested his forearms on his knees, hands clasped together, and held her gaze in his. As much as he hated to dwell on his hesitation earlier, she needed to understand what she'd done for him. She needed to know she was a hero, not someone to be blamed for a situation outside of her control. "I was in a car accident a month ago. You probably already know that."

The slight tilt of her head confirmed she'd read all about his reasons for being here.

"When that van slammed into the car, it took me right back to that place. Right back to being trapped in a car where someone's dumb ass actions might take my life. I panicked. Twice. Once while driving, then again when you tried to get me out of the car. Giving me your hand, giving me something real to grab on to, it snapped me back to where I needed to be. You saved me."

Tears filled her eyes, and she sunk her teeth into her bottom lip. "PTSD is a bitch, isn't it?"

He blew out a long breath. "Yeah, it really is."

Hurried footsteps came toward them, and Cruz appeared with the utensils needed to eat.

Brooke flipped open the lids of the take-out boxes. "You're in for a real treat. Wade's fried chicken is legendary."

The scent of garlic and butter and everything comfort food made saliva pool in Lincoln's mouth. His stomach growled, reminding him he hadn't eaten since breakfast. He'd devour the food Wade brought over for dinner and then go back to his cabin. Sleep wouldn't come easy, and it wasn't the pain thudding against his skull or mounting questions that would keep him awake. It was the unwanted attraction for Brooke brewing in his gut.

His life was already complicated enough. The last thing he needed was a woman with a crazy ex making things worse.

7

B rooke sat behind her desk in the lobby and willed her ass to move from the comfortable, cushioned chair. Climbing out of bed when her alarm blasted had proven difficult, but she had to get on with her day. Even if every muscle in her body screamed at her to stay home. She had a business to run, and nothing Shay did would keep her from fulfilling her dreams.

Even running her off a mountain.

A quick call to Cruz earlier gave her no new information. The van was stolen, no clues on who'd taken it, and the vehicle hadn't turned up since yesterday. Cruz had every officer in the area on the look-out for the van, but she wasn't holding out hope.

Cruz still hadn't touched base with Shay. He'd called the number she'd given him, but no one answered. Frustration pounded along with every heartbeat. Cruz would reach out to Shay's father today, something the mayor of their small hometown would hate. Mr. Lawrence refused to believe his son was capable of any wrongdoings, even when the evidence had placed him in jail. He wouldn't be any help to Cruz.

Which left one more person to call. Her mother.

Brooke tapped the tip of her index finger against the edge of the desk and stared out the window. Gray skies settled in for the day, a perfect reflection of her current mood. Speaking with Mama was never fun, and usually consisted of either joyful proclamations of love finally found or tearful stories of another tragic rejection. Every call ended with pleas for money and a request to come see Brooke.

Money Brooke would gladly send if it meant keeping Glenda Mather from setting foot at Crossroads Mountain Retreat.

Wanting to get the inevitable over, she scooped up her phone from beside the computer and locked herself into the breakroom. She didn't need anyone overhearing her conversation. Not even Zoe knew of all the trials she'd endured with her mother, and she planned to keep it that way.

Sinking into an overstuffed chair with a view of the rain sliding down the window, she placed the call and braced herself.

"Hey there, Brookie." Her mom answered after the first ring, as if she'd waited by the phone, expecting a call.

Brooke cringed at the nickname. It didn't matter how much time passed, the sound of the childish name always made her feel small and beaten down. "Hi, Mama. How are you?"

"Oh, I'm doing so well, honey. It's so good to hear your voice. And I just have the most wonderful news! I met a man. A real nice one this time. Not like those other jerks I always seem to find." Excitement mixed with the familiar southern drawl.

Brooke tucked her feet beneath her and rolled her eyes. *Here we go again.* "I'm glad, Mama. But I have a question. Have you talked to Shay at all lately?"

"You're not going to ask me about my man?" A small pout accentuated the words. "We haven't spoken in weeks, and all you want to do is talk about the man you couldn't nail down?"

She sucked her teeth and squeezed the phone. "He almost killed me, Mama, and I had the good sense to finally walk away. Now, please tell me. Have you spoken with him?"

"Of course I have." Glenda giggled like a schoolgirl, not the forty-five-year-old woman she was. "He moved back to town about a month ago. Saw him at the market, and we got to talking about how if things were different, ya'll would be almost to your two-year wedding anniversary."

"Oh, Mama. You didn't." She fell back against the chair, tilting her head to the ceiling. "You remember how he put me in the hospital, right? Why in the world would you speak to him?"

"That was a long time ago. He told me how much he's changed and wanted to reconnect. He asked for your number, so I gave it to him. Did he call? What did he say? Tell me everything!"

The excitement in her voice made Brooke's insides curdle. Just once she'd hoped she hadn't been right—that her mother wouldn't have done the worst possible thing. Glenda had always championed Shay, even when she'd spied the bruises he'd left on Brooke's skin. Shay's family came from money, which she viewed as her own personal triumph. If her daughter married rich, Glenda would have an unending source of cash.

It didn't matter if Brooke was slapped or mistreated from

time to time. That's just the way the world worked for Glenda Mather.

"We haven't spoken, and I'd appreciate if you steer clear of him when you see him. He's dangerous."

"Oh, you've always been so dramatic." The suck of Glenda taking a drag from a cigarette filled the line. "Shay was always a nice boy."

She shook her head, words escaping her as she pictured her mom sitting at the kitchen table with one leg crossed over the other and a cigarette hanging between her fingers. "Do whatever you want. I don't care. Just keep me out of it."

"Well don't get all pissy. I haven't seen him in a few days anyway." A hacking cough interrupted her.

Interest piqued, Brooke straightened. "Is that not normal? How often have you been seeing him since he moved back to town?"

"I mean, his daddy got him a job at the market. Didn't I mention that? He's managing the place. He's had a tough time apparently, trying to get his life back on track after what happened. You should be grateful he doesn't hold it against you. But when I told him all about that fancy retreat of yours, he really perked up. He's a good manager. Might be able to help you at your own place."

Anger pushed her to her feet. She'd spent her whole life listening to her mother's nonsense. Hell, watching the abuse she'd endured and making excuses for her asshole boyfriends was what led Brooke to think her own abusive relationship was normal. But she didn't have to listen to it anymore, and she didn't have to let her mom take her down the same twisted path she'd chosen to walk herself.

"I don't need Shay's help. I need him to stay out of my life. I don't want anything to do with him, and I don't want you putting my name in your mouth around him. Do you understand?"

"Fine. If that's what you want. But can I tell you about Rick now? He's just so handsome and sweet. Works at the factory outside of town. Makes a real good living. He's gonna take care of me."

Brooke's patience was too thin to sit and listen to her mother ramble on about her new crush. "I'm glad, Mama, but I have to go. I'll call soon."

"Wait! Brookie! My hours were cut and I'm having a real hard time paying my bills this month. Rick said he'd help, but it's just too early to take that kind of money from him. Any way I could borrow a little cash? I'll pay you back this time. I promise." The last words came out on a shrill whine.

Brooke hung her head. A part of her wanted to slam down the phone and refuse to give Glenda another penny. She was only enabling her, continuing to support bad habits that would never change as long as Brooke continued to bail her out.

But the other part—the little girl inside her that just wanted her mother to love her—couldn't refuse Glenda's requests. Couldn't stop the hope buried deep inside her that one day, her mama wouldn't want anything from her. Just her love.

"Sure, Mama. I'll put a check in the mail today." Disconnecting, she sank back into the chair and watched the slow drips of rain morph into a downpour. Her heart ached. Not only had her mother slipped Shay information and a way to contact her, but by telling him how well Brooke was doing with her new business, she'd handed him the motivation he needed to finally seek his revenge.

～

LINCOLN MOVED AS FAST as his aching body would allow him through the fat drips of rain and darted inside the lodge. Sitting at his cabin all day wasn't for him. He'd hounded Cruz all morning, each phone call or text reminding him that Cruz was handling things. Lincoln wasn't here to work —he was here to keep focused on the goal. The goal of getting back on the job.

What sick twist of fate had landed him in the middle of an investigation that he wasn't allowed to work?

He needed to do *something*. He had no idea what all lay hidden in the lodge, but Brooke had mentioned a hot tub the day before and he intended to use it.

With his gym bag high on his shoulder, he scanned the deserted lobby. His wet sneakers squeaked against the gleaming mahogany floors. Water dripped from his jacket, leaving small puddles in his wake. He headed for the desk where Zoe had checked him in, but no one sat in front of the computer.

Turning a wide half-circle, he searched for anyone to help him. He hadn't been anywhere but this main room and didn't know where anything was located. Remembering Julia had turned down the right corridor the night Cruz dropped her off, he ventured to the left. A sign for the locker rooms loomed ahead, and he quickened his pace. He headed for the men's room and found an empty locker to hold his stuff, then changed into a pair of swimming shorts and shoved his feet into flip flops. Following the scent of chlorine, he nodded silent greetings to a couple of men he passed and pushed through a door to a pool.

Not too bad.

The four-lane lap pool was housed under a glass ceiling with windows for walls, as if trapped inside a giant green-house. White and black tiles lined the floor. Heated moisture hung heavy in the air and filled his lungs. One woman swam in the pool, her arms cutting into the water with each stroke. She was so graceful, her movements effortless.

Reaching the end of the pool, she lifted her head from the smooth sheet of water and brushed soaked strands of hair from her face. Brooke grabbed the handles of the ladder and emerged from the pool like the fantasy woman from *Christmas Vacation*. Her one-piece bathing suit—the same color red she usually wore on her lips—rose high on her thighs. And dipped low in the front, her breasts threatening to spill from the wet fabric.

He swallowed hard and averted his gaze. Last thing he needed was for Brooke to catch him gawking. Turning his back to her, he surveyed the rest of the area. The hot tub Brooke had mentioned the night before sat in the opposite corner of the room beside a narrow, wooden box. Probably a steam room. His muscles practically vibrated at the idea of soaking in the hot water.

"Hey, Lincoln. How are you feeling this morning?"

He turned toward Brooke and bit back a groan. She stood beside the pool with her wet hair thrown over her shoulder, squeezing water from the strands. He fought every instinct to roam his gaze up and down her body, locking his eyes on hers instead. "Sore. I remember you mentioned something about a soak in a hot tub last night. Thought I'd head over and try the same thing out myself."

"Do you mind if I join you?"

"Not at all." He offered her a tight smile then hurried to jump into the burning water. He closed his eyes as he sank in deeper, the jets pumping against his skin. A tiny splash sounded, indicating Brooke had entered and it was safe to open his eyes.

She plunged into the water and sighed. "This is heaven."

Brooke might be in heaven, but being so close to a barely clothed, beautiful woman he had no right touching was closer to hell for him. He found a spot on the window behind Brooke and kept his gaze fixed to it. "This place is really something. Not what I had in mind."

She tilted her head to the side. "Didn't you look up pictures online?"

He shook his head. "I had my mind made up I didn't want to come. Didn't matter what it looked like. Maybe I wouldn't have been so hesitant if I'd known what I was walking into."

She smiled, understanding lighting her eyes. "I hear that a lot, and I'm glad people are happy with what I have to offer once they get here. This place is special to me. My goal is for every person who stays to feel the same."

"How did you end up here? In a place like this?" He couldn't help a quick peek at her flushed skin. "You always like the mountains?"

"Always." A wistful quality threaded through her voice. "My grandfather owned this place years ago, but back then it was a youth camp. I came every summer. When he died, he left me the land, along with every penny he'd ever saved. I was barely a teenager then and didn't know what I wanted to do with the place until life threw me a curveball."

"Ah, you got one of those hurled at you, too, huh? The ex?" He wanted to know more about her, hear her story, but he didn't want to pry or ask too many questions. Opening up to strangers wasn't high on his list for his brief stay here, he would be nothing more than someone who'd passed through. Even if they had almost died together.

She tapped the tip of her finger on her nose. "You guessed it. I mean, I knew what I was walking into with him. Hell, I followed right along with every pattern I'd ever seen growing up. What I didn't expect was being left with no job, no dream, and no future. I poured my soul into this place, and it brought me back from the dead. If I can help do the same thing for others, everything I went through would be worth it."

The sincerity of her words pressed against his chest. She'd been in his shoes, more or less, and came out the other side in a better place. He hoped the same would be true for him. Only he wanted to be back in a uniform a few hours away in Nashville. "I'm not sure what I can do here that will convince my captain I'm ready to get back on the force."

She winced. "I still didn't show you around. You up for a tour after the soak? I know you're probably sore, but I promise to take it easy on you."

Her sentence brought to mind a dozen different scenarios that didn't involve a tour. Blood pumped through his heated veins. He had to get the hell out of here before he said something he'd regret. "I'd like that. Might as well do it now."

Climbing out of the hot tub, he grabbed a towel and wrapped it around his waist. "I'll meet you in the hallway outside the locker rooms." He didn't spare her a glance as he marched to the locker room and headed straight for an ice-cold shower.

8

"R eady?"

Relief mixed with disappointment in Lincoln's gut at seeing Brooke dressed in track shorts and a tank top. Even though the shorts sat high on her thighs, showing off toned legs, and her top clung to her chest, the image of her in her siren-red bathing suit would be seared in his brain for eternity. "Let's go."

Brooke clapped her hands then rubbed them together. "We're already in the fitness wing, so why don't we check out the gym?"

"Sounds good." He didn't want to admit it, but that was the only place he really wanted to be. The daily exercises he'd been given by an occupational therapist back home could be done in his cabin, but his body craved a high-intensity workout he could only get at a gym.

He walked beside her down the wide corridor, following behind as she entered a fitness center that made drool threaten to pour from his open mouth. "I know where I'll be for the rest of my stay. This is impressive."

"Thanks. I spend a fair share of my own time here."

Brooke moved further into the room, extending a finger to different sections of the space as she walked. "We have the basics. Free weights. Treadmills. Any lifting machine you could need. A personal trainer is available, as well as classes in the separate rooms along the back."

He followed each flick of the wrist and dip of her chin as she pointed out every piece of equipment. The whine of a treadmill hummed, and he could see a glimmer of a small group doing some sort of exercise in one of the rooms with a circular weight that looked like a steering wheel. Probably some fitness crave he'd rather stay far away from.

"Towels there. Dirty ones get put in the baskets. Fill station for your water." She spun toward him, her finger now aimed at his chest. "Which reminds me. I have a welcome basket at the front desk for you. Water bottle, list of activities and classes, contact list, and dining room schedule. Sorry I didn't get it to you when you checked in, but..." She pressed her lips together, quirking up an arched eyebrow.

He chuckled. "I was late. I get it."

"Exactly." She grinned. "Nothing more to see here, so let's move on."

He turned on a groan, not really caring about anything else besides this area. He didn't want to do the yoga his brother tried or any other alternative medical practices, but he didn't want to offend Brooke. "Sure."

"Can't muster up more enthusiasm than that, huh?"

"Sorry." He wrinkled his nose and waved a hand over his head. "Whatever you have to show me out there doesn't interest me. But I'll go see it."

She rested a hand on his arm. "You never know what you'll end up needing while you're here. Something new might surprise you. At least this way you'll know where to find everything."

His stomach dipped like he'd taken the first hill down a roller coaster. He was afraid that the only thing he'd want after today was more time with Brooke. "Lead the way."

He kept his comments to himself as she walked him up to the third floor and showed him the therapy rooms and meditation spaces. An art class was taking place in what looked like his high school art room, men and women splashing bright, bold colors over canvases. The views would be nice to look at, but no way he'd sit cross-legged on the floor singing kumbaya with a bunch of strangers or express his feelings through painting.

Ok, so that's not what people were doing. Everyone they crossed paths with—whether staff or guest—had a ready smile, and no one danced naked around a candle or held hands in prayer. But the only thing that interested him on the upper level of the building was the wood-paneled study lined with books and a quiet place to relax.

"That's everything inside." Brooke swung her gaze to the window. "The rain's slowed. The trails will be a little muddy, but I can show you some of the things we offer outside. That might be more your speed. Then we can come back and grab lunch before I set you loose."

"Are you sure you have time? I hate that I'm taking up your whole morning."

She shrugged. "I need to keep busy. If not, I'll just go crazy waiting to hear from Cruz."

He ran a hand through his hair, somehow still surprised at how long it had gotten. "I get that. All I want to do is throw myself into the investigation headfirst, but my idiot brother keeps reminding me that I'm not currently working."

Laughing, she kicked a foot forward and ran the toe of her sneaker over the burgundy rug covering the wood floor. "Your brother's not an idiot."

"You don't know him like I do," he said, softening his words with a smirk. "But I'm game for heading outside."

"Good. I need to stop by the kennel and grab Wyatt." She glided down the stairs as she spoke.

"Kennels?"

"For the therapy dogs. Wyatt is mine, but he insists on spending a chunk of his day with the other dogs. It gets a lot of his energy out and gives me an excuse to visit all the other animals."

"Huh, now that's something I'd like to see." The thought of sitting for a therapy session with a psychologist or whatever wackadoodle the retreat provided made his skin itch, but therapy dogs were an entirely different story. His work schedule had been too hectic the last few years to own a dog of his own, but he'd always loved animals.

Another reason all the mounted heads at the bar had creeped him out.

Brooke paused and aimed a grin his way. "I thought the only place you'd be is the gym?"

Shrugging, he continued down the curved stairway that led to the back of the main room of the lodge. "I guess petting some dogs while I'm here won't hurt. Yours is cute as hell, but I always feel like he'll eat my hand if I get too close."

She laughed, the sound loud and unexpected from such a small person. "Wyatt's a sweetheart unless you try to hurt me. Then I make no guarantees he won't go for the hand."

A deep, urgent voice reached his ears and had Lincoln halting at the bottom of the stairs. A voice he recognized as well as his own. "Why's Cruz here?"

Brooke patted her sides. "I don't have my phone on me. Do you? Maybe he called one of us about Shay?"

He shook his head and hurried toward his brother. "I have mine. I would have felt it vibrate if he'd called."

Cruz stood next to a large man whose beard made Lincoln's look like a joke. Cruz had a notepad in hand, writing as he nodded and listened to the frantic statement from the guy who looked like he belonged on that paper towel commercial. Red flannel shirt pushed up to his forearms covering a heather gray t-shirt with the logo of the retreat etched across the middle.

Brooke stepped around Lincoln and rested a hand on the man's bicep. "Chet, what's wrong?"

The man towered over her, but his watery brown eyes and slumped shoulders made him appear much smaller. He clasped his beefy palm around his other wrist and rubbed his thumb against his skin over and over again. "It's Julia. She didn't come home last night. She won't answer her phone. I got a bad feeling and called Cruz this morning."

Lincoln stepped closer, joining the conversation. "Any luck finding her, Cruz?"

Cruz locked tired eyes on him. "No. But we found her car in the woods. No sign of her."

BROOKE FOUGHT to keep her composure as she sat beside Chet in Julia's room on her neatly made bed and kept his hand squeezed in hers. His muscles trembled beneath her firm grip, and his shallow breaths told her that he was close to losing his cool. Chet worked hard every single day to keep his PTSD under control, and fear for his cousin threatened to snap his very thin leash.

"Officers in the tri-county area are doing everything they can to find Julia. Have you tried calling any of her friends? What about other family close by she may have reached out to?" Cruz asked.

Chet rubbed his thumb over his wrist and shook his head. "She doesn't have many friends. And no family around but me. I'm supposed to keep her safe. I brought her here to keep her safe." He wedged his head between his hands and rocked back and forth. "She has to be okay. This can't be happening again."

Her heart crumbled to her feet. Chet's departure from his job as a police officer mirrored hers more than any other employee at the retreat. His tragedy hadn't come in the form of an accident on the job or a career-ending injury. His personal life had gone up in flames when his wife and child were ripped away—leaving a broken man who struggled daily to keep his demons from dragging him back into hell.

Not knowing what else to do, she wrapped her arms around Chet. "Everything will be fine. Cruz will find her. I'm sure this is all a big misunderstanding." Even as she said the words out loud, she didn't believe them. Coincidences didn't exist in her world, and Julia being attacked by a stranger at the bar right before being taken from her car had to be connected.

And that stranger could very likely be Shay, sweeping back into her life to do whatever he could to wage psychological warfare on her. Breaking into her cabin, leaving messages, and now messing with one of her employees. If he was responsible for taking Julia, he'd crossed a line there was no turning back from.

Lincoln stood in the middle of the doorway with his hands shoved in the pockets of his gray jersey shorts. "Where was she headed last night?"

"Chill N' Grill. For dinner." Chet kept rocking, his words coming out short and choppy.

Lincoln dipped his chin, eyes narrowed as he took in the dorm-style room. "Could be the same guy from the other night. Maybe his pride was injured, and he's been on the lookout. Would make sense for him to stake out the place he met Julia. Especially if he's not from around here."

Chet dropped his hands and straightened. "Who? The guy who hit her? She said it wasn't a big deal. Some guy she thought she'd recognized from college who took things too far." He jumped to his feet and his long legs ate up the space in the small room as he paced from wall to wall. "I knew I should have done something—pushed her for more information. I just let that bastard slink away and didn't do a damn thing."

"We're trying to find him. Have been since Saturday night," Cruz said.

Chet stopped and braced a palm against the wall. "Do you know anything about who this guy is?"

Swallowing hard, Brooke clasped her hands in her lap. "I think my ex-fiancé has come back. He broke into my cabin, and I think he's the one responsible for the accident Lincoln and I were in yesterday. He's lurking and he's dangerous, and I'm so sorry that Julia has gotten caught up in whatever it is he's trying to do."

Chet smacked the heel of his hand against the wall and hung his head, his shoulders moving up and down as he took in large gulps of air.

Brooke flinched. "I should have told everyone to be on the lookout. Should have let everyone know what happened to my cabin and been more transparent about the accident. I just wasn't ready to reveal all the ugly truths of my past. To rip open a healing wound for everyone to see. I should have—"

Facing her, Chet held up a hand, his wide brown eyes impossibly sad. "No apologies. They won't do anything to help Julia, and there's no reason for them. Not now. Not ever. We just need to focus on how to find this bastard before he hurts my cousin."

She sniffed back all the brewing emotion threatening to break free. Chet was right. They all needed to focus on one goal—bringing Julia home. "Did you call Shay's father? Have any other leads?"

Cruz sighed. "You were right. Mr. Lawrence is a dick. Refused to give me any information. Said he'd sue if his son was arrested based on false allegations and police corruption again. I also tracked down his place of employment and spoke with his boss. Shay hasn't shown up for work in three days."

The news didn't surprise her but still sat heavy in her chest.

"Where exactly was the car found?" Lincoln asked.

Cruz cast a sideways glance to Chet then back to Lincoln. "I can't give you information on the case, man. You know that."

Chet growled, the sound far more menacing than anything Wyatt ever managed. "Tell him whatever the hell he wants to know. I don't care about the bureaucratic bullshit. The more minds on this the better. Julia would agree."

Cruz sighed and rubbed a hand across the back of his neck. "We found her car off the road a few miles from here. No sign of struggle. Rain washed away any tracks or tread marks."

"Is your ex familiar with the area?" Lincoln shifted his attention to her.

She shook her head. "Not that I'm aware of. We're from a small town outside of Gatlinburg. About an hour away. As far as I know, he's never stepped foot in Pine Valley or anywhere close by."

"So we need to look at rentals, motels, and even camp-grounds he could be staying. Somewhere close. Somewhere he could walk from to get here. He wants to be close to keep an eye on Brooke. That's probably how he got to Julia. Saw her leave and pulled some trick to get her to stop." Lincoln screwed his lips to the side. "Does your ex camp? Could he have a site set up in the woods?"

Despite the seriousness of the situation, she couldn't help but snort out a humorless laugh. "No way. He always hated the outdoors— his big dream was to live in some fancy city. Always wanted to be a part of something bigger."

Lincoln raised his brows. "Really? The guy from the bar in the cowboy hat?"

She thought back to the security footage at the bar and the view of the man in the van. She'd had the same thought —Shay had never been one to wear a cowboy hat. But maybe he'd wanted to blend in. Or maybe he'd changed more than she'd thought possible in the time they'd spent apart. Which meant he could have a number of new skills and tricks she was oblivious to.

Fear washed over her. She'd been foolish to think she had the advantage because she knew Shay so damn well. In reality, she didn't know who he was now at all. And there was only one way to learn everything she needed to know.

Shrugging, she bounced her gaze around the room until she settled on Lincoln. She'd only met him a few days ago, but something kept drawing her back to him. Kept pushing her to trust him. "I've never known Shay to wear a cowboy hat or trek through the mountains, and I'd never imagined he'd kidnap someone he'd just met. But a lot has happened since the last time I spoke with Shay. I can't say for certain what he would or wouldn't do. All I know is he's dangerous and has to be found."

She drew in a deep, shuddering breath. "I need to call him and get some answers." Her soul trembled at the idea of speaking to Shay, but it had to be done. It could be the only way to find him and bring Julia home safe.

9

Brooke ventured to the back deck in need of privacy for another phone call she didn't want to make. It seemed pushing down her past was no longer an option. She settled onto a rocking chair tucked into the far corner, away from a few guests seated with cups of coffee, taking in the view. Cruz stayed inside with Chet, but Lincoln followed her and stood at the railing, staring out into the lake.

Appreciation warmed her from the inside out. He hadn't said a word, just walked beside her and offered his silent companionship—his strength. Something she needed in spades to press the call button and wait for Shay to answer.

"Brooke? Is it really you?" Weariness seeped through Shay's gravelly voice.

Bile surged in the pit of her stomach. "It's me."

Shay's sigh blew through the speaker. "It's good to hear your voice. I'm so glad you called."

"Why do you want to talk to me? Why did you break into my cabin and leave that save-the-date card? Why did you take Julia?" Her voice shook, her volume increasing with each word until Julia's name came out on a shriek.

"Wait, what? Who's Julia?"

"Oh my God, you don't even know her name! What's your big plan here, Shay? What are you trying to accomplish?" Fury pushed her to her feet. "You need to stop this. Whatever the hell *this* is."

Lincoln turned worried eyes her way, and she gave a tiny shake of her head. He nodded then twisted back toward the view of the lake.

"Listen, I was an idiot to break into your cabin. And I brought that card because I was feeling nostalgic and just wanted to talk to you. But I don't know anything about some woman named Julia."

His lies made her cringe. He'd never been one to fess up to his wrongdoings. Always thought whatever he did was well within his rights. But this time, he'd gone too far. The only way to get any answers from Shay was to force them out—to catch him red-handed. To do that, she needed to get the snake to leave whatever hole he'd slithered into to. "Where are you now?"

"I'm staying at this place close to you. I really hoped you'd agree to talk. To see me."

Lincoln was right. Shay had chosen to stay somewhere near the retreat to keep an eye on her. Not like that surprised her. If he'd fallen into some kind of delusion that she would want him back, even after nearly killing her twice now, his perceived claim on her would ignite his possessiveness. "Tell me where you're staying, and I'll come see you." Her heart pounded. She had no desire to come face to face with him but getting to him meant getting to Julia.

"You don't want to come here. It's a dump. Can we meet

somewhere else? There's a little diner I found that's not too bad, outside of town. Mel's or something."

Mel's was close to ten miles away and in the middle of nowhere. Locals were the only ones who usually ate there, and mostly during hunting season. Hunters who'd spent hours in the woods often stopped in on their way back to town. "Mel's is fine. I can be there in twenty minutes."

"I'm so glad we're doing this. I've missed you."

His enthusiasm made the bile slosh around in her stomach. She disconnected and joined Lincoln by the railing, taking a second to let the warm summer breeze bring drips of cool rain to her burning skin.

"Are you okay?" Lincoln asked, his voice low and gentle.

"No, but this isn't about me." She focused on the surface of the water. The dots from the rain morphed into small rings, growing wider and wider as they rippled across the surface. One drop led to another and another until they overlapped and consumed everything nearby. Just like her spiraling life.

"Did he say anything about Julia?"

"Claimed not to know her, but he lies. All the time. He agreed to meet me at Mel's, a secluded diner outside of town. Not too far from here." Turning to rest her back against the railing, she caught a glimpse of Chet inside. She'd go and confront Shay for him—for Julia. They didn't deserve to get sucked into her mess. She had to make things right.

"I'm going with you. Cruz will want to be there, too." Lincoln mimicked her movement, and his arm rested against hers. "My guess is you won't talk Chet into letting you out of his sight, either."

She shook her head. "It's too risky. If he knows three

men are with me, especially a police officer, he won't show. I'll go alone. I can handle him."

"Not going to happen. Cruz and Chet can stay here, but I'm with you. You said it yourself, you don't know how much this guy has changed. You already know he's dangerous, and in my experience, being in jail makes men even more dangerous. No matter how much time they spent there."

His insistence brought a smile to her lips. She'd spent her entire life taking care of her mom, then using whatever skills she had to keep her own head above water. She'd never had anyone vow to remain by her side, to help her in a tough situation. As much as she wanted to argue and claim she could handle her problems, knowing he'd be near when she came face-to-face with Shay made a little of her anxiety dissipate.

She bumped against him. "You're right. Going alone wouldn't be smart. Thank you."

He stared down at her and grinned. "Really? That easy for you to agree I'm right? I like this side of you."

She pressed her lips together to keep a laugh from spilling out. "Watch yourself. Now let's go let Chet and Cruz know the plan."

"You're going to be fine, you know."

She angled her head up to take in his kind blue eyes. His light brown hair skimmed the top of his shoulders, and the familiar desire to feel the coarse hair on his chin against her skin had her fisting her hands at her sides. "How can you be sure?"

He swept a hand through the air as if pushing back an imaginary curtain. "This guy tried to knock you down before and look what you created. You're a strong woman. You won't let him take this, or anything else, away from you. You won't let him inflict pain on anyone else. You'll stand up for you and Julia and any other woman he's mistreated."

Tears filled her eyes and she swallowed hard to keep them from sliding over her lashes. "Damn straight. Now let's go nail this bastard."

LINCOLN GLANCED out the dirty window into the parking lot of Mel's Diner. He sat in a vinyl booth, keeping one eye on Brooke sitting at the counter and one at the entrance of the parking lot, waiting for Shay to show up. Cruz parked in the far corner, demanding to be there so he could make the arrest. Brooke agreed, as long as he didn't show up in his cruiser and stayed out of sight.

"Still not here?" Brooke swiveled in her stool and peered outside the window.

"Not yet." He cast her a quick glance then let his gaze roam over the rest of the empty diner. The room, barely bigger than a small kitchen, housed a 50's style-counter with a handful of booths. Mel, the owner, whistled from his visible spot in the kitchen. Grease stains marred the off-white walls and busted linoleum lined the floor. "Please tell me we don't have to eat while we're here."

Brooke laughed then glanced over her shoulder toward the whistling. "You better hope Mel didn't hear you. He'll force feed you his famous venison stew. And trust me, you won't be mad about it."

He snorted and shifted on the cracked seat to keep a better eye on everything. "How are you holding up?"

"Like I'm about to jump out of my skin." She tapped her toes against the floor as if her words spurred on the motion.

"Can't blame you." He shoved a hand through his hair

then rested his elbow on the back of the booth. He wished he could wipe all the fear and worry from her eyes, but the best he could do was try to keep her mind busy while they waited for Shay. "How long have you been friends with Cruz?"

She pinched together her face, his question clearly catching her off guard. "A couple years. He came up to the retreat and introduced himself when he got word about what I was doing. Even before the doors opened. He welcomed me into the community, and everyone else seemed to follow suit."

"Sounds like Cruz. He's always been the one to open up to people. Always wanted more than just big arrests or an important desk. He wanted to find a close-knit community that looked out for one another. I'm glad he's found that here."

She smiled, the fear fleeing from her face for a beat. "Pine Valley has a way of making strangers family. That's something that'd been missing from my life since my grandpa died when I was a girl."

His heart lurched. She'd confided that her grandfather died but hadn't mentioned any other family issues. Only that she'd witnessed the same cycle of abuse she'd fallen into. He and Cruz might differ over the type of lives they wanted to live, but he couldn't imagine not having his brother in his corner. Hell, he was lucky. His mom could be a little overbearing, but he never doubted how much she loved him. Especially after his dad was killed in the line of duty. "You don't have any other family?"

Lifting a shoulder, she stopped kicking her foot against the floor. "My mama still lives near Gatlinburg. We talk every couple of weeks, but she never was the kind of mama who baked cookies and made sure I did my homework. She had me when she was sixteen. Just a kid herself, really. She did her best, but she's never been there for me the way I needed. The way I wanted."

"I'm sorry." His words were inadequate, but they were all he had to offer.

Mel ambled through the doorway of the kitchen with a plate in each hand, his bulky frame teetering from side to side with every step. The flickering light bounced off his bald head and wrinkles creased over wrinkles on his ancient face. "If ya'll gonna sit in here, you might as well eat some pie." He slid one plate over the counter toward Brooke then headed in Lincoln's direction. "I'll grab drinks. What do you want? Coffee? Whiskey?"

Lincoln doubted Mel's Diner had a liquor's license, but that wouldn't stop him from taking what was offered. Especially if it meant calming his frazzled nerves. "I'll take that whiskey." The old man set a slice of cherry pie in front of him, and Lincoln reached for the bundle of silverware wrapped in a napkin.

Mel grunted, dipped his chin, and retreated behind the counter. "What about you, Ms. Mather?"

"Water's fine, Mel. Thank you."

Lincoln dug into the pie and the tart cherries burst on his tongue. "Shit, this is good."

"Shit?" Mel returned with a short glass of amber liquor. "Hope that's not what it tastes like."

"No, sir. Tastes amazing. Thank you," Lincoln mumbled between bites.

Mel retreated into the kitchen without another word.

"Wade might make the best fried chicken around, but his pie doesn't hold a candle to Mel's." Brooke wrapped her lips around her fork then pulled it out slowly.

Was the woman trying to kill him, eating her damn pie

like that? He cleared his throat and stared down at his own plate. "Will your boyfriend be upset you prefer another man's pie?" As much as he tried, he couldn't hide the bite of jealousy in his question.

Brooke made a face as if she'd just smelled a skunk. "Boyfriend? What in the world are you talking about?"

"Wade. He rushed over after he found out about the accident with his all-mighty chicken." Okay, so he had to admit Wade's chicken was amazing. But that didn't mean he had to like the man or his relationship with Brooke.

Not like he had any right to be jealous. Brooke was an attractive, interesting woman, but nothing else was between them. And as much as he'd love to have a quick tumble in the sheets with her, Cruz would kill him for screwing around with a friend.

Brooke pointed her fork in his direction. "Wade treats every woman he meets like that. He's a helpless flirt and a good friend. Nothing more."

He peeked out the window, rain drizzling down the clear glass, and searched for another car besides Cruz's truck still tucked away at the back of the lot. Nothing. "Whatever you say. None of my business."

Brooke hopped off her stool. "Trust me, Wade will be a bachelor for life. I have no interest tying myself to a man who's not planning to stick around. Excuse me for a second. I need to use the restroom. If anyone comes in, just pretend like you're here for the pie."

He took a sip of his whiskey then savored another bite. He couldn't place the feeling that overcame him at learning Brooke was unattached, but he didn't want to dwell on it. Whatever he was feeling didn't matter. He was in town for two weeks, and she'd just told him she wanted a man who planned to stick around. That definitely wasn't him.

A shrill scream raised the hairs on his arms, and he jumped to his feet. He ran the short distance to the woman's room and slammed open the door. The door bounced off a wall of the single-user bathroom. The light was off, but he could still make out the single toilet and sink. No one was inside.

"Brooke!" He yelled her name, praying to hear her voice.

Pivoting, he turned toward the men's room and crashed through the door.

Nothing.

He spilled back out into the hall and ran down the short corridor. An exit sign glowed red above an entry at the back. He bolted toward the door, using his momentum against the thick silver bar to push it open. He hurried down the two steps and found himself surrounded by trees. Rain beat down on him. He stilled, listening for signs of movement and studying the dense woods.

Brooke was nowhere to be found.

10

———————

Brooke struggled to breathe. Shay kept one arm hooked around her neck and squeezed her windpipe. The other firm hand stayed clamped over Brooke's lips as he yanked her through the maze of towering trees. The metallic taste of fear coated her tongue. Her feet peddled like a cartoon character to keep up with his frantic pace, moving her further from the back door of Mel's Diner.

The sound of Lincoln calling out her name reached her ears. Shay whipped her behind a thick trunk and pinned her against the rough bark of a pine tree. Her chest rose and fell with each frantic breath.

Lincoln's panicked voice called out, and she opened her mouth on another scream, but no sound penetrated Shay's palm.

"Be quiet," he whispered in her ear.

His hot breath against her skin made her cringe. Damnit to hell and back, she should have known he had a trick up his sleeve. She never should have let him pick the place to meet.

"You're going to take a little walk with me and then we

can talk. If you try to alert your friend, I'll make sure Julia suffers the consequences. I left her back in my room. Poor thing is terrified. I'd hate to tell her you're the reason I'm so damn frustrated. You know how I get when you push my buttons."

Sweat collected on her palms, combining with the rain dripping from the trees. She needed to stay calm. If Shay was with her, he couldn't hurt Julia. But she couldn't anger him and then let him get away. She was only too aware of the pain he could inflict when upset.

Swallowing back tears, she nodded and rested a hand on his arm. She widened her eyes and locked her gaze with his. His jet-black hair was longer than he used to wear it, the ends curling around his ears. Crows-feet marred the corners of his eyes, making him appear older than his twenty-nine years, and his cheekbones protruded from his thin skin.

Gone was the youthful roundness and bright flash of humor that she remembered. The boyish charm that had tricked her into thinking she was falling for a sweetheart instead of a monster.

He dropped his hand from her mouth, circling his palm around her wrist instead.

"I won't make a sound. I promise." She engaged all her past training to keep her voice even.

A grin split his face before he leaned forward and pressed his lips to her mouth. "I knew you'd come around. Knew you'd understand why I did all of this. It's just because I love you so damn much. Come on. I need to get you away from here so we can talk." He yanked her forward, pulling her around by her wrist.

She chanced a quick glance behind her but couldn't see Lincoln. Did he charge into the woods in a different direction to try and find her? Or maybe he went to Cruz first?

Regardless, she needed to let them know where she was the best way she could. Dragging her sneaker on the ground, she left a broken trail through the fallen leaves and dirt. Now all she needed was for Lincoln to follow it.

The rain slowed, but the sprinkling of water from the outstretched leaves soaked her shirt. Mud coated her shoes and flicked up her calves. The sun was hidden behind a sea of thick clouds, leaving her skin chilled. Shay hauled her deeper into the forest, and a million questions zipped through her brain as her feet struggled to keep up. "Where are we going?"

"Not much farther," he said, his focus zeroed ahead.

Hesitation had her pulling against his grasp.

He spun around, brows pulled down low. "What's wrong? Just keep walking a little bit longer. Then we can sort everything out."

"In the middle of the forest? There's nothing back here. Why can't we just return to wherever you're staying, let Julia go, then we'll figure out what to do from there?" Her composure was slipping, her confidence at her decision to follow him deeper into the thicket of trees dwindling. Sweat tickled the back of her neck, and her vision blurred through the drops of rain shaking down from the trees. Images of the last time she was alone with Shay went off like bombs in her head—each reminder setting off sparks of phantom pain through her psyche.

Dropping his head, he grimaced and buried his hands in the front pockets of his jeans. He kicked a stone with the tip of his cowboy boot. "Look, I lied. I don't know who this Julia chick is. I just needed a reason for you to come with me without that jackass following."

She reared back her head. Her mind spun like a drunken ballerina. More lies. She squeezed her eyes shut, trying to figure out what to do. What the right next step was. "Why are you doing this to me again? Why can't you just let me go? You almost killed me that night—would have if the police wouldn't have shown up. Does that even bother you?"

"Of course it does. I hate that you made me act like such a heathen." He took a step toward her.

She stepped back, sadness pooling in her chest over what a fool she'd been to let Shay manipulate her for so damn long. "What about yesterday when you ran my car off the road? What did *I* do to you then? Tell me, how was shoving my SUV down a mountain my fault?"

The sound of rustling leaves reached her ears, as if someone moved quickly through the forest. But she didn't react. Didn't want Shay to take his undivided attention off her. *Please Lincoln, let that be you and not a black bear coming for me.*

"I didn't cause you to have an accident."

She snorted. "And you also didn't break into my cabin and leave a save-the-date card, right? Why cross out the date? You claim to want me back—to love me. A giant red X across our wedding date doesn't exactly scream romance."

He fisted his hand in his hair and twisted his lips into a snarl. "I love you, but I'm still mad as hell. You got me locked up. Cost me my job, my future. That date...it was supposed to bring happiness and now it just pisses me off." He dropped his hands and stared at her with rounded eyes. "I want to start over. Erase everything in the past. Even the memory of June 3rd and what could have been."

His ramblings made no sense, but they never really did. Shay always bounced from thought to thought, lie to lie, spinning whatever web he could to confuse her and push his twisted agenda.

A loud twig snapped. Shay lunged for her, grabbing her

arm and pulling her in front of him like a human shield, his forearm across her neck.

She gripped his arm and clawed at the thick muscles locked around her throat. Fear dotted her vision. He would choke her right here in the woods and leave her dead body to be found.

Lincoln weaved through a cluster of trees, running toward them. He slowed as he approached, his jaw tight and narrowed eyes hard as rocks. "Let her go."

Relief at seeing Lincoln's face slowed her rapid heartrate. For once, she didn't have to face Shay alone. But she still needed to get away from him before he went too far.

"I don't know who you are but mind your own damn business. She wanted to come with me. Tell him, Brooke."

"Give it up, Shay. Lincoln won't let you walk away, and another officer is nearby. This won't end well for you." She wasn't sure where Cruz was, but no doubt Lincoln alerted him to the situation. "Tell us where Julia is."

"You'll never find her." He snarled in Brooke's ear. "I won't tell you shit. Not unless you come with me, and this guy walks away."

Brooke's mind waded through all the bits of information Shay had given. Each statement contradicted the next. She couldn't tell fact from fiction, but she was certain she couldn't go anywhere with him.

Tightening her grip on his arm, she dropped all her weight toward the ground.

Shay stumbled forward, and his arm loosened from across her throat.

She ducked her head, freeing herself from his hold. She launched to her feet, desperate to escape the monster who'd almost taken her life. She surged forward, and a hard yank to her hair pulled her backward.

Growling, Lincoln charged.

Shay wound her long ponytail around his fist. He slammed her head against the trunk of a tree before throwing her toward Lincoln and taking off into the forest.

Stars burst between her eyes. Pain exploded and nausea pitched in her stomach. Her knees gave out and she fell to the ground.

Lincoln's strong arms came around her, catching her before she hit the forest floor. She clung to him, her breaths hitching in her throat, making it hard to breathe.

He settled on the ground, never letting her go. "I got you. You're okay."

She buried her face in his neck, wincing when the tender spot on her head connected with his collarbone. "Go after him." She fought hard to get the words out even though the idea of him leaving her on the cold, wet ground was almost more than she could bear.

"No way. I won't leave you. Cruz can track him while I get you to the hospital."

She touched trembling fingers to the tender spot in the side of her forehead. "No hospital. I'm not even bleeding. I just want to go home."

Keeping her tucked against him, he rose to his feet and cradled her like a child. She wrapped her arms around his neck, and despite the trauma and the pain, a sense of safety and security overcame her.

For once in her life, she'd finally found someone to take care of her in exactly the way she wanted. Not by taking charge of her life or trying to be her white knight. But by showing up and being by her side. An overwhelming urge to cry had tears stinging her eyes. Because the man who'd finally stepped up was the one man who'd walk away in less than two weeks and return to his life far away from her.

Pent-up energy and a need to break Shay's nose had Lincoln struggling to sit on the sidelines. While Cruz and the local police scoured the area around Mel's Diner, he sat beside Brooke in her cabin and promised her Shay would be caught soon.

He could tell she didn't believe his bullshit any more than he did, but what else was he supposed to do? Brooke had been through hell the last two days, not to mention the physical stress and trauma she'd endured. The last thing she needed was to be out in the damp woods, searching for hours for signs of where Shay was holed up.

And the only way to keep Brooke from storming from her cabin and joining the search party was to sit with her.

"Are you hungry?" Needing to move, he rose and made his way to the kitchen that mirrored the one in his cabin.

Sitting on an overstuffed, cream-colored chair with her knees tucked to her chest, she shook her head then winced. "No way I could eat anything right now. But feel free to make yourself anything you want."

His own stomach pitched with anxiety, but he needed to keep himself busy. He spotted a single-cup coffee machine that used the little pods on the counter. "What about some coffee?"

She wrinkled her nose. "No, thanks. But tea would be nice."

He clapped his hands then rubbed his palms together. "Tea it is." Opening the cabinet above the coffee machine, he found the little plastic pods—divided into flavored coffees and teas. "Any requests?"

"Decaffeinated. I don't think my nerves can handle the buzz of caffeine right now."

He grabbed the pod, located a purple mug that read *Dog Mom,* and figured out the right combination of buttons to press in order to make the damn thing work. "You really should have one of these in all the cabins. That instant crap is disgusting."

A spark of mischief flashed in her tired eyes. "If I did that, most people wouldn't venture up to the lodge to get their morning fix."

Crossing his arms over his chest, he leaned against the counter and waited for the tea to stream into the mug. "So, it's a strategy, huh?"

"Exactly."

The door swung open, gaining his attention, and her dog ran into the room and jumped onto Brooke's lap. She cringed but wrapped her arms around his furry neck and rested her head against his. Zoe hurried in behind the dog, closing the door on the splatter of rain slanting inside. "Thought you'd want your buddy, so I swung by the kennel and picked him up. Tucker said you can leave him at the kennel any time, or he can stop by and grab him if Wyatt needs to get some energy out."

"Thank you." Brooke gave Wyatt another big squeeze before letting her arms fall to her sides.

"Should he be sitting on your lap? He has to weigh about as much as you." Lincoln slid out the now-steaming mug and set it on a glass coaster beside Brooke. "And who's Tucker?"

She smiled up at him. "You try and tell him he has to get down."

Lincoln snorted, not willing to try and move the giant ball of fur.

"Tucker's in charge of the Kennel. Used to be on the K-9 Unit before an accident led him here." Zoe took a seat on the ottoman in front of Brooke's chair and frowned. "Have you heard anything from Cruz or Chet?"

Brooke's smile fell. "Not yet."

"I can't believe this is happening," Zoe said. "How's Chet holding up?"

"He's losing his mind, and I don't blame him." Brooke shifted so Wyatt sat beside her then curled her palm around the mug. "Then for Shay to bounce back and forth between admitting to taking Julia and claiming to not know who she is. He's so infuriating."

Lincoln retraced his steps back to the kitchen and prepared a cup of coffee for himself. Brooke might not want the caffeine, but he'd need it to get through the rest of the day. "Zoe, can I get you anything?" he asked as the machine chugged to life once more.

"No, thanks. I don't have a lot of time. Just want to check in before heading into town. Is there anything I can do for you?"

Brooke shook her head.

Zoe glanced over her shoulder at Lincoln. "What about you?"

"I'm good."

Exhaling a long breath, she swept back onto her feet. "Sorry I have to run, but you look like you're in good hands."

The side of Brooke's mouth hitched up even as her gaze dropped to her tea. She offered Zoe a wave then lifted her mug to her lips.

Lincoln waited for Zoe to leave before he reclaimed his spot on the couch. Wyatt lifted his head, studying Lincoln's every move. He extended a hand to give the dog a chance to sniff him, then smoothed a palm over his soft fur.

"See. I told you that your hand would be safe."

He huffed out a laugh. "This time."

Any hints of amusement vanished from her face. "You don't have to babysit me. I'm fine. You have other reasons for being at the retreat besides making sure I'm all right."

A pinch of guilt squeezed his chest. "I'm not leaving you. Not again. If I would have stayed by your side earlier, Shay wouldn't have taken you. You wouldn't have been hurt. I should have known something was off. Should have sensed it."

"Shay's smarter than I gave him credit for," Brooke said. "He saw me come in with you and waited in that hallway until I was alone. When he dragged me outside, he used my weak spots. He knew if he threatened Julia, I'd do whatever he said. He's always known how to get what he wants. And now, he has his sights set on me."

Lincoln stared into the black coffee, his thoughts as jumbled as his emotions. Shay might have his sights on Brooke, but he wouldn't get his hands on her again.

At least not if Lincoln had anything to say about it.

11

Darkness washed over the porch of Lincoln's cabin, the hour late and the sky dark under a blanket of thick clouds. He'd spent the rest of the day with Brooke, unwilling to leave her alone. Especially when Cruz delivered the news that Shay was still at large.

Brooke had been visibly shaken when Cruz mentioned a tent set up a few miles from Mel's Diner. She'd been wrong about Shay's willingness to camp in the wilderness.

But Lincoln meant what he said. He wouldn't leave her until Shay was caught and Julia came home. Even if that meant sitting on his porch in the middle of the night, standing guard from a few feet away while Brooke got a good night's sleep.

Leaves rustled in the distance, and Lincoln jumped to his feet and squinted to study the thick brush around Brooke's cabin. He grabbed a flashlight and headed down the stairs, not trusting the sound to be only the breeze pushing around the outstretched limbs. With one hand on the sidearm tucked in his waistband, he moved quietly between the two structures—toward the noise.

A flash of movement caught his eye. He gripped the butt of his gun as a ball of cream-colored fur jolted through the brush. Wyatt moved low to the ground, teeth bared and the hair at the back of his neck pointed toward the sky.

Lincoln stopped and raised his hands as if in surrender. "Hi, boy. It's okay. I'm not going to hurt anyone. It's me, Lincoln." His heart pounded, the sound thudding against his eardrums, as he waited to find out if Wyatt would attack.

Wyatt straightened, wagged his tail, and charged with what Lincoln swore was a smile on his mouth. He stood on his back legs, placing his front paws on Lincoln's chest, and licked his cheeks.

Laughing, Lincoln reared back his head. The dog was cute, but he didn't want Wyatt's tongue anywhere near his face. Hell, he wasn't sure he wanted that tongue on him at all.

"I'm so glad I have such a good guard dog." Brooke's throaty chuckle quickened his pulse.

Lincoln scratched the dog's head and lifted his gaze to Brooke's front porch. She stood with her arms wrapped over her middle, keeping a thin red robe tucked around her.

Damn, what was it with her and that color? Siren's red. He'd never see it again without thinking of her.

Taking a step back, he let the dog's front paws drop back to the ground. "Don't be mad at him. He just knows one of the good guys when he sees him."

"Or he remembers the peanut butter you gave him earlier tonight." Shadows hid her delicate facial features, but there was no denying the amusement in her voice.

He rocked back on his heels. "Could be."

She started toward him, and a gust of wind whipped her hair across her face. Unfolding one arm from around her stomach, she tucked the strands behind her ears. The end of her robe flapped open, revealing the lacey tank top and skimpy shorts raising on her thighs underneath. She righted her robe, but not before the image was burned into his mind's eye.

God, now he'd never sleep. Knowing what she wore when lying in bed. Alone. Her cabin so damn close.

Stopping beside him, she tilted her head to the side, causing all the strands she'd just tamed to tumble over one shoulder. "What are you doing out here?"

He shrugged and studied the lake. "Couldn't sleep."

"And you heard my dog going outside to pee from inside your cabin while you couldn't sleep?"

He scrunched his nose, not wanting to admit to keeping an eye on her from his porch, but realizing she already knew the truth. "What can I say? He's a noisy rascal."

She huffed out a breath. "You don't need to keep watch. I'm fine."

Facing her, he took in the tight lines around the edges of her mouth and bags under her eyes. "Then why aren't you asleep?"

She sighed, her shoulders heaving up and down with the motion. "I just can't. Not when Julia is out there somewhere. Not when I know the type of pain Shay could be inflicting on her. I hate that we can't find him. It shouldn't be this hard."

"Shit like this never seems to be easy." She didn't respond, so he stood and listened to the sound of the lapping waves as they broke on the shore. Wyatt rubbed against his legs, nudging his hand with the top of his head to get some attention. "You should try to get some rest. Even if you can't sleep, close your eyes for a bit and let your body heal."

"If I head back inside, will you do the same? I'm not the

only one who needs rest." The side eye she gave told him that she already knew the answer to her question.

"If I tell you yes, will you believe me?"

She laughed, the sound weaving itself deep inside him. "Not at all."

"Then I guess we're at an impasse." No way he'd retreat into his cabin for the night. Too many things could happen that he couldn't hear from inside the thick walls. He refused to drop the ball again.

She swung her mouth to the side as if in deep thought. "We can't stand out here all night, so why don't you come inside? It's silly to be alone in our own cabins, on edge over every little noise."

A ball of excitement dropped straight to his toes. He cleared his throat, needing to push away the desire at the thought of spending the night with her—seeing her first thing in the morning. Even if nothing sexual happened, no matter how badly his body screamed to at least see if Brooke had the same reaction to him, staying with her all night was a kind of intimacy he seldom experienced with a woman. His dedication to his career had left a string of one-night-stands behind him and nothing more. "Are you sure? If I fall asleep on your couch, I might keep you awake with my snoring."

She raised her brows. "I thought you didn't plan to sleep?"

His jaw dropped and heat engulfed his body. He'd have to jump in the damn lake to cool himself off before he took her up on her invitation. It'd be hard enough to keep his hands to himself without her innocent words giving him the reaction of a horny teenager.

Slapping her hands over her mouth, a tiny squeak

leaked through her lips. "Oh, my God. I didn't mean that like it sounded."

"Don't worry about it. I know what you meant." He grazed a palm over her shoulder and gave a little squeeze. "Come on. Knowing our luck lately, it'll start raining again while we're out here."

Relief curved her lips. She patted the side of her thigh, Wyatt taking it as some kind of signal and falling into step beside her.

Staying in place, he watched her for a moment while he tried to calm his racing heart. He would keep his hands to himself, stay on the couch, and be there just in case she needed him. Nothing else. His intentions were purely for her safety and to encourage her to get a little sleep.

Hurrying along behind her, he shook his head at his own bullshit. He was falling for this woman faster than her SUV had hurled down the side of a mountain. He just hoped he wasn't in for another crash landing.

Brooke smoothed a hand over her hair, wishing she could disappear into the bathroom for a quick second and swipe on mascara or add a touch of blush. But no way Lincoln wouldn't notice if she emerged with fresh make-up.

Not like it mattered what she looked like. It was the middle of the night and they both needed to try and sleep. Nothing else. No matter how much her body craved his touch. No matter how curious she was to feel the difference between his smooth, shoulder-length locks and abrasive facial hair.

The hinges of the front door squeaked. Lincoln stood in

the doorway. Wyatt pranced in a circle in front of him until he bent down and scratched the dog behind his ears.

"You've made a friend for life." She snapped her fingers, gaining Wyatt's attention. "Go to your bed, buddy."

Tail still wagging, Wyatt trotted to his plush bed set up beside the fireplace.

"Impressive." Lincoln finally took a few steps inside, the soft glow of the single lamp highlighting the subtle blond strands in his light brown hair.

Unsure of what to do, Brooke headed for the couch. He might have said he wanted her to sleep, but no way could she lay in bed while he lingered in her living room. "Thanks. I did most of the training, but Tucker helped a lot. He's like that dog whisperer guy. I'll take you down to the kennel tomorrow so you can see how the dog therapy works, and you can meet Tucker."

He strolled to the mantle and ran a finger along the thick wooden beam. "You don't have to do that. I can find it myself. You have enough going on without having to be my personal tour guide."

She ignored the sting of disappointment. Lincoln was here because he'd been through a severe trauma while in the line of duty. He wouldn't get past that and reinstated if he kept spending all his time with her.

"Is this your grandfather?" He gestured toward a framed photograph.

She smiled. "That's him. I was about ten when that picture was taken. We'd just taken first place in a canoe race across the lake. All of my best memories are with him."

He lifted the frame and studied the picture for a beat before returning it. "I was close to my grandfather, too. My whole family was a mess when he died. My mother especially. We'd lost my dad a few years prior, so it was really hard to lose her own father."

"I'm sorry. That must have been difficult." Even though sympathy pooled in her gut, she couldn't help but be envious. When her own grandfather passed, she'd had no one to help her process her grief. Her mama was too angry that she hadn't received any money to comfort her daughter. Her grandfather had passed everything down to Brooke.

Something Glenda never failed to remind her of when Brooke hesitated to give her money.

Tucking in his lips, he crossed the space and sat on the opposite end of the couch. "We got through it, but I'm sure you don't want to hear about any of that."

She shifted to face him, propping up one knee on the soft cushion while her other foot stayed pressed against the floor. "I'd like to hear more about what made you decide to come here, if you don't mind sharing. I could use a distraction right now."

He mimicked her pose then hooked an arm over the back of the couch and blew out a long breath. "I told you about the car accident."

"That much I'd read in your file." Each guest supplied information regarding why they'd chosen—or been forced—to come to the retreat. Some people needed to heal physically before returning to work, others emotionally, while most needed to work on both aspects of their well-being. A few, like her and most of the staff, would never wear a uniform again and needed an escape and chance to wrap their minds around such a huge loss. "But why did you choose this specific place?"

He wrinkled his nose and rubbed a hand up and down the back of his head, tousling his long strands. "My captain gave the order to get my head on straight while my hand healed. Cruz mentioned this place, and it seemed as good as any."

She arched up a brow and grinned. "You mean it seemed as horrible as all the rest?"

A low rumble of laughter shook his chest, the sound as smooth and sweet as honey. "Something like that. But if Cruz was close, all the better. We don't get to see each other as much as I'd like. This would kill two birds with one stone."

"Has your hand gotten any better since the accident?" She asked, dipping her chin toward the hand resting on top of his thigh.

He made a fist, wincing when it didn't tighten all the way. "A little. I have exercises from my occupational therapist I do every day. But it's still not where it needs to be. I can't grip my gun properly or pull the trigger tight enough."

"I understand how frustrating that can be. Keep working on improving your strength. That's all you can do."

Relaxing his hand, he nodded and turned his gaze to the unlit logs in the fireplace. "As much as it annoys me, the hand is the easy stuff. I can do something to fix the problem. I can act. The other stuff is harder."

She scooted forward, leaning close to hear his quiet words. Wrinkles deepened on his forehead and a vacant stare—similar to the one he'd had when trapped in the SUV —haunted his expression. The urge to ask questions sat on her tongue, but she didn't want to push.

"The guy's still out there. The one who slammed into my cruiser and messed up my life. I couldn't get out of the car and chase the bastard down. He disappeared into a crowd of people and hasn't turned up since. I couldn't stop him— couldn't put him in a cage where he belongs." Blinking, he smoothed the tortured lines of his face. "I keep imagining all the things he could be doing right now. All the people he could be hurting."

Wanting to comfort him, she slid her arm over the back of the couch until her hand touched his and linked their fingers. "You did what you could, and when you're back in Nashville, you can find him and finish the job."

Flipping over his palm, he squeezed her hand. A hint of sadness glazed over his bright blue irises. "The entire police force is searching the city and nothing. The guy just vanished. I can only hope that means he's laying low for a while. Keeping out of trouble. I arrested his drug supplier, but that doesn't mean he doesn't have connections with another. Not to mention the domestic violence hits the asshole has on his record. He could have returned to the backwoods town he'd ran from as a troubled teenager—out of my hair, but also out of reach with no way to stop him from finding a new supplier and hitting the streets again."

She grimaced, the idea of any person enduring abuse at the hands of a loved one hitting way too close to home. "Guy sounds like a real peach."

He grazed his thumb over her skin, sending shivers of delight through her entire body. "A kid is dead because of the drugs he sold him. Good kid, too. Had his whole life taken away from him because he made one mistake—was a little too curious for a taste of the wild side. It's not fair." He ran a shaky hand over his beard.

"That's the one part about the job I don't miss. Knowing so many criminals worked the system or walked away from a crime, and I couldn't do anything about it. Could never hold every one of them accountable."

"That is a hard pill to swallow," he said. "But this one impacted me more than the rest. And the fact that he's still out there really pisses me off." He fisted his hands, grimacing when he couldn't tighten his injured hand.

She dipped one corner of her mouth. "I'm sorry." The words wouldn't do a damn thing to help him, but it was all she had to offer. "I wanted a distraction and made you talk about something that's just bringing you down."

He lifted a shoulder. "That's why I'm here, right? To open up about all this shit?"

"I thought you were here to spend all your time in the gym and ignore everything else?" Teasing, she offered him a small smile.

"Someone told me I might be surprised about what I find here, and I think she might be right." He dropped his gaze to her mouth.

Instinct had her licking her lips. She wanted nothing more than to lean forward and sample a taste of Lincoln, but what was the point? He'd be gone in a little over a week. Not to mention how unprofessional it would be to get involved with one of her guests. Curse her damn luck that the only man after Shay to inspire a fluttering of emotion inside her would be out of her life so soon. She couldn't risk her battered heart with a man who was nothing more than a casual acquaintance.

Even if her heart screamed that Lincoln Sawyer could be so much more.

Sliding out her hand from under his, she stood and averted her gaze. If he could somehow see how badly she wanted him—and act on it—she'd never be able to resist. "It's getting really late. I should try to sleep."

"Okay. Do you mind if I crash on the couch? I'm not sure if I'll get any shut eye here or not, but no way I will back at my cabin. Not with everything that's going on, and even though you say people here don't lockup, having a deadbolt that doesn't lock keeps me on edge."

She frowned. "Your locks should be fine."

"The wood on the doorframe is splintered," he said on a shrug. "The lock doesn't have a place to stick in the wood. I just figured it wasn't a big deal for ya'll to fix."

"We might be trusting around here, but we don't expect that out of everyone who stays here. Especially guests who've endured trauma. I'll put in a maintenance order to get it fixed right away. I don't know how that was overlooked when your cabin was prepared." A twinge of unease tickled her spin. Could Shay have tampered with more than one cabin? She'd have to make sure none of the other homes had any issues.

"Thanks, but I plan to stick by your side anyway until Shay is caught. That is, if you don't mind my staying."

Gratitude for his chivalry battled with a need to get far away from him for the sake of her own sanity. "Sure. Is the blanket thrown over the couch enough for you? I can grab a pillow from my bed."

He yanked the throw pillow from behind his back. "This is fine and so is the blanket."

Not trusting her voice, she dipped her chin then retreated to her bed in the far corner of the room. For the first time since moving in, she cursed the lack of walls in the studio-style home. She might be in the furthest spot in the room from Lincoln, but he was still so close she could hear his every movement as he tossed and turned on the couch. Burrowing under her blanket, she closed her eyes and tried to ignore the need pulsing in her core.

And tried to forget that a man she was falling hard for was mere feet away, and there wasn't a damn thing she could do to keep him around.

12

Something cold pushed against Lincoln's hand, jerking him out of a deep sleep. He sat up, heart pumping wildly at the unknown sensation, and found himself eye-to-eye with the most pathetic stare he'd ever seen. A high-pitched whine poured from Wyatt's mouth, and his tail whipped so hard across the floorboards, it kicked up stray bits of dust.

Lincoln stretched his arms above his head and scanned the room. The clock on the cable box blinked 6:00 a.m. Brooke lay curled on her side in the corner of the bed. A slim calf poked out from under the covers, and his throat went dry before focusing his attention back on Wyatt. "What do you need, boy?" he asked in a whisper.

Wyatt turned his head toward the door then back to Lincoln.

He groaned, his tired and stiff muscles not ready to face the day. But he couldn't lay here under the dog's watchful eyes and not offer him the relief he needed. Rubbing his palms over his scruffy cheeks, he sighed and clamored to his feet. "Okay. Let's do this. Just let me get my shoes."

Shaking his head, he found his discarded sneakers by the front door and jammed his feet inside them. Why was he talking to the damn dog? Must be the fact he'd only managed to get three hours of sleep. After Brooke had hurried to bed, he'd laid awake forever talking himself into staying put. He'd wrestled with the idea of following her and acting on the impulse to take her in his arms and kiss the hell out of her.

But what would be the point? They'd share one unbelievable night together, then he'd be gone and she'd be alone. Again. He couldn't do that to Brooke. She was special, and the woman had been through enough shit in her life that she didn't need him adding any more complications. Especially now.

Not to mention the way she'd practically ran from him when he'd pushed things too far last night. But man, she made it so damn hard to keep his distance. Something he needed to be more mindful of in the next few days. He still wanted to stay close in case Shay struck again, but he had to be more careful about revealing the way she made him feel.

Being as quiet as possible, he opened the front door and stepped onto the porch with Wyatt pushing past him. He kept an eye on the dog as he pranced around the grass along the front and side of the cabin. The sun had penetrated the thick clouds and warmed the faint coolness that had lingered the day before. He might not have gotten much sleep, but it'd be enough to get him through the day. Hell, he'd survived on much less.

Once Wyatt finished his business, he bounced back up the porch steps and trotted to the closed door. He glanced behind him at Lincoln.

"Wow, you're demanding, aren't you?" Growing up, he'd never had a dog but loved the expectant way Wyatt looked at him, as if Lincoln were here for the sole purpose of doing as the dog wished. And seeing how the big furball had roused him from sleep at 6:00 a.m., that might be exactly what ran through Wyatt's mind.

Opening the door, the scent of fresh, strong coffee assaulted his still-sleepy senses. Brooke stood with her back to him as she waited for a mug of coffee to fill. Rich, brown hair tumbled down her back, tousled and messy in a way that made him want to fist the strands in his hands. She skimmed one bare toe over the side of her leg, and God help him if it wasn't the sexiest sight he'd ever seen.

Pressure built in his chest, and he rubbed a hand over his heart. Damn, he had it bad. Not wanting to startle her, he cleared his throat. "Morning. How'd you sleep?"

"Better than I expected." The machine made a hissing noise as the last bit of water seeped out, and Brooke turned toward him and offered the mug. "Yesterday you drank it black. Is that okay, or do you want cream or sugar?"

What he wanted was to set the steaming mug on the kitchen counter, haul her ass back to bed, and savor a glimpse of her delicious body beneath the tank top and shorts she'd worn to sleep. Instead, he accepted her offering and took a quick sip of the piping hot liquid in order to pull himself together. "Black's fine."

"Did Cruz call at all?" She asked and prepared the machine to make another cup of coffee.

"I didn't get a chance to check my phone. Your dog was pretty insistent I let him outside as soon I woke up." He scooped his phone off the end table where he'd left it the night before. "No calls or messages." Content to watch her, he settled into a chair tucked behind the kitchen table.

She opened the fridge and pulled out a bottle of liquid creamer. "Sorry about that. I can be a pretty deep sleeper.

He probably tried to wake me, then ran to you when I didn't budge."

Stretching out his legs, he crossed them at the ankles and took another sip. "Not a problem. Whatever I have to do to stay on his good side."

"Between the treats last night and letting him pee this morning, I think you're safe." She doctored her coffee then replaced the creamer in the fridge. "Are you hungry? I don't have a lot here but could manage something if you want breakfast."

"I'm good." There was only one thing she could offer him right now to curb his appetite, and it had nothing to do with food. He really should get the hell out of here and never look back, but for the life of him he couldn't peel himself off the chair to leave.

Squeezing her eyes shut, Brooke's shoulders fell and she scrunched up her nose. "Breakfast. Oh man, why didn't I think about Chet needing help this morning? The last thing he needs to worry about is cooking."

Lincoln lowered his mug to the table. "The guy was a mess yesterday. Is there anyone around who can cover for him?"

Brooke opened her eyes wide and lifted her lips in a smile that didn't hold one ounce of joy. "Me."

Of course she'd offer, even with her own past returning to blow up in her face. "What time is breakfast served?"

She flicked her gaze at the clock on the stove. "In about an hour."

"Then we better hurry up and get to the lodge." Standing, he gulped half the contents of his mug then winced as it burned all the way down his throat.

She cocked her head to the side, eyes narrowed. "We?"

"You don't think I'm going to make you cook for

everyone alone, do you? I know how to crack an egg or two. I'll shower and dress and meet you back here in fifteen minutes. Does that work?"

Her wide smile stayed in place, but this time there was no denying the happiness that poured from it. "Well, all right then."

He cast her a brief salute then hurried to his cabin. Keeping his distance while living yards away from Brooke wasn't possible. He'd just make sure to keep a tight leash on any feelings brewing, help keep her safe, then leave when his time here was done.

His only fear was that when his two weeks came to an end, leaving Brooke behind might be more difficult than he expected.

BREAKFAST at the retreat was a pretty low-key affair. With only a dozen guests, Brooke didn't want a full menu, but wanted options if they chose to come to the dining hall for food.

She'd lucked out when Cruz introduced her to Chet. He was an amazing chef and loved to bake. He claimed spending time in the kitchen—especially baking—helped him deal with his PTSD. So every morning a small buffet was available for the guests at 8:30 a.m., with Chet highlighting a different feature each day.

Today, the smell of homemade cinnamon rolls straight from the oven wafted through the hallway from the kitchen. The scent of vanilla icing and warm cinnamon usually made Brooke's mouth water, but not this morning.

This morning, the inviting aroma surrounded her like a

cloak of sadness instead. Reminding her that Julia wasn't here to plate the pastries.

With Lincoln by her side, she entered the kitchen and her heart dropped to the floor at the sight of Chet's watery eyes and broken spirit. He sat on a stool pushed against the steel counter in the middle of the room.

Zoe lifted a pan of pastries from the oven and slid it onto the counter. She wiped the back of her forearm over her brow and threw an oven mitt beside the pan of rolls. "Morning. Didn't expect to see you here, Brooke. Hi, Lincoln." A smirk played on her lips for a beat as she eyed him.

Brooke crossed the room to Chet and wrapped him in a hug, wishing she could absorb all his pain. "We thought we'd stop in and help get breakfast served." Keeping her hands braced on Chet's biceps, she pulled back and dipped her chin to lock her gaze with his. "How you holding up?"

He pulled in a shuddering breath. "Not good."

"Have you spoken with Cruz this morning?"

Chet shook his head.

"You don't need to be here right now. We've got this covered." She swept a hand through the air, unable to hide a smile at Zoe whisking a bowl of eggs with a white apron wrapped around her black yoga pants and Lincoln digging for something in the industrial refrigerator.

Chet lifted his large shoulders. "What else am I supposed to do? Just sit around and wait to hear something? I'll go crazy if I don't do anything."

Sliding her palm down his arm, she found his hand and squeezed. "I get that. But just know we're all here for you. For whatever you need."

"'Preciate that." Slowly, he pushed himself to his feet. "But right now, I need to make sure everyone has enough food to eat."

"Tell me what you need me to do."

The next thirty minutes Brooke worked alongside the makeshift kitchen crew, preparing breakfast and placing it in the dining room. She'd never again take for granted the meals she ate. Cooking had never been her thing, and now she remembered why. After the buffet was broken down and the kitchen cleaned, she slumped against the counter and shoved a cinnamon roll in her mouth.

Lincoln took a spot beside her, leaning against the counter and hooking his mouth into a grin. He wiped a thumb over the corner of her mouth. "You missed a little icing."

She eyed the drip of white frosting on his finger and the urge to lick it off had heat creeping up her neck.

Lincoln sucked the icing from his finger, and Brooke almost melted.

Zoe threw a dish rag into a pile of dirty towels. "I need to get going. If there's anything else I can do, call me."

"Thanks for everything, Zoe." Chet sank back onto the stool and leaned his forearms on the smooth silver table. "All of you. You don't know how much your help means." His voice cracked, and he dropped his head into his hands.

Zoe rubbed a palm over his shoulder, gave a little wave, then disappeared from the room.

"I need to get these towels in the wash and grab the dirty laundry from the gym and pool too." Brooke scooped the soiled linens into her hands and glanced at Lincoln. "Thank you. For everything." She wanted to tell him to go find something useful to do for himself—something to improve his mindset, maybe hit the gym. But the idea of him not being by her side made a hollow pit inside her open up. A feeling that both fascinated and terrified her. *Was she falling for him?* She eyed him from the side, the thought both terrifying and exciting.

Lincoln nodded then shifted his gaze to Chet. "You want to go for a run? I'd love to get outside and don't know the lay of the land. Would be nice to have someone with me."

Brooke fought the urge to throw the towels in the air and wrap her arms around Lincoln. She didn't want Chet to be alone but didn't want to make him feel as though she were altering her schedule. He'd hate that and insist she stop watching over him like a child. But if a guest needed assistance, Chet would be hard-pressed to deny the request.

Even if all three of them knew Lincoln just wanted to be close to the big man too, not wanting him to be left alone to wait for answers.

Chet scratched the dark whiskers on his chin. "I could probably do that. I'm not much of a runner though."

"That's fine," Lincoln said. "I'm a little out of a shape these days. How about I get changed really quick and meet you back here?"

A sharp rap on the edge of the door caught her attention. Cruz stood with his cowboy hat wedged in his hands, pressed against his heart with the weight of the world evident on his shoulders. The deep lines around his tightly pressed lips didn't bode well. "That run's gonna have to wait. I'm afraid I have some bad news."

Brooke wrapped her arm around the crook of Lincoln's elbow and held her breath. "What is it?"

Cruz drew back his shoulders as if summoning more strength than his body held and met Chet's wide, terrified eyes. "I'm so sorry, Chet. Julia's body was just found. She's dead."

His words fell into the room like a grenade, exploding the lives of everyone inside. Brooke's legs threatened to buckle, and she leaned against Lincoln to keep herself upright. A wave of grief washed through her, pressing against her organs and making it hard to breathe. Julia was so young, had so much life ahead of her, and now she was gone. Ripped away from her family and friends, and for what?

Unable to face the horror on Chet's face, Brooke dropped her gaze to the floor. Her past had stormed back with a vengeance, but this time Shay wasn't just after her. This time, he'd killed an innocent girl.

Because of Brooke, Julia was dead.

13

Lincoln poured through the case notes Cruz had handed over as they made their way to the crime scene. He could give two shits if he wasn't a part of the Pine Valley Police Force, no one would keep him away from the spot in the woods where Julia Holmes' body had been dumped.

Luckily for him, no one on the small force—or the heartbroken chef—argued about the big-city cop pushing his way onto the investigation. He had far more experience working suspicious deaths than any other officer in Pine Valley, and he'd use it to find justice for Julia.

Cruz pulled into a parking lot surrounded by trees at the entrance of a city park. He slid his cruiser into an empty spot next to another cop car and sighed as he unhooked his seatbelt and rubbed his fingers over closed eyelids. "I can't believe this is happening."

Lincoln flipped to the next page of notes, wanting another look at Shay's criminal record. Besides the domestic abuse and brief stint in jail for almost killing Brooke, the guy's rap sheet was pretty damn clean. "Stuff like this is always a hard pill to swallow. All we can do now is make sure whoever did this is caught and punished for his crimes."

Cruz dropped his hand to the steering wheel and aimed his hard stare out the windshield. "Don't worry about that. I'll make sure Shay Lawrence doesn't ever see the light of day."

"Dude, I get the anger and frustration you're feeling right now, but you need a clear head to do your job. No assumptions. No thinking you have the details all figured out before we work the scene. That's how things get missed."

Cruz swung his slack jaw and narrowed eyes at Lincoln. "What the hell does that mean? You think I'm messing this up? That because I'm not some fancy Nashville cop anymore I can't nail the bastard who came into *my* town and killed an innocent girl?"

Biting into his cheeks, Lincoln kept a firm grip on his temper. Not only did he understand the whirlwind of Cruz's emotions right now, he felt them. Each and every one. Ever since they were kids, he and Cruz could always tune into what the other felt. And in this instance, not only was the stupid empathetic bullshit messing with his senses, but he had his own shit invested which raised the stakes. "Knock it off. You're angry. I'm angry. Hell, I'm sure the whole damn town is angry. And we all should be. I'm saying you need a clear head and open eyes for what we're about to walk into."

His words were true, and Cruz knew that even without the lecture, but Lincoln also couldn't ignore the pressure squeezing his gut after finally getting his hands on Shay's record. Was the man violent? Absolutely. Did his past show he was capable of hurting a woman? Without a doubt. But what was the point of kidnapping and murdering a woman he'd just met?

He'd keep his doubt and questions to himself until after seeing the crime scene. Cruz was wrapped up so tight in this case, Lincoln didn't want to pump anything else into his head. He wanted his brother to come up with his own conclusion about what was happening. And Lincoln would do the same.

Cruz tightened his jaw. "You're right. I'm sorry. This is just a whole new level for me. Our town is quiet. Shit like this doesn't happen here. At least not since I've been around. And this isn't some woman I've never met. I knew her, damnit." His voice cracked and he drew in a shuddering breath.

A stab of regret pierced Lincoln's chest. How could he be so stupid to not understand the depth of Cruz's pain right now? He rested a hand on his brother's shoulder. "It's not the same, man. You couldn't have stopped what happened to Julia any more than you could have stopped what happened to Diana."

Cruz slumped against the seat, his chin tipped toward the ceiling. "I should have been able to get to them both before the worst happened. I failed Julia just like I failed Diana, and they're both dead because I couldn't do my job."

Lincoln had tried for years to help Cruz see that it wasn't his fault that his fiancé died. The robbery they'd walked in on had shocked them both, and Cruz couldn't be responsible for the stray bullet that took Diana's life. Diana's death was what pushed Cruz into moving away from Nashville—claiming he needed somewhere a little slower-paced to hang his hat. Wanting a small town where he could do his job without the pressures that came with every damn day in a uniform in a city the size of Nashville.

And now, five years later, he faced the death of another

young woman. A woman who was close to the same age Diana had been when she'd died.

"This isn't on you, any more than Diana getting shot in that convenience store is on you. But just like with Diana, we can work together to find the bastard responsible and lock him up. As long as you're up to it."

Cruz didn't respond for a long beat, then finally opened his eyes, grabbed a duffle bag from the backseat, and gripped the door handle. "I am. Let's do this."

Lincoln nodded and pushed out his door to meet Cruz at the front of the vehicle. The rain from the day before was gone, but a lingering humidity made the air thick and sticky. The sun beat down, making the pavement the shining spot of light amidst the shadows beneath the thick canopy of leaves surrounding the parking lot.

"She was left up the trail a little ways." Cruz dipped his head toward one of several signs marking the different paths for hikers and tourists to enjoy along the rugged Smoky Mountains.

Lincoln studied the area as they trudged up the hill on the dirt path, searching for anything that was out of place or could be a clue to explain how Julia ended up in the middle of the woods. A dip in the trail led them to a spot of activity that stood out in stark contrast to the calm of nature around them. Yellow crime scene tape weaved between trees, marking off the area from any hikers who might stumble along. A grim-faced officer stood just off the path, either to block the view from anyone approaching or because he couldn't face what was behind him.

The yellowish tinge to his baby-face made Lincoln bet on the latter.

"Beau." Cruz dipped his chin. "Thanks for blocking off the area."

"The least I could do, Sir. No one's been back here since you left, and the coroner is on her way. She said she might need help transporting the body to her van." Beau kept his face lax, but a slight tremor shook the last part of his statement.

"Not a problem." Cruz tilted his head toward Lincoln. "This is my brother. Officer Lincoln Sawyer out of Nashville. He has more experience than any of us on these kinds of cases, and he's offered his assistance."

Beau turned large green eyes filled with sadness and a hint of fear his way. "Nice to meet you. I'm eager to help any way I can."

Lincoln tucked in his lips, impressed with the young man's demeanor despite the gruesome circumstances. "Keep doing what you're doing, Officer."

Cruz swung his bag off his shoulder and dug his hand inside. He pulled out a couple pairs of latex gloves and handed over a pair.

Lincoln stuffed his hands into the stretchy material, inhaling the familiar scent he'd never thought he'd miss so much, then crouched low to study the ground. "Did anyone make note of the tracks found leading up to and around the body when they got here?"

"Only one set of footprints was found when I arrived this morning, and they matched the tread marks from the hiker who found her."

Lincoln swept away leaves and underbrush as he approached the body. "Could Julia and the killer have gotten to this site from any other way, or is the path the only option?"

"Hard to tell," Cruz said, staying close to his side. "A rock-faced hill slopes down the mountain on the south side of where the body is. Chances are pretty low they climbed up that way, but I wouldn't be surprised if time of death is earlier than the time she was dumped here. I don't think this is the kill site."

Lincoln had assumed as much but wanted to wait to get cause of death before working with the theory Julia was carried to this spot after her death. "What about coming down the path from the opposite end? Not from the lot where we parked."

"Not impossible for him to approach from that way but would have been one hell of a hike. Only other place for him to leave a vehicle would be another entrance to the park, which has to be close to twenty miles away, up and down some pretty difficult terrain."

The buzzing of flies vibrated his eardrums. He steadied his nerves as the putrid stench of death invaded his nostrils. Julia's lifeless form lay face-up on the ground, eyelids closed.

Lincoln's feet turned to lead, and all the air left his lungs. An image of another body, another life taken too soon, swept into his mind's eye and threatened to suck him back into a vortex of darkness.

"What's wrong?" Cruz narrowed his gaze, a hint of worry shining through his blue eyes.

Lincoln knelt and examined Julia's hands. "Her lips and fingernails are blue. Consistent with an opioid overdose."

Cruz rubbed the back of his neck. "You think she died of an overdose?"

"Can't say for sure until we get the autopsy, but there are no other marks on her. No death wound." He stood, his mind spinning. Leaning to the side, he studied the exposed veins that lined the inside of her arm. Clean with no marks on one arm. Tilting to the other side, he nodded toward the telling sign of a needle mark on her inner forearm. "Track mark. Only one."

"So, what? Shay grabbed her from her car, gave her drugs, then dumped her here? That doesn't even make sense."

"We need to look at Julia's past. See if there's a history of drug use. Just because there aren't any other track marks doesn't mean she hadn't experimented with other types of narcotics. My gut says Julia didn't do this to herself, especially with the bruising on her neck that appears to be from a taser, but we need to be positive." Lincoln stole another glimpse of Julia. Drug use wasn't consistent with what he knew of Shay's past, but they were way too similar to another criminal who was holed up somewhere in Nashville. A man who gave tainted drugs to the unsuspecting just to keep his profits high. "Either Shay Lawrence is playing a sick game with all of us, or he isn't the one who killed Julia."

A CRACK SEVERED Brooke's heart in two as she stood beside Chet in the morgue while he made a positive identification of Julia. There hadn't been any doubt of who Cruz found in the woods, but protocol had to be followed. And no way in hell would Brooke let Chet stand alone in a cold room and look into the lifeless eyes of his cousin.

Chet brushed a gentle hand over Julia's cheek while tears fell down his face. "She had so much to offer. So much to look forward to. How could I let this happen?"

Pressure threatened to burst through Brooke's sinus cavity as she struggled to hold back her own tears. Now wasn't the time to fall apart and wallow in the guilt eating her from the inside out. Now was the time to stand tall, be strong, and show Chet the support he desperately needed. "This isn't your fault."

"It sure as hell feels like it." His shoulders trembled as he tried not to break down. "Look at her. How could someone do this?"

"I don't know. It's all so senseless." Brooke didn't want to look at the scab on Julia's lip that would never heal, from where she'd been struck at the bar, or the new marks on her neck. Marks that were consistent with being caught off-guard with a taser.

So impersonal.

So calculating.

Her mind raced as she mentally flipped through everything she knew about Shay, as well as everything she'd learned during her time in uniform. Shay had come close to ending her life, so she didn't doubt his ability to lash out. He was a hot-head with a violent streak. A man who acted on impulse then fell to his knees to beg forgiveness. Could he really carry out such a cold-hearted plan?

"I'm so sorry, sweetheart. I should have protected you." Chet placed a kiss on Julia's forehead then headed for the door. No words were spoken until he climbed into the passenger side of his truck, Brooke sitting behind the wheel. "I need a drink."

"I know just the place." Turning over the engine, she pulled away from the county morgue and headed for the Chill N' Grill. The restaurant would be empty this time of day, and Wade had a much better selection of alcohol then she did. Not like it mattered to Chet. Nothing would take the edge off losing Julia.

Ten minutes later, Wade stood behind the bar, wiping down glassware. His eyes widened, then filled with a glassy sheen he quickly sniffed away.

Chet climbed onto a stool and dropped his clasped

hands onto the bar, rubbing his thumb over the thick skin of his wrist.

Brooke sat next to him, wanting so badly to consume his pain—pain that should have been heaped on her shoulders alone. Not Chet's, who'd already lost so much. Not Julia's, who didn't deserve to have her young life cut short.

Wade set a shot glass in front of her and then crouched to grab a bottle of whiskey from under the bar. He filled each little glass then poured one for himself. He lifted the glass in the air. "To Julia."

Brooke and Chet followed suit. "To Julia."

Brooke swallowed the liquor in one gulp and winced as it burned all the way down her throat.

Wade refilled Chet's glass and offered him a tight smile. "I'm so sorry, man. Let me know if there's anything I can do."

Chet tipped his head back in acknowledgement, his stony stare aimed straight ahead.

Wade flicked a concerned look at Brooke, then returned to wiping down the beer glasses.

A vibration in her pocket alerted her to a call. She jumped off her stool and fished out the phone. "I'm going to take this call over in the corner. I'll be right back."

Chet grunted and shot back the whiskey.

Keeping one eye on Chet, Brooke answered the phone. "Hello?"

"Hey, Brooke. It's Lincoln. Do you know where Chet is?"

Despite the sadness pulling down her heart, the deep timbre of Lincoln's voice brought a small smile to her face. "I'm with him at the Chill N' Grill. He needed a drink after identifying Julia."

"I bet, and I hate to do this, but Cruz and I need to talk to him. Can you drive him back to his place?"

The tightness of Lincoln's words set her on edge even

more. "Sure. What's going on? Are you okay? Did you find something?"

A beat of silence passed. "Something about the crime scene felt off to me. I'm not sure if I trust my judgement. I need to bounce some things off you when you get here."

"Okay. We'll be right there." She disconnected and hated the excitement over seeing Lincoln again brewing inside her. Excitement was the last thing she should be feeling when a good friend was so broken, and a young woman was gone forever.

14

Exhaustion like he hadn't experienced in over a month—not since he'd been forced to take a leave of absence while his hand healed—weighed down on Lincoln. He loved his job but hadn't missed the heaviness of a case that he couldn't quite figure out.

Especially when a murderer was on the loose, running free until he could put every little piece of the puzzle together.

He sat at the oval kitchen table in Chet's one-bedroom apartment—a cabin turned duplex tucked back in the woods—and flipped open the file he and Cruz had put together after leaving the crime scene. A part of him wanted to hide the pictures taken of Julia, but he'd ask Chet if he preferred to see them or not. Not much could be worse than seeing the poor girl on a cold slab of metal in the morgue.

Brooke leaned toward him, taking in the handwritten notes.

He covered them with his arm, blocking her view.

She scowled. "You're not going to let me see what you and Cruz found? Why did you want me here then?"

"I want your take of what's going on. You, Cruz, and Chet." He dipped his head toward each of them as he spoke their names. "We all have personal ties to this case. I don't want to fill your head with anything until I see things from your own viewpoint."

"There's a lot of people working this case right now," Cruz said. "But you're the only one who has a history with one of the suspects."

Chet raised his hound dog eyes from the glass of water gripped in his palm. "Suspects? I thought ya'll knew exactly who did this. You mean to tell me it could be someone else?"

"Every case needs to be approached without assumptions. This isn't any different." Lincoln focused on Chet, needing him to open up, but not wanting to push him too far. Cruz had filled him in on the man's past—the tragic death of his wife and child years before. Dealing with such a hard blow again had to be soul-crushing. "Chet, is there anyone at all Julia had issues with?"

He shook his head. "Not that I recall. She hasn't been in Pine Valley very long. Moved here after school was over. She needed a job and thought being at the retreat could be fun. Brooke was kind enough to let her stay at the lodge. I don't think she's even made many friends outside of work."

"We need the names of the employees she spent her time with." Cruz slid a pencil and paper over the table toward Chet.

A deep frown pulled down Brooke's mouth, and wrinkles creased her furrowed brow. "You think someone who works for me could have done this?"

"Like I said, we need open minds to see every angle," Lincoln said. "What about before Julia moved here? People from her school she didn't get along with? An old boyfriend who she may have argued with?"

Propping his elbow on the table, Chet rested his head in his hand and rubbed his fingers over the bridge of his nose. "We already went over this when you found her car. No boyfriend, few friends. Even back in school in Nashville, she was a serious student who didn't take any risks. Studied hard and stayed out of trouble. What's the point of doing it again?" He shoved an angry hand through his hair.

Lincoln's gut clenched. So many coincidences crossed his path with those he found himself surrounded by. But Nashville was a big city, and the chances of a student at a prestigious university crossing over to the sketchy areas of East Nashville he worked in were slim to none. "We could have missed something." Lincoln met Brooke's hard stare, the churning of her brain clear as day behind her brown eyes.

"What do you think we missed? Something stood out to you. Something has you doubting Shay is the one behind this."

Her ability to read his mind had him drawing in a sharp breath. He couldn't tell if it was because of her past experience on the job, or because after only a few days she knew him so damn well. Either way, it was time to get her take on what happened to Julia. "I want your impressions before we go over what's in the file."

She rounded her eyes and fiddled with the edge of the table. "I'm not sure what you want me to tell you. I didn't see Julia before she was at the morgue."

Sensing her hesitancy, Lincoln covered her fidgeting fingers with his hand. "I want to know what your gut instinct was when you saw her. What went through your mind?"

Chet shot to his feet and slapped the glass of water from the table. "Shit. What the hell is this about? You want to know what went through Brooke's mind when she saw my murdered cousin? You want to know what went through *my* mind when I saw Julia on that slab? I can tell you right now. Outrage. Horror. Guilt. God almighty, how will this help find the asshole who did this to her?" His voice caught and tears rimmed his dark lashes, hovering over the edge.

Cruz rose and placed a hand on Chet's shoulder. "Why don't you and I get some fresh air?"

"Fine." Chet stalked across the kitchen to the back door, yanked it open, and stormed outside.

"Good idea," Lincoln said. "Looks like he needs a little more time before he jumps into this."

Cruz nodded then hurried out the door, closing it tight behind him.

Brooke dropped her head in her hands, and her shoulders shook on a sob. "I'm sorry. I've been with Chet all morning. I couldn't fall apart in front of him. Couldn't just let go for a second. He deserves so much better than this. Julia deserved so much better than this."

Lincoln slid his chair as close as he could and wrapped an arm over her shoulder, guiding her head to lean against him. "You're right. They both deserve better, and we will make sure that Chet gets justice for his cousin."

She buried her face in his neck and let the tears fall, soaking into his shirt. "That will help a little, but it won't bring her back. He'll never get over this."

The truth of her words fisted around his heart. He hated she was right—hated knowing the same was true for Cruz. Cruz would live with the pain of Diana's death for the rest of his life, just like Chet would carry the pain of losing Julia. "He might never get over it but knowing the person responsible for ending her life is in jail will help him live with it."

Sniffing back her tears, Brooke straightened and wiped her face. "Why don't you think it's Shay?"

He rested his hand on her knee, needing the contact from her as much as she needed it from him. "I promise I'll tell you every single thing Cruz and I have discussed, but first I want to know your thoughts. What did your gut say when you saw Julia in the morgue?"

She nibbled on her bottom lip. "I can't be certain Shay killed Julia, and that scared the crap out of me."

"And what did you see that made you pause and reconsider who's guilty?" He already knew the answer but needed her to confirm his own theory.

She slid her fingernail over the edge of the table. "There's no doubt Shay is abusive and dangerous and capable of hurting someone to the point of death—or near death in my case. But..." She lifted unsure eyes his way.

"Take your time. I know this isn't easy to talk about." He hated pushing her. She'd spent years healing and trying to put her past behind her. Now she was being forced to face it head on.

Wrapping an arm around her waist, she splayed her hand over her side. "Whenever Shay hit me, it was because he was mad. Something would set him off, and I'd take the brunt of his anger every time. Like most abusers, he'd claim I made him act that way. I was too loud, too needy, too messy. After he'd lash out, he'd cry and promise to change. Even the last time when things went so far, he was pissed I finally had enough and left. If he couldn't have me, no one could."

His blood heated, and he rubbed his palm over her knee. Regardless of if Shay killed Julia or not, the guy was still a bastard who should be locked up. Still a dangerous man with an agenda who needed to be found. "Crimes of passion. Crimes of impulse. No planning. No calculations. Just act and react."

"Exactly. Whoever kidnapped Julia set a trap. Took their time. So impersonal and cold. Unlike anything I experienced with Shay." Fear dilated her pupils. "But if Shay didn't kill Julia, who did?"

Lincoln didn't have an answer yet, but he wouldn't stop digging until he figured it out.

BROOKE THREW her head back on the headrest of the desk chair and closed her eyes. Hours of sitting in the conference room, speaking with employees about their relationship with Julia, caused a dull ache to beat against her forehead. She'd worked alongside Lincoln as they made their way down the list Chet gave them. The list was long. Julia might not have worked at Crossroads Mountain Retreat for long, but she'd made a huge impression on everyone who knew her.

Each new face she spoke with was filled with despair.

Each new face demanded answers.

Not one person raised an ounce of suspicion from Brooke.

Righting herself in her seat, misery added ten pounds to her shoulders. "What do we do now? We spoke with everyone Chet listed. It's clear no one we just talked to hurt Julia."

Lincoln tapped the tip of his pen against the conference table. "Agreed. Did she interact much with the guests? Have you ever had any issues with anyone giving employees a hard time?"

"No. Never any issues. And she spent most her of time in the kitchen—away from the guests."

He pushed back against his chair. "I have to let Cruz know we came up empty."

"Did he get ahold of my old Captain?" She'd offered to contact her former boss from the police force in her hometown, but he'd wanted to speak with the man himself.

"Yeah. He's got everyone in town looking for Shay, but no one's seen him." He scratched the back of his ear like an irritated dog chasing a flea.

Something had triggered Lincoln—made him fidgety like he didn't fit in his own skin anymore. After she'd opened up to him about her doubts regarding Shay, Chet and Cruz had come back in and they'd sprang into action. A new intensity was wrapped around Lincoln's shoulders, as though the fight had become more personal, and she had to find out why. "We haven't gotten a chance to talk about the crime scene."

He tossed his pen and it skidded across the table.

She raised her brows, waiting for him to say something. He'd made it clear in his time here that sharing his emotions wasn't easy—hell, the man balked at taking classes or participating in any group outing since he'd been here. Not that he'd had the time to try anything. Between his vehicle being vandalized, falling off the side of a mountain, and rescuing her from her ex, his few days at the retreat were pretty much all taken up by her.

And damnit if she couldn't bring herself to feel even a smidge of guilt.

"I had the same thoughts as you even before I got to the crime scene. Just reading Shay's record. Things don't add up. The only abuse or aggression he's displayed is toward you. I understood how he could have used Julia against you. Taken her and guilted you to go with him, just like he did at the diner. Even if that fell out of his pattern. But this." He waved a hand over the file in front of him. "Killing someone he didn't know. Why? What's the pay off? How does this help him achieve his goal of getting to you?"

She shrugged, wishing she had answers. "I don't know. Maybe to throw us off? If we're chasing our tails, searching for someone else who killed Julia, that lets him fly under the radar."

"Does it though?"

Pinching the skin of her forehead, she sighed. "Not really. We're still searching for him, and now we're even more pissed. Looking harder than before. Do you think he could be escalating? He spent time in prison. That could have hardened him, pushed him into acting more brazen. Using whatever he deemed necessary as a tool for his personal gain." She winced at the idea of Julia being a tool —a simple pawn in a game in which Brooke was the prize.

He lifted his hands then quickly dropped them to rest on the sides of the chair. "It's possible."

"But something else is making you think not probable."

His gaze sought hers, and he dipped down his eyebrows. "How can you read my mind like that?"

Smirking, she held his gaze and tingles of excitement burst in her tummy. "Spill."

"Something at the crime scene really hit me." He flipped open the folder and slid out a picture of Julia's lifeless body. "From what we know, Julia has no history of drug use. She even was tested at school in order to compete on the swim team. But the blue on her lips and on her fingers indicates a drug overdose. Not to mention the track marks on the inside of her arm."

Brooke swallowed hard, the image of Julia's drained

body strewn in the woods difficult to take in. "But the marks on her neck are consistent with a taser."

"True. My gut says she didn't willingly take drugs with whoever grabbed her."

Unable to tear her gaze from the picture, she ran her finger over the glossy paper. "What does that mean?"

Lincoln rubbed circles against his temples. "I'm not sure. I could be reading into something that means nothing. I'm spinning my wheels, feeling like I've just been dumped down a damn rabbit hole with no way out. But something isn't sitting right."

She hated to admit it, but the giant shit storm that had blown into town the same day Lincoln had shown up in Pine Valley had left everything a jumbled mess with no clear direction on how to wade through it. "I need to give my brain a break."

Lincoln snorted. "I wish I could."

"What do you do when you need to get out of your own head?" She'd love to hit the gym or even head up to the third floor and see if any of the therapy rooms were in use. Maybe not a discussion group, but an art class or even meditation. But something told her Lincoln wouldn't be game for alternative therapy right now.

"I run."

She mentally cringed. Running would kill her knee, but if that's what Lincoln needed, she'd suck it up. "Okay then. Let's hit a trail. The sun's out and the fresh air will do us some good. I can grab you some clothes we keep on hand for the staff if you don't want to head back to your cabin and change." She rose, unwilling to wait for an answer before springing into action.

"I don't know." He rubbed the back of his neck, indecision clear in his aquamarine eyes.

"I won't take no for an answer." Extending a hand, she scooped up the contents on the table and shoved the file under her arm. "I understand things haven't gone as planned since you got here, but you're supposed to be working on you."

"But—"

"No buts. You came here stressed and hurting, and everything that's happened since has only added to that. You can take twenty minutes to clear your head. It might help you see things from a different angle." She fisted her hand on her hip. "I'm sure Cruz would agree."

Lincoln rolled his eyes and kept his lips firmly together.

Fine. She'd bust out the big guns. "Please, Lincoln. For me. I could really use a few minutes to gather my thoughts. A run will help us both."

His lips tilted upward. "Are you making that up because you think I won't say no?"

She shrugged.

"Fine. A quick run."

She fought a grin as she tipped her head in agreement and headed out the door. Life might be falling apart around her, but she'd somehow tumbled into an easy rhythm with a man she barely knew.

With a man she'd give anything to know more.

15

Т

he sun beat down in Lincoln's eyes, and he squinted against the harsh afternoon light. Brooke waved an arm high above her head, directing him toward where she stood at the far edge of the parking lot. Heat shimmered off the black tar in waves, and he hurried to join her near the shaded trees.

He still couldn't believe he let her talk him into going for a run. Even if she might be right about needing to take a second to just let his mind work while not focusing so hard on the facts spilling over in his brain.

Brooke smiled wide as he approached. "The clothes fit you well."

Pulling at the hem of the T-shirt, he glanced down at the familiar logo most of the staff wore. "Not too bad."

With her hands extended toward the sky, Brooke stretched from side to side. A black brace wrapped around her right knee.

"Bad knee?" As he closed in on thirty-two, his body ached in ways he'd never experienced after a hard workout.

But so far, besides the hand injury, he'd been lucky not to have any permanent injuries to contend with.

Cringing, she dropped her arms and scrunched up her nose. "Another one of Shay's parting gifts. He stomped on my kneecap and busted it pretty bad. Never healed completely. One of the reasons I couldn't go back to work in a uniform. Couldn't pass the physical. My boss said I could work a desk, but what's the fun of that? I wasn't made for paperwork. I was made for this." She smiled and gestured around her.

His injured hand pulsed at the idea of not being able to return to work because he couldn't regain all his mobility. How far and fast he could run wouldn't matter if he couldn't squeeze a trigger. Not like that stopped him from bringing his Glock along for the run. His aim might suck, but he didn't want to be caught unprepared. "Sorry to hear that, but it looks like you made the right decision by starting something new."

"I think so."

Doubt crept into his mind. He didn't want her to be in pain because this was the only option he'd given her to get his mind off the case for a few minutes. "Are you sure you're up for a run? We can try something else. Hell, I'll even do that yoga shit if you'd prefer." Lord almighty. Had he really just offered to take a yoga class?

A spark of mischief glowed from her pointed glare. "Trust me. Yoga will never be my thing. I'd rather take my chances on a trail any day. We just might have to cut it a little short."

He lifted his leg, grabbing his ankle and pressing the bottom of his foot to his ass to stretch his quads. Dropping his ankle, he repeated the motion with his other leg then filled his lungs with a deep breath. "I'm ready when you are."

Brooke took off down a trail wide enough for them to run side-by-side. She kept her pace slow and steady.

He studied the woods while they jogged, letting his mind wander to different areas they passed—the moss-covered ground, a scurrying squirrel, the song of a nearby bird. The pace quickened, and his chest heaved in a familiar motion. His muscles burned after not being pushed the last couple days, but he matched his stride with Brooke's. Beads of sweat trickled down the sides of his face as he ran up an incline, the motion like moving through quicksand.

Damn, it felt good. He ran a few miles most mornings but was lax with his workouts ever since the accident. Too depressed and filled with self-pity to put in the work and get his ass in gear. He hated to admit it, but Cruz was right to push him into coming to Crossroads Mountain Retreat.

Things might not have gone the way he expected, but that didn't mean it hadn't given him what he needed. Meeting Brooke made him realize a whole life waited for him. A life outside of the job. Returning to a uniform was still his plan, and he had no clue what he'd do if that plan didn't come to fruition, but for the first time the idea of a different future didn't scare the hell out of him.

The trail turned around a bend and a clearing parted the trees, providing a picture of the lush green peaks of the mountains. Lincoln slowed his gait before coming to a stop. He pulled in lungsful of air and wiped his brow with the back of his hand.

"You okay?" Brooke asked through ragged breaths beside him.

"Yeah, it's just..." Words escaped him, so he pointed toward the vista that had stopped him in his tracks.

Brooke's shoulder brushed up against him. "It's beautiful, isn't it?"

He turned toward her, taking in the profile of her pert nose and full lips. Her long hair was pulled into a high ponytail. "It really is."

She faced him, a small smile playing on her lips and questions lingering behind her eyes. "What? Do I have something on my face?" She ran her fingers over her high cheekbone.

He shook his head and a weird ache spread through his chest. "You really are something." Taking a chance, he reached for her hand and linked his fingers in hers. A part of him hated how right it felt, how she fit so damn well.

Another part wanted to jump and scream out a whoop of joy. Even with all the chaos around them. Even with the turmoil that hadn't left his gut since seeing Julia's blue-tinged lips and fingernails. This moment was more than he'd ever imagined possible. A beautiful, kind woman who intrigued him and was smart as hell. A woman who made him reevaluate what he wanted out of life.

A woman he should run far away from because falling for her meant giving up everything he'd worked for his whole life.

She ran her tongue over those red lips of hers and every thought that invaded his mind the last twenty-four hours disappeared in a flash. Unable to help himself, he took a step toward her.

Her eyes widened, and she dropped her gaze to his mouth.

He raised his free hand to graze his thumb along her jawline. "I really want to kiss you." The words came out on a growl.

A tiny sigh seeped through her parted lips. "No one's stopping you."

He lowered his mouth to hers and the sweet taste of her soft lips filled his senses. Erasing the space between them, he wrapped an arm behind the small of her back and pressed her against him.

With one hand still clasped in his, she hooked her arm around his neck and deepened the kiss.

Warmth exploded in his core. The urge to carry her to the grassy knoll and peel off her clothes had him pulling away. His chest heaved, passion threatening to burst from him, and he rested his forehead to hers to gain control of himself. "Thank you."

A huff of laughter barked from Brooke, the same huge sound that surprised him every time. "Thank you? Really?"

He chuckled, unable to take his hand from the thin strip of skin on her back. He mentally slapped himself. Never had a woman rendered him such a freaking idiot.

A distant thud, as if something was being struck, was carried to him on the breeze, and he straightened. "Did you hear that?"

Brooke tilted her head to the side. "Might be from the archery area."

"Archery? I'm sorry, did I come to a retreat for law enforcement or Summer Camp?"

The wicked gleam was back in her eyes, and she stepped toward the noise. "Lincoln Sawyer, I have a feeling you have no idea what you signed up for."

He couldn't stop the wide grin from taking over his mouth as he tightened his grip on her hand and followed behind the most fascinating woman he'd ever met.

THE *THUNK* of an arrow hitting a target matched the deep thud of Brooke's heart as she led Lincoln around the bend toward the cleared patched of land used for different group outings. She hadn't thought to check the scheduled activities for the day when she'd picked a trail for their run. She'd been surprised Lincoln had agreed to step away from the case for a few minutes and just leapt into action. At least coming up on the group outing would give her a chance to show Lincoln more of what the retreat had to offer.

Summer Camp activities and all.

"I told you this place was a children's summer camp when my grandfather owned it. I decided to keep some of the same things I loved so much as a kid. Our wilderness expert teaches archery, hatchet throwing, and handles the shooting range. She also leads overnight camping excursions and gives instructions on survival skills." She had to concentrate on the sales pitch she'd repeated a hundred times so as not to let the lingering sensation from their kiss steal her ability to form sentences.

"Hatchet throwing?" The inflection of his voice revealed his skepticism.

She threw him a sideways glance. "Ever try it?"

"Can't say that I have." He tightened his grip on hers. "But I've tried a few new things since I've been here."

"Like thanking the woman you just kissed?" She couldn't stop the girlish giggle from falling over her words. Oh crap, that giggle sounded just like Mama.

The thought threw an ice-cold bucket of reality on whatever just happened with Lincoln. Her good friend was in a living nightmare, her ex was stalking her and was possibly now a murderer, the threat of an unknown enemy lingered at the fringe of all their lives, and here she was kissing a handsome man on the mountain.

What the hell was she thinking? Shame filled her. Forgetting her responsibilities to traipse around with a man was something Glenda would do. Not her. Her number one rule was to do the opposite of what her mama did. Not fall all over herself because some guy had just kissed her senseless.

Forcing a smile, she slipped her hand from his and quickened her pace. If she could get Lincoln interested in whatever Grace was doing with the other guests, she could make some kind of excuse and head back to the lobby. Then she could find Chet and see what needed to be done to help Cruz. "Everyone should be just around this corner. We cleared a bunch of trees to make a section for all the outdoor fun we offer." The cheerful clip to her words was so false she had to fight not to wince.

The path widened and a clearing appeared. A large, rectangular building dominated the area, the metal siding different than any other building at the retreat. Brooke hated the metal shingles, but Grace insisted the shooting range be made from the ugly gray material. A shed was set up close to the trio of targets for the archers, a thick white line marking off where to stand on the opposite end. "What the heck? Where is everyone?" No way she mistook the sound of the arrow. Could someone have taken a shot when they passed by, leaving the area before she and Lincoln arrived?

Thunk.

An arrow sank into the target twenty feet away, but no one was there.

"Where'd that come from?" Lincoln scowled and turned in a circle.

Shaking her head, she surveyed the area. "The axe throwing is on the other side of the building, but no one could shoot from that far away. They'd have to be in the woods."

A distant whistling sound grew closer as it whizzed by her ear. An arrow speared the ground by her feet, and a hard ball of fear sat heavy on her chest. Someone was watching them. "Run!"

With Lincoln by her side, she took off in a sprint for the safety of the evergreens. Her lungs burned and her knee throbbed. But she kept pushing. Harder and faster. The manicured grass morphed into thick weeds and patches of dirt as she wove between the trees.

Thunk.

Another arrow, this time piercing the rough bark at her side. Her pulse jumped against her throat. Someone was hunting her down like a deer in the woods.

The now-chilling whistle of an arrow came closer and fell to the ground at her feet. "We might be getting out of his range. We have to keep moving." Her breath heaved but she kept pushing her pace fast.

Weeds and underbrush swept against her ankles as she pushed deeper into the woods, Lincoln at her back. She skirted between the trees, not wanting to walk in a straight path and using the barriers as protection against the unknown attacker. The sun couldn't leak through the towering mangle of limbs and leaves, casting them in shadows. Her thighs burned as she kept her footing on the steady incline.

She stopped, holding up a finger for Lincoln to do the same. She trained her ears to listen for an approaching madman or whirl of more arrows. "Maybe we lost him?"

Lincoln braced his hand against a thick tree trunk and darted his gaze around.

Bang!

A bullet lodged into the mossy base of a tree two feet to her left. Terror grabbed at her throat and squeezed. They hadn't lost anyone—the psychopath had just traded the bow for a gun.

16

Lincoln dropped to a crouch and pulled Brooke down. Her body molded against him, and her warm breath skimmed across his face. The smell of her sweat mixed with her strawberry shampoo and the sap from the towering pine that hid them. Keeping her pressed against the rough bark, he shielded her from the threat which he still couldn't see. He searched through the shifting shadows, listening for approaching footsteps or animals running in the opposite direction of whoever chased them into the woods.

"We need to move." Brooke whispered the words, but there was no denying the panic and fear in her voice.

He glanced over his shoulder. The forest was thick behind them. "Any trails up there?"

"No." She mouthed the word and darted her rounded eyes in every direction.

Grimacing, he weighed their options. Adrenaline might be coursing through his veins, but both of them had used a lot of energy on their run. Venturing deeper into the woods, where no marked paths or trails waited, wasn't appealing. If they got lost, they'd be screwed.

"Lincoln." A tiny whine lengthened his name. "Let's go."

Bang!

Another bullet splintered the wood of a fallen branch feet away. Fleeing now made them huge targets. He couldn't put Brooke at risk like that. He reached around to the back of his waistband and grabbed his gun. The familiar weight loosened a bit of tension in his shoulders.

"What are you doing?" Brooke hissed.

"He's close. If we run, we get shot. Not to mention getting lost in the woods. Stay behind the tree. If he keeps pushing up the mountain toward us, we'll see him. Then I'll make him pay." He flexed his fingers, and jolts of pain tugged his nerve endings. Gritting his teeth, he strained against the invisible force controlling his muscles.

A twig snapped, and a squawking bird flew from a nearby tree. Lincoln held his breath. A faint rustling pricked his ears.

Brooke's gaze burned a hole in his forehead, but he couldn't allow himself to focus on her. Not when letting his concentration wander from the subtle sounds of approaching footsteps could mean not reacting in time to save their asses.

Bang!

The trunk shuddered, and Brooke shrunk as low to the ground as she could get.

"Shit. The sonofabitch is fast." He chanced a peek around the tree just as the flash of metal from a gun whipped around the low branches of a skinny evergreen. "He's close."

He heaved in and out, breaths trembling. He could do this. The asshole was well within reach. All he had to do was get his hand to do one simple task. A task he'd trained for almost his entire life. His hand had to work. It wasn't only his life that depended on it.

Lincoln wiggled his fingers against the handle, willing his tendons to stop throbbing. Willing his mind to stop thinking for one damn minute and just let his body act. His brain spun in loopy circles and black spots dotted his vision. Numbness crept along his fingers. The lack of feeling in his limb made pressure crowd his chest. He squeezed his eyes closed and tried to even his breathing, but a fog clouded his brain.

"Lincoln. Look at me."

He blinked before focusing on Brooke.

She covered his hand with hers then gently took the gun from his grip.

Defeat crushed down on him. He couldn't do it. Couldn't make his body do what it needed to keep them safe. Couldn't force the doubt and pain from his thoughts.

He'd failed himself and Brooke.

Brooke trained the gun in front of her and whirled around the tree. She shot once, twice, three times.

A deep scream echoed through the surrounding trees.

Lincoln sank to the ground and covered his ears with shaking hands. Anxiety swelled inside him. His heart pitched up his throat and his palms grew sweaty.

Another shot. Close. Too close. Footsteps pounded against the ground. Leaves brushing away.

A warm touch on his arms had him opening his eyes. Brooke's face hovered inches from his.

"We're okay. Whoever it was just ran. I shot him, but not sure where." She pressed a palm against his jaw.

He reared back. He didn't deserve her gentle touch or kind words. He was a coward, unable to fight against whatever had just wound around his mind like the coils of a poisonous snake.

"We need to get down to the shooting range. There's a phone in there. We'll call Cruz and get a team to search the woods. Maybe he left a blood trail to follow." She stood over him, offering a hand.

He tightened his jaw and pushed against the base of the tree to get to his feet. Humiliation burned his neck, creeping into his cheeks. He couldn't look her in the eye. Fury at his own ineptitude beat a steady rhythm against his temple, and he fisted his left hand. He wanted to slam it against something, release the pent-up anger. But what good would two injured hands do him?

Concern wrinkled her brow, and she placed a palm on his chest, keeping him in place. "Are you all right?"

He swatted away her hand and stalked forward. "I'm fine. Let's just get the hell out of here. Cruz needs to get guys up here now." He swallowed around the annoyance clawing at his throat. He shouldn't need his brother to sweep in and do a job Lincoln was perfectly capable of doing.

Well, used to be capable of doing. Now he couldn't even attempt to pull the trigger of his own gun without freaking out. What the hell was that? He'd experienced PTSD, flashes of panic where his body froze, but never anything so intense. Never felt as though everything inside him was on the edge of exploding.

Brooke fell into step beside him, weaving through the trees toward the clearing. "You don't have anything to be ashamed of. This stuff happens. Especially the first time back in a situation like this. Your body and mind just aren't ready yet. That's why you're here."

Stopping, he turned hard eyes on her. "I don't want to hear it right now, okay? I'm here because I didn't have a choice. And from where I'm standing, I'm still just as messed up as I was when I arrived."

"But you haven't even—"

"Just stop." Shaking his head, he shoved a hand through his hair and continued down the hill. "I don't want to talk. Let's just get to the phone and call Cruz. That's all that matters right now."

The urgency to get away from Brooke and the mortifying scene they left behind kept his pace quick and mouth shut. Once they were back at the lodge, he had to decide what to do next. It was clear that staying at the Crossroads Mountain Retreat wasn't the right move. He needed more help than Brooke could give him.

TENSE SILENCE FILLED the small office attached to the shooting range. Brooke eyed the clutter sprawled across Grace's desk in the windowless room, fighting against the urge to straighten up. Paper targets riddled with holes and pictures of guests enjoying the outdoors were taped all over the cinderblock walls. Only an oval table separated Lincoln from her, but the space between them seemed so much farther. The glass of water beside Brooke remained untouched. The terrifying events of the past hour replayed in her head. Her heartrate had finally returned to normal, but a new ache pulsed in her chest that had nothing to do with fear. Nothing to do with being hunted down like a scared animal.

No, it was Lincoln's dismissive attitude that left her feeling defeated. Once Cruz had arrived with a team of officers, Grace volunteered to take them into the mountains. She was a skilled tracker, and if Brooke wounded her attacker enough to draw blood, Grace had the best chance of following the trail. Brooke wanted to stay close in case she was needed, and Lincoln sat hunched over in a plastic chair, refusing to speak.

Not like there was much to say anyway. He made it clear coming here was a mistake, and she couldn't blame him for his conclusion. She'd taken up all his time, and although she'd thought he'd enjoyed spending time with her, that obviously wasn't the case.

The door swung open. Grace walked in, her long dark hair in a braid thrown over her shoulder and dirt smeared on her gray T-shirt. Cruz followed behind her, closing the door before turning exhausted eyes on Brooke then flicking his gaze to Lincoln.

"Did you find anything?" Brooke asked, although the defeated expressions both Cruz and Grace wore told her everything she needed to know.

Grace sighed and skirted around the messy desk to drop down into her chair. "I found some drops of blood. We followed it until the trail turned cold. There's too much area to cover for the few of us."

Cruz tossed his hat on the small table by Brooke's water glass. "He has to be close. He was on foot, with no sign of a vehicle. I have officers searching the closest state and city parks for the white van. Maybe we'll get lucky. He might be too injured to make it back to wherever he left his car."

"Did you put a call into the local hospitals?" Brooke asked. Chances were someone smart enough to keep them all running in so many circles wouldn't be stupid and show up at a hospital for care. But stranger things happened.

"Done. I'm securing a chopper to canvas the area." Cruz flicked a finger toward the water. "Can I get some of that? It's hot as hell out there."

Brooke lifted the glass she hadn't taken a sip from.

Accepting the cup, Cruz took a large gulp then set it back on the table. "Lincoln, can you help with the chopper? You have more connections than I do."

Lincoln grunted.

Brooke lifted her eyes to the ceiling. Lincoln had acted like a sullen child since she'd slipped his gun from his hand. The man was obviously dealing with a panic attack, and she hadn't had time to talk him down before grabbing the gun and saving their asses. If he couldn't see that—if he was the kind of man who couldn't handle a strong woman taking charge—then he definitely wasn't the man for her. In the moment she'd had nothing but empathy for him, but now that time passed and he still refused to speak, she was too pissed to be understanding.

Cruz cut his gaze to her. "What the hell's wrong with him?"

Pressing her lips together, she held back the words she really wanted to say, instead offering a small shrug.

"Dude, don't do that shit. If you want to know what's going on, ask me. Don't bring her into this." Lincoln kicked his legs in front of him and let his head loll back.

"Bring her into what? A conversation?" Cruz shook his head, disgust evident in his curled lip. "Whatever crawled up your ass, it's time to yank it out. Shit's getting real, and I need you."

Lincoln shot to his feet and flexed his right hand. "You don't know what the hell you're talking about."

Brooke fixed her gaze on the motion of his fingers, and a pinch of pity squeezed her gut. She let her own irritation and personal feelings get in the way of giving Lincoln what he really needed—her understanding. "It's been a long couple of days. We're all on edge. Let's just relax for a minute."

Lincoln snorted.

"What the hell is your problem?" Concern leaked through Cruz's annoyance.

"My problem is I froze, okay? I can't do my damn job. I couldn't keep us safe." Lincoln slumped against the wall. "I had the gun, I had the shot, and I couldn't do it. And it wasn't just my hand." He touched his fingertips to his temple. "My mind, man. Everything was shaky, and I couldn't catch my breath. I couldn't concentrate on anything."

The urge to comfort Lincoln surged through Brooke, but it wasn't the time to rush to his side. His earlier words still cut deep, and she needed to take a step away and let him figure out how he could help himself. To work through his issues and set himself on the right path. Their days might have been steamrolled by Shay, and possibly some other lunatic, but when this nightmare was over Lincoln would have to turn all his focus on himself.

"Sounds like a panic attack to me." Grace propped an elbow on her desk and twirled the end of her braid around her finger. "Ever have one before?"

Closing his eyes, Lincoln rubbed his forehead. "Never like this."

Cruz rested a hand on Lincoln's shoulder, dipping his chin until Lincoln opened his eyes and caught his stare. "That's why you're here, man. I shouldn't have accepted your help with this case. There's a reason your boss wanted you to take some time. Your physical injury will heal, you'll make sure of that, but it's what's in your head you need to deal with. And since you've been here, all you've done is take on other people's problems. I should have realized what you were doing."

Brooke bit her lip, hating the crushing guilt pinning her down. Shay had left her shaken, and she'd clung onto Lincoln and his offer to stay by her side until Shay was caught. Now she realized Lincoln had latched on to an opportunity to push aside his own demons. Not because he wanted to help her, but because he didn't want to deal with his own problems.

But she couldn't get caught up in her injured pride. She had a job to do, and the main part was providing Lincoln with tools to help dig himself out of his emotional turmoil. "You still have time here. We offer plenty of classes that could help you. You just have to find the right one."

"I don't want to talk right now. Not to anyone. I need... time." Lincoln dropped his gaze to the ground.

His words were like one of the arrows they'd ran from right to the heart, but she wouldn't let him see how his dismissal hurt. "I understand."

Grace stood, her towering height making Brooke feel small from her seat at the table. She anchored her hands on her hips. "Ever throw a hatchet?"

"Who? Me?" Lincoln eyed Grace with interest.

Grace chuckled. "Yeah. You. I know what these two have done. But if you're looking for a way to get out some pent-up emotions and don't want to sit down with a shrink, it could help more than you imagine."

Lincoln twisted his lips, as if mulling over the idea. "Worth a shot."

Brooke's stomach dipped, and jealously ebbed through her. Swallowing past the lump in her throat, she fixed her attention on Cruz. "I need to get back to the lodge. Can you take me in your golf cart?"

Cruz nodded. "Sure thing. I need to get going, too. Grace, can you get Lincoln back to the lodge when you're done here?"

"Absolutely."

The cheeriness in her voice constricted Brooke's muscles. What a ridiculous reaction to a friend doing her job and helping a guest through a hard time. She offered a tight smile to Grace and pushed through the door into the warm sunshine. She had more important problems to deal with than Lincoln Sawyer, and she didn't need him to keep her safe. She could do that all on her own.

17

A weird knot formed in the pit of Lincoln's stomach as he watched Brooke leave the office. She hadn't given him so much as a wave before leaving with his brother. Not that he blamed her. From the moment she'd taken charge on the mountain while he shook like a damn leaf, flames of embarrassment had nearly consumed him.

Besides, his brother was right. He'd jumped on the chance to immerse himself in a crime that wasn't his problem so he didn't have to deal with his issues. Issues that clearly wouldn't go away by ignoring them. He was still reluctant to try any of the kumbaya treatments the retreat offered, but if he could throw something sharp and dangerous and get the same results, all the better.

"I want to stop by the lockers next to the targets for archery before we head to the hatchets," Grace said, opening the door and stepping out in front of him. "I need to know if someone took one of my bows." She gestured behind the long rectangular building that housed the shooting range.

"You think the guy could have brought his own bow?"

He walked beside her to check the storage, even though he didn't understand her reasoning. It would only make sense that the bow and arrows were taken from here.

"I guess I should rephrase that. I want to know *how* someone took one of my bows." She glanced over her shoulder with hooked brows. "I always keep the equipment shed locked. Did someone get a key or bust the lock?"

"Good points." He surveyed his surroundings. The archery targets he'd spied when first coming into the clearing were yards away, the metal shed close by.

Grace marched ahead and lifted the busted lock from the door. She slipped it off the handle and opened the shed, pulling on a dangling string. Light splashed down on the stifling space.

Lincoln clasped his hands behind his back, happy to stay out in the sunshine. Two people inside the shed would be a little too suffocating for him. After being trapped inside a totaled car for hours, he'd rather avoid tight spaces.

"One missing bow. Several arrows," Grace called out. "If Cruz is lucky, they can pull some prints off the arrows he found or maybe the door."

Lincoln grunted. He wouldn't bet on finding anything useful. The criminal they were dealing with knew what he was doing. Leaving behind incriminating evidence would be a rookie mistake.

Grace stepped out of the shed with a hatchet in each hand. The sun reflected off the sharp metal. "Take these." She passed them over then retreated back into the stuffy metal box.

Lincoln rubbed his thumbs over the smooth wooden handles. The ends of the axes were thick enough that he didn't have any trouble wrapping his palms around them.

Their weight felt good—his primal instincts were kicking into high gear.

Grace reemerged with two more hatchets and kicked the door shut behind her. "Remind me to put in a maintenance order for a new lock."

Her request had him stealing a glance at the leggy brunette with twigs caught in her hair, probably picked up from tracking a madman through the woods. "Wasn't aware I worked here."

"Hmm."

Her noncommittal noise raised his ire. "What?"

"Nothing. It's just Cruz made it sound like the stick up your ass was due to the panic attack. Not sure why it's still up there." She pointed her weapon to the left, away from the archery area and shooting range. "We need to hike up a little toward the tree-line."

He couldn't help the chuckle pushing up his throat. "You complain about a stick up my ass then in the next breath give me directions with your hatchet. I don't know if I should be irritated or amused."

"I didn't complain about the stick. Trust me. I get it. I've had my own fall from glory. Took me years to find my footing. I was a grouch during that time, too. Cost me a hell of a lot, but that's a story for another day." Stopping beside a wide stump, she smirked and sunk the sharp edges of the blades in the wood. "And like you so aggressively told Brooke. You don't want to talk."

He winced. "I wasn't aggressive. I just...I don't know. What happened back there with Brooke...I didn't handle it well, okay?"

"Not my problem. I don't do the talking thing, either. That's why I'm out here. I like the woods and the quiet. Nature's my therapy. Now, face the target."

Aggravation had him squeezing the handle. The muscles in his right hand pulsed, but his grip remained firm. He hadn't meant to snap at Brooke, hell, the woman saved his life. He just needed to get over his bruised ego, and he couldn't do that with his brother and a stranger in the room staring at them. "I'll clear things up with Brooke."

Grace took the axe from his left hand and pressed her lips together. "I don't really care. Now, like I already said, face the target."

Blowing out his frustration, he did as she said. Thick stumps were hoisted on top of stands, the smooth sides painted with bullseyes circling the middle. He didn't have to explain anything to this woman, so why did her opinion of how he treated Brooke bother him so much?

Maybe because Brooke might think the same thing. That he was a misogynistic asshole who didn't want a strong woman helping him. But his reaction didn't have anything to do with Brooke. He was pissed at himself. Brooke was just the unlucky recipient of his anger.

Grace cocked her hip, letting the hatchet she'd grabbed from him dangle at her side. "Hold the handle like you would a hammer, keeping the blade aimed down. Look at your target, pull the axe over your head, and throw toward the bullseye. Easy as pie."

"Pie, huh? I never understood that expression. What is that even supposed to mean?" He shifted the weight of the weapon, bouncing it up and down. Pain seared his hand. He gritted his teeth, needing to prove himself capable.

"Not really sure. Quit stalling and give it a try. Sometimes it helps to scream when you release the axe."

With the axe pulled over his head, he glanced at her. "Seriously? Screaming helps hit the target?"

A sad smile lifted her lips. "Not the target. Yelling helps unleash all that pent-up emotion."

The idea was nonsense, but what the hell? He opened his mouth wide and let out a deep, primal scream that vibrated his core. He whipped his arm forward, letting the axe fly through the air.

The death grip squeezing his chest loosened a fraction. He closed his eyes, and the slight breeze skimmed his face. The laughing eyes of the man who got away slammed against his mind's eye, flashes of memories assaulting him.

Ian Samuels.

He'd chased the sonofabitch for months, gaining a front row seat to the death and destruction he left in his wake all in the name of greed. He'd preyed on the young and naïve. The drugs he sold taking more lives than Lincoln wanted to remember.

But he did remember. He remembered all of them as they played like a damn movie trailer across his memory bank. Every face. Every grieving parent. Every person he disappointed because he couldn't nail the asshole down.

Grace placed another hatchet in his hands. "Do it again."

Opening his eyes, he repeated the same motions, grunting out another yell as the weapon flew from his hands and hit the target. More memories assaulted him. More sensations gripped him, stealing his breath as events played out in his brain. Ian in the car in front of him, speeding through traffic. Lincoln training his gun out the window and aiming at a tire to slow him down. Then the sound of metal on metal, his car collapsing into itself, pain ripping through his body as he watched Ian drive away. Still out there. Still dangerous.

He hunched over, forearms on thighs, and the scream grew louder. Deeper. Crushing his lungs as it poured through his mouth like overflowing sewage needing to be purged. Unshed tears burned his eyes and a release loosened muscles he'd held bunched so tight.

Closing his mouth, he straightened and breathed in the clean mountain air. His chest heaved in and out as he struggled to keep his composure. He searched for the target and grinned.

Bullseye.

His aching hand shook as he held it out to Grace. "That felt damn good. Let's do it again."

THE SCENT of dogs and a hint of lemon cleaner greeted Brooke inside the kennel. Other people might turn their nose at the slight musty odor, but she took a deep breath. Her day had gone from bad to tragic to terrifying. Nothing would wash away the horrors of the day, but there was one surefire way to at least lift her spirits for a few short moments.

A low half-wall separated the large, open play space from the narrow entryway. Multi-colored leashes hung from mounted hooks. Dark stained shiplap covered the room with black wrought-iron forming the cages—lined one after the other with small black mats that said *Woof* in front of each little door.

The sound of kibble hitting a bowl echoed off the pitched ceiling, and Brooke rounded the half-wall to find Tucker getting the food dishes ready for dinner. Five sets of brown eyes stared at her, tails wagging, but not one dog stood or barked.

Except Wyatt.

He jumped from a dog bed in the corner and bounced

toward her. His tongue lolled from his open mouth, and he whipped his tail from side to side.

Brooke crouched low and opened her arms, hugging him close. His soft fur tickled her chin, and she pressed a kiss to his forehead before standing. "Hey, Tucker. Thanks for keeping Wyatt all day. Things have been crazy."

Tucker set down the bag of food and faced her. Specks of yellow shone through the green of his eyes, and his blond hair spiked as though he'd just ran his hands through it. "Are you kidding me? Keeping him is the least I can do. Are you okay?"

She huffed out a humorless laugh. "No, but I'm more worried about Chet."

"Chet will get through this. It'll hurt like hell, but he will." Tucker scratched the side of his arm, and she couldn't help eyeing the intricate tattoos that circled his bicep. "He's crashing at my place tonight, though. I'll keep an eye on him."

"I'm surprised he agreed to that. Chet loves his solitude, especially in hard times." Wyatt nudged her hand with his wet nose, and she ran her fingers over his furry head. "How'd you convince him?"

Tucker grinned. "I told him I'd bring my ass up to his place in the woods with all the dogs if he didn't stay with me tonight. He knows I'd do it too, and the chaos would drive him nuts."

Brooke smiled and shook her head. "You're shameless."

His grin deepened, causing dimples to sink in his cheeks. "Gotta use what I've got."

"Good point."

All traces of amusement fled his face. "You need anything else? You can crash at my place, too."

His kindness warmed her. "I'll be fine. Just want a giant

glass of wine and some peace and quiet. If I hurry, I can catch the sunset."

He nodded, the worry not leaving the firm set of his stubbled jaw. "Call if you change your mind."

"I will. Now get to work. Those pitiful dogs are looking pretty hungry." She tilted her head to the line of cages and the obedient canines waiting with tongues lolling for their food, then waved before heading for the door with Wyatt at her side.

The kennel was close enough to her cabin that she opted to leave the golf cart behind. She grabbed her backpack from the floor of the cart, threw it over her shoulder, and hurried to the path along the lake. She tried to relax and enjoy the sights that normally soothed her, but each subtle sound set her on edge. She hated this. Hated not being comfortable in her home. Hated not feeling comfortable in her own damn skin. But how could she not let paranoia overwhelm her with Julia's unknown killer at large?

Brooke took the corner around the edge of the lake, Wyatt strolling along beside her, and her stare went straight to Lincoln's cabin. The way the sun sat low in the sky cast shadows over the home. No lights shone through the windows or movement that would clue her into Lincoln's presence.

She shouldn't care about where he was or who he was with. Hopefully he had found something useful during his time with Grace that spurred on an excitement to try more types of therapy. She'd already come to the conclusion that getting involved with him was a bad idea, so his attitude earlier shouldn't bother her.

But damnit, she *was* bothered. Maybe her raw nerves and the heightened emotion of the last couple days were to blame. It would make sense that the high intensity caused her to misinterpret what she was really feeling—had her mistaking gratefulness at him being there for feelings toward him.

Determined not to dwell on Lincoln, she tore away her gaze from his temporary place. The thought of wine had her picking up her pace toward home. The faint creaking of a rocking chair reached her ears. Something in the air shifted, and Wyatt pressed closer to her side with a growl in his throat.

Was she paranoid or was someone watching her? She searched the thicket surrounding her house. Nothing moved or caught her gaze. She approached her porch with caution, and her heart all but stopped.

Shay slowed the gentle motion of her favorite rocking chair and rose to his feet. His hands hung at his sides and the outline of a gun against his dirty jeans shined like a silent warning. "Welcome home, Sweetheart. We have a lot to catch up on."

18

Brooke took mental stock of anything she could use against Shay. Her phone and water bottle, along with a change of clothes, were all safely tucked into the backpack hooked on her shoulder. No way she'd be fast enough to dig through the bag, find her phone, and make a call before Shay used the weapon hanging at his side.

"I can see those wheels of yours spinning from all the way up here. Don't do anything stupid. I'd hate to have to put a bullet in that mutt. Just come inside so we can talk." Shay didn't make any movements, and his voice was calm—too calm.

Anger gritted her teeth. She rested a hand between Wyatt's perked-up ears, not wanting him to charge up the porch steps and get hurt. If Shay did anything to harm one hair on her dog's head, she'd tear him apart limb by limb with her bare hands. "You're crazy if you think I'm stepping inside that house with you."

Shay scratched his cheek and took a step forward. "I don't see how you really have a choice."

"Are you going to kill me like you did Julia? Like you

tried to do in the woods this afternoon? I don't understand why you keep insisting we speak when all you've done is try to hurt me." She hated the crack in her voice but being so close to Shay brought up so many emotions.

"I didn't kill anyone." He stomped his booted foot against the floorboards of the porch. "It's all one big misunderstanding. Damnit, if you'd just let me talk. Let me explain how this all happened. Then you'd get it through that thick head of yours. You'd see what I've been going through. What I've put up with just to get you back."

"I don't care what you've gone through. I care about all the bad decisions you've made. I care about Julia and the life you stole."

Shay raised the gun and aimed it at Wyatt. "Enough! You're always talking. Always pushing my buttons. For once in your life, just keep your mouth shut and do what I tell you. Get. Inside. Now."

Her mind whirled. If she went in the cabin with him, chances were slim she'd ever make it back out. If she stayed out on the path, he'd shoot her dog—her best friend. She held up her hands. "Okay. You win. Let's talk."

Smiling, Shay lowered his gun.

"Wyatt, go have fun." She barked out the command and prayed Wyatt listened.

Wyatt took off, running along the lakeside path in the direction they'd just come from. Tucker had taught Wyatt all sorts of tricks, his favorite being told to go have fun. Wyatt understood that meant it was time to see his friends. She'd never used the command when she needed her dog to get help, but she was certain he'd obey.

Shay smirked and descended the first step, leaning heavily on the railing. "Great guard dog."

"He's just a puppy." She tried to keep a casual tone. If

Shay suspected she'd just sent her dog for help, there was no telling how he'd react.

"Whatever. Just get inside."

She was pressing her luck, but she couldn't go with him. Not inside. Not on the porch. Not within reach of his iron fists. She'd rather he shot her outside her cabin than find herself trapped with him again. At least a gunshot would draw the attention of anyone nearby. "No."

He worked his tongue over his gums, causing a ripple in the skin around his lips. "No?"

She stood her ground, chin high and heart pounding.

A growl as scary as Wyatt's emanated from Shay, and he limped down another step. Pain contorted the lines of his haggard face. The dull light exposed his rough shape— worse than he'd been just the day before. Deeper lines crossed his forehead and larger circles engulfed his menacing eyes. He leaned against the railing as though he couldn't keep himself up.

She glanced down at his leg. A large hole tore through the side of his jeans and crimson stained the light blue denim. "How's the gunshot wound? You need to get that cleaned up. Turn yourself in so you can get to a hospital."

"I didn't get shot."

His refusal to admit to the truth had nervous laughter bubbling from her throat. "You're unbelievable. Just admit to what you did. Take responsibility for once in your life. This isn't going to end well for you, so you might as well give up."

"Never. I'll never walk away from you. Not until you're either mine, or I see everything taken away from you like you took everything away from me." A tremor shook his hand, making the gun bounce against his side.

She struggled to get ahold of her anger. Making him mad wasn't wise. She just needed to buy a little time and hope that Tucker was still at the kennel. He'd be concerned if Wyatt came back without her. Then help would come and Shay would be caught. She just needed to keep her cool.

"Which is it? You want me back, or you want to destroy me? It can't be both, Shay. You say you've changed. That if I just talk to you, I'll understand why you've done the things you've done. But standing here, spitting out threats because I'm not falling in line, is not showing me you're a different man from the one I knew two years ago."

He pinched together his face, eyes closed and lips pursed. "You just drive me so crazy. Being near you scrambles my brain. I've been so close, right under your nose, and couldn't touch you. Couldn't be with you. Do you know how hard that's been? How it's twisted me up inside?"

His revelation sent chills shooting up her spine. How long had he been watching her? How close had he been? How many times had he violated her privacy when she hadn't even been aware? Disgust slid down her insides.

Shay was so far gone. He'd crossed from abusive asshole to psychotic stalker and murderer. She couldn't reason with him. She eyed his injured leg again and weighed her options. Her words and pleas wouldn't sway him, but she might be able to match him physically. He wouldn't expect her to fight back—she never had before.

But one question loomed large. Could she get the gun from him before he shot her?

WIND BLEW through the open sides of the golf cart, and a grin of satisfaction pulled at Lincoln's lips. A sense of peace settled on his shoulders. It'd been years since he'd unraveled the tangle of pent-up emotions and aggression. He'd always locked it up tight, ready to move on to the next case. The next victim. The next problem. Examining what each assignment heaped on to his mental state meant toppling over the psychological game of Jenga he'd been playing for most of his life.

But now, after spending time in the woods with Grace, he'd released a shitload of animosity. He wasn't stupid enough to think he'd fixed all his issues, but it was a good start. The experience opened his eyes to the idea of trying something else tomorrow. Maybe even a therapy session was in his future, or god forbid, a yoga class.

Brooke would love to see that.

He winced at the thought. He'd been an ass and hoped Brooke would hear him out. He'd just have to make sure she listened when he showed up at her door and groveled. He didn't know what was between him and Brooke, but he didn't want it to end with him treating her poorly because he was ashamed of his own failure.

The spare cart Grace let him use bumped down the same path he'd ran earlier with Brooke. He grinned, forgetting how much fun it could be to do something as simple as drive too fast in a golf cart.

A dog charged through a cluster of mighty Oaks and cut him off. He stomped on the brake and veered off the path, cutting a line across the grass. He lurched forward, the steering wheel slamming against his chest, pressing against the tender spot from the car accident. "Shit."

Woof! Woof! Wyatt barked in front of the cart. He stood tall, his ears pointed toward the sky, and the fur at the nape of his neck at attention.

Lincoln jumped onto the ground and rushed to Wyatt's side. God, he'd be in deep shit if he hit Brooke's dog. "You okay, boy?"

Woof! Woof!

"What's wrong?" He tried to pet Wyatt but the dog took a step back, swinging his head to the side. Lincoln glanced in the direction Wyatt seemed to be looking but nothing was there. "What is it?"

Wyatt growled, backing away, then barked once again.

Lincoln blew out a frustrated breath. He felt like he was talking to Lassie, trying to figure out the location of the boy who'd fallen down the well. A sense of unease skittered over his skin. He might have only known Brooke a few days, but he knew how much her dog meant to her. Wyatt running around alone, out of sight from Brooke's cabin and barking like crazy didn't sit right.

He ran back to the golf cart and patted the seat beside him. "Come on, boy. Let's go." Wyatt leapt onto the cart, and Lincoln sped down the hill. When he reached the parking lot to the lodge, he whipped toward the back and bumped along to the path around the lake. He took the corner too fast, causing the cart to tilt. He hooked an arm over Wyatt's middle to keep the dog from spilling out.

The sun dipped behind the mountains, and two figures dotted the path close to Brooke's cabin. He pressed the gas pedal to the floor, urging the cart to move faster.

Wyatt barked, a low growl following deep in his throat.

Lincoln squinted, the shadowy figures indistinguishable against the darkening sky. But he didn't need much light to recognize Brooke's petite frame and long, flowing ponytail. "Brooke?" he yelled.

The second, taller figure glanced his way. Dark hair curled around the man's ears. Dirt smeared his clothes.

Shay. Fear spiked in his gut.

Shay darted to the side of her cabin and into the woods.

Brooke ran toward Lincoln, glancing over her shoulder

every few steps. "Shay. He ran into the woods. He was at my cabin when I got back and has a gun."

Lincoln parked the golf cart a few feet from Brooke's cabin and jumped out. "That bastard just showed up?"

Brooke gripped the side of the cart and nodded. "We need to go after him."

All the peace he'd found flew right out the window. His instinct was to race after Shay and ram his fist in the asshole's face. But Shay had a gun, and Lincoln had already failed to pull a trigger today. His hand wasn't ready to take the needed shot, and he had to be man enough to admit that to himself. "No. We need to call Cruz."

Brooke's terror-filled eyes widened. "But he doesn't have much of a head start, and his leg's injured. I think from where I shot him earlier. We can catch him."

Lincoln took a steadying breath, needing to be logical in a situation where all he wanted to do was act on impulse. "He's got a gun, and he's already proven he's unstable. I can't shoot, and you can't put yourself in his path. Not when there's no telling what he'll do, and the sun is about to set. Cruz will come and search the woods. It's the safest option."

Wyatt jumped down and barreled into Brooke. She crouched and rubbed her hand over his side. "Good boy. You're getting one hell of a treat when we get inside."

Lincoln rubbed the back of his neck. "So that's what that was about. Your dog was a barking lunatic. I thought I was crazy to think he was trying to tell me something. Turns out, he was."

Brooke lifted one side of her mouth and stood. "I told him to go have fun. I expected Tucker to come, but he must have already left the kennel. I'm glad he found you."

"Did he hurt you?" Lincoln grabbed his phone while he

asked, needing to keep his hands busy so he didn't reach out and touch her.

She wrapped her arms over her middle. "No. Just scared me half to death."

Lincoln placed the call and tightened his jaw as he waited for Cruz to answer.

"Hey, man. How you doin'?" Cruz asked.

"Okay, but Shay was at Brooke's place. He took off in the woods. He has a gun. Brooke can't go after him without backup, and I can't give her what she needs." Pressure mounted in his lungs, but not because he couldn't charge up a mountain with the confidence that he could assist in bringing down Shay. Because his words forced him to acknowledge how much he wanted to give Brooke everything she needed—everything she wanted from life.

"Sonofabitch." A weariness weaved through Cruz's voice. "I'll be right there. Can I talk to Brooke?"

"Hold on." He activated the speaker button and held out the phone for them both to hear.

Brooke leaned toward the speaker. "Hi, Cruz."

"Are you all right?" Cruz asked.

"Fine. Just shaken up." She glanced up and connected her eyes with Lincoln. "Your brother showed up just in time. Scared Shay. He took off behind my cabin."

"Did he say anything useful?"

She rubbed her hands against her arms as if to warm herself from some unknown chill. "He told me he's been close for a while. That it's been tough not to touch me." Her voice cracked and tears filled her eyes, making them sparkle like the shimmering surface of the lake.

Screw it. He still had amends to make to Brooke for his earlier behavior, but he couldn't stand by and watch her struggle. He erased the distance between them and wrapped an arm over her shoulder. Wyatt stayed firmly planted in front of her.

She offered him a small smile before she continued. "I think he's close. Maybe a spot in the woods. A tent or an old hunting blind or shack he's found to hole up in. He's hurt, so he won't get too far."

"You two hold tight. I'm on my way." Cruz disconnected without a goodbye.

Keeping Brooke close, Lincoln pocketed his device. "I know it's hard not to act right now, but it's the best option."

She didn't respond.

Pivoting, he faced her. The tears were gone, replaced by the hard glint he'd witnessed earlier when she'd left the shooting range. He drew in a breath and steeled his resolve. "Brooke, I'm sorry about what happened earlier."

She took a step away, causing his arm to fall from her shoulder. "Mmm-hmm."

"I have no excuse for being such a jerk, but if you're willing to listen, I'd love to tell you some things that might shed some light on my behavior."

"Sounds like an excuse to me." She tilted her head to the side, one perfectly sculpted brow raised.

She wasn't making this easy for him, but at least she hadn't sent him packing. "Maybe it is an excuse, I don't know. I just want to talk. Give me five minutes. Please."

Her slight nod had relief pooling in his gut. Five minutes might not be enough to dig himself out of the gigantic hole he'd made, but it was a start. "Thank you. Can we talk inside? It's not safe just standing out here. No telling where Shay ran to."

Without a word, she turned to the cabin with Wyatt at her side. She glanced over her shoulder with a hesitancy he hated to see lingering in her brown eyes. "Come on. I was going to pour a glass of wine."

Smiling, he followed her inside. A lunatic might be scouring the woods, watching him, but Lincoln wasn't half as scared of Shay as he was of what was about to happen next. Brooke Mather would either accept his apology or send him away with a broken heart.

19

Closing her eyes, Brooke braced her hands against the edge of her butcher block countertop and said a quick prayer for some Zen. She still couldn't wrap her mind around Shay showing up on her porch with a gun. Just in case the plea for calm didn't work, she grabbed two large glasses and filled both more than halfway with blood-red merlot.

Blood.

A shudder ripped down her spine at the color of the wine. Shay's blood had stained the wide planks on her porch. A permanent reminder of him invading her personal space—forcing himself into her life. Her nerves shook and energy zigzagged through her body. As much as she wanted to charge into the forest and find Shay, Lincoln was right. Calling Cruz was the best option. Especially with night approaching.

Securing a stemless glass in each hand, she headed for the leather couch. Lincoln still stood by the closed front door, as if unsure if her invitation to come inside was real. Good. Let him squirm. He'd shown a side earlier that made her want to slam the door shut on any lingering feelings for him. His apology was appreciated, but his words wouldn't erase the memory of how he'd behaved.

She set Lincoln's wine on the coffee table and settled back into the corner of the couch, feet tucked under her and glass cradled in her lap. Wyatt walked in a small circle on the floor in front of her and curled into a ball. No, she didn't want to hear anything else from Lincoln, but she also didn't want to be alone. Not after being ambushed at her own home. Not after Shay fled, his location unknown.

Taking a sip, she let the dry wine slide down her throat. She grabbed a cashmere throw off the back of her sofa and draped it across her legs. At the sight of Shay, a chill had crept over her skin that she hadn't been able to escape.

Keeping her gaze on Lincoln, she tipped her chin toward the second glass of wine. "Either you're going to drink that or I am." She wouldn't offer comforting words or encourage him one way or the other. She'd asked him inside and already said she'd hear him out. The rest was up to him.

Lincoln kicked off his tennis shoes and rounded the side of the couch, opting to sit on the chair to its side. He leaned forward and kept his gaze fixed ahead of him. "Like I said, I'm sorry for being an ass."

"I don't remember the word ass being used, but that's a pretty accurate description." She studied the uneasiness in his tapping toe against the rug. It was clear this wasn't a situation Lincoln was used to, and she respected him putting himself out there. She just wasn't sure how much she was willing to forget. She'd heard a million apologies from Shay over the years. Each one filled with lies and insincerity. She'd learned the hard way words didn't mean a thing without action.

He snorted out a laugh and finally glanced at her. "I shut

down. My body. My mind. Everything. The last time I held a gun in my hand, things didn't go well. I didn't get off the shot needed to stop a criminal before a car smashed into my cruiser. The guy I was after got away, and I knew this time if I couldn't get my shit together, it could mean one of our lives."

His words softened her, but what he experienced in the woods didn't mean he could treat her poorly. "I sympathize for your panic attack or whatever you want to call it. I've had them myself, and I know how difficult it can be. But that didn't give you a right to treat me like dirt. To snap at me then dismiss me. I did what I had to do, and if you're too threatened by a strong woman to accept a little help, I don't know why you're here—sitting in my cabin—to begin with."

He hung his head. "You're right. You saved us, and I acted like a child. My failure to do what I was trained to do hit harder than I expected. Made me realize my future isn't clear. I might not get reinstated on the force. That thought knocked me on my ass, and I took my frustration out on you. I never should have done that."

She dropped her hand to the side of the couch to pet a snoring Wyatt. Lincoln's words rang all the right notes, but if she was being honest with herself, she had some confessions to make as well. "You were right, though. I shouldn't have recommended we go for a run. I never should have let you distract yourself with my problems. You're here to work on you, and if I would have let you do that, you might have already started the process of healing. Lord knows you wouldn't have been forced to deal with struggles you weren't ready to face."

"If it hadn't been you, I would have found something else. My walls have been high ever since I arrived. I didn't think anything here could help, so why bother trying? I was my own worst enemy, and it took losing my shit in a life and death situation to show me what a stubborn jackass I was being."

Empathy washed through her, clearing away most of her anger. "I'm glad you realized that. Did Grace slap you upside the head when I left? She has a knack for getting the stubborn guests to come around."

He grinned. "She definitely made her thoughts clear, not like she said anything I hadn't already figured out. I wanted to run back here sooner and talk to you, but I got pretty caught up with what we were doing out there."

The ridiculous stab of jealousy came back with a vengeance. She hid her disdain at the idea of Lincoln and Grace having fun—alone in the woods—behind another sip of wine. "How was the axe throwing?"

Leaning back against the chair, he scratched his jaw. "Unlike anything I've ever done. Shocked the hell out of me. She told me to scream when I threw the damn thing. I thought she was nuts, but when I did, it unleashed all this stuff I've carried around. Something about letting go of the hatchet and yelling at the top of my lungs let all the crap trapped inside come out."

"It's a good feeling. Most of the guests start with the physical stuff. An intense workout with the trainer who breaks them down a bit, throwing an axe or using a bow with Grace, or releasing some tension at the shooting range..." She wrinkled her nose. Damnit, things were going so smoothly. Bringing up shooting a gun was the last thing Lincoln needed. "Sorry. I didn't mean to be insensitive."

A smile touched Lincoln's mouth, and he shifted from the chair to the couch. He slid next to her and rested a hand on her knee. "Please. Don't apologize. I acted like a dick and now you think you need to be careful about what you say in front of me. I hate that. I'm fine...well at least I think I will be."

Lifting her hand from Wyatt, she rested it on top of Lincoln's and offered a reassuring squeeze. Her life might be a disaster right now, but this was why she was here. To help people find their footing. To show them all the tools available to help them.

Lincoln moved the pad of his thumb over her skin. "Today opened my eyes to a lot of things. Some good. Some bad. But one thing I know for certain. While I'm here, I want you by my side. I want to tell you what I tried, laugh when you watch me make a fool of myself in yoga, and have someone safe to confide all my fears to. I want you to push me. To continue to help me be a better man."

His words made moisture pool at the corners of her eyes, but one thing he said echoed in her ears. *While I'm here.* A part of her rebelled against the idea of standing beside him and giving him so much of herself when he would only be here for a short time.

But the other side of her screamed to let herself go for once in her life. To not worry about turning into her mama. To be in the moment and enjoy what Lincoln could offer her, even if the moment would be way too short.

She leaned forward into his warmth, his rugged smell, and pressed her lips to his. She'd take the time he offered. Even if when he left, she'd be picking up the pieces of her broken heart.

JOY SWOOPED in and filled Lincoln's chest until he was close to exploding. He wrapped his arms around Brooke and held her close. He moved his lips against hers, slow and tender.

Never had he imagined she'd not only accept his apology but end up kissing him. He might have said he wanted her by his side while he was at Crossroads Mountain Retreat, but if she wanted him around afterward, he'd have a hard time walking away.

Which left him far from the city he loved.

A thought for another time. For now, all he wanted was to taste the sweet wine from Brooke's lips and feel her soft body move against his.

She pulled away and the prettiest pink stained her cheeks, her always-present red lipstick smeared.

He pushed aside a lock of hair and cupped her jaw in his palm. "You're so damn pretty."

The pink on her cheeks flamed brighter. "You're not too bad to look at yourself."

He grinned, feeling like a stupid teenager, and covered her mouth with his again. Her tongue brushed against his lips, and he opened his mouth, welcoming her like the sun on a rainy day. She tasted like wine and a hint of coffee and something else entirely Brooke. The combination went straight to his head.

Needing to be closer, he pulled her ass onto his lap while her legs rested beside him on the couch.

She giggled. "I need to put down my glass or I'll spill everywhere." She leaned forward to set her drink beside his on the coffee table, making her slide against his growing arousal.

He ground together his teeth and gripped her hips, keeping her locked in place.

She turned wide eyes his way and the sexiest smirk played on her lips before she dove toward him, her mouth devouring his.

An urgent knock beat against the door.

Lincoln groaned.

"Just ignore it," Brooke whispered. "Whoever it is will go away."

He chuckled and grazed his hands up and down her sides. "I would if Cruz hadn't said he'd be here to discuss what happened with Shay."

Brooke huffed out a long breath then pressed her forehead to his. "How can you make me forget everything else that's happening around us so easily?"

He shrugged. "It's a gift."

She maneuvered off his lap and hurried to the door.

Lincoln stayed where he was, needing a minute to let the blood flow back through his body and erase the evidence of how turned on he was. Screw Shay for being such a pain in his ass. Lincoln had never wanted a woman the way he wanted Brooke. A deep, carnal need to be with her ebbed inside him. But finding Shay came first. He'd have the rest of the night to show Brooke how much he wanted to be with her, and nothing would stop him.

Brooke peeked through the window beside the door then opened it wide with a smile on her swollen lips. "Hi, Cruz. Has anyone found anything?" Breathlessness lifted her words in a way that had Cruz arching his brows.

"How are you?" Cruz glanced to Lincoln with questions clear as day in his eyes. "Both of you."

Lincoln shifted his package and satisfied his gym shorts wouldn't expose what he and Brooke had been up to, stood and faced his brother. "We're fine. Just shaken up this guy keeps slipping away."

Cruz lowered his cowboy hat and crushed it between his hands. "That's why I'm here. I wanted to check in on you, but we also found something in the woods. An old outbuilding draped with a camouflage tarp. Shay wasn't there, but pretty sure that's where he's been holed up this whole time."

Brooke wrapped her arms around herself and shook her head. "I would be surprised he lasted in the woods, but after seeing the tent by Mel's Diner, I should have expected a temporary setup that gave him easy and quick access."

Lincoln skirted around the back of the couch to get to Brooke's side. He secured an arm around her shoulders. He didn't care about the concerned set of Cruz's mouth, he wanted to be there for Brooke. Especially for disturbing news like this. "How do you know Shay was using the space?"

Cruz sighed. "We found pictures and notes. Some old clothes, as well as more save-the-date cards with threats scribbled across them. I don't know if he planned to plant them places to scare you or what, but they certainly point a finger at Shay. We dusted for fingerprints, so we'll know for certain soon."

"But he's not there? Was there blood in the building?" Brooke asked, her body shaking.

"No, and no," Cruz said. "We're still on the lookout for him, and it's too dark now to spot traces of blood that could be on the ground—even with lights. I'll comb the area tomorrow with Grace and see if anything else turns up."

Brooke dropped her arms to her sides and stood tall. "I want to see it."

Cruz winced "Why? It will only creep you out."

She pressed her lips together and fisted one hand on her hip. "Seriously? I need to know what he's been doing out there. Need to see how close he's been. Besides, maybe he left something behind that tells me something it might not tell anyone else."

"She has a point." Lincoln hated to admit it, but getting

Brooke's eyes on the hole Shay kept crawling back to could give them some clue to Shay's current whereabouts.

"Okay." Cruz's concession came out on a long breath. "But not until morning. I have an officer standing by to make sure Shay doesn't try to get back in the structure tonight. Everything will still be there when the sun is up, and with Shay still at large, it will be safer in the daylight."

Brooke twisted her lips to the side as if deciding if she agreed with Cruz's logic.

"Makes sense," Lincoln said, not giving her a chance to argue. "I'll make sure Brooke is safe tonight."

Cruz narrowed his gaze, his jawline hard as stone.

Lincoln tensed his muscles to fight against the urge to squirm. One quirk of the lip or wrong movement was all Cruz needed to understand what was happening between him and Brooke, and it wasn't any of his business. Even if Brooke was a good friend that Cruz felt protective of.

Brooke dropped her gaze to the floor, but not before a hint of a smile glowed on her face.

"Fine," Cruz said. "I'll come by in the morning to get you both. If Shay comes back, call me."

Lincoln pivoted to Brooke's side to open the door for Cruz. "Will do. G'night."

Cruz hesitated in the threshold, shooting Lincoln one last warning look before jamming his hat back on his head and hurrying down the porch steps.

Lincoln closed the door and faced Brooke.

She fell against him while a fit of laughter shook her body. "Sorry. This isn't funny. But the look Cruz gave you. Like he'd chop something off if you didn't keep your hands to yourself." Straightening, she wiped tears from the corners of her eyes. "I've never had a big brother before, but I'm guessing that's how they're supposed to act when looking out for their sisters."

He rolled his eyes. "No, that's how *my* brother acts when he's on his high horse."

She tilted her head to the side. "And do you plan to take his warning looks seriously? I mean, maybe I should stop and consider why Cruz would be upset about us spending time together."

"Don't you dare." Crouching low, he picked her up and threw her over his shoulder as he took off for the bed.

Brooke's laughter erupted once more until he laid her down on the soft blanket and hovered over her. All amusement skittered from her features, and she propped herself up with her elbows.

The subtle movement made her breasts jut forward and his mouth go dry. He lunged, trapping her delicious mouth with his. He roamed his hand under her shirt, along the smooth skin at her sides.

She moaned and molded herself against him.

Shay might be lurking around, but tonight, Lincoln would erase the name of every man from Brooke's thoughts. He'd show her all night long how a real man treated a woman he was falling in love with.

20

The morning sun leaked through the flimsy white curtains covering the window behind Brooke's bed. She stretched her arms over her head, and her muscles hummed with satisfaction. Images of the way Lincoln had taken her body to heights of pleasure over and over again filtered through her brain. A soft purr vibrated her throat, and she reached for him.

Her hand patted the soft sheet beside her. Frowning, she pulled her blanket above her bare chest and sat. Her cabin was empty, only the gentle hum of the refrigerator filling the quiet space. Her heart dropped. Last night meant more to her than a quick lay, and she'd assumed it meant more than that to Lincoln. Had he fed her a line of bullshit to get her into bed, then took off before the sun came up? Had she not learned her lesson after always believing the man she loved had changed, only to prove time and time again he was the same bastard he'd always been?

Her breath stalled, and she smoothed her palm over her aching chest. Lincoln wasn't a man she loved, he was a man she respected and liked and wanted to spend time with. He was a man she hated to think about not seeing every day. He was...sonofabitch.

Falling in love so damn quickly wasn't possible, hell she'd known Shay for years before the first ping of love took hold. But the tugging in her chest that longed for his presence told a different story.

The front door swung open, and Wyatt ran inside with his tail wagging and tongue hanging out the side of his mouth. Lincoln stepped in behind him and closed out the blinding sun with the door. "You're awake." He beamed, not even his full beard hiding the width of his smile.

Relief loosened her muscles, and she ran a finger along the sensitive spot on her jaw where the thick hair on his face had rubbed against her skin the night before. "I am."

"I planned to get the coffee made and maybe scramble some eggs to surprise you with, but your dog had other ideas." Lincoln dropped a duffle bag on the floor and stalked toward her, his grin morphing into a smirk. "But if you want to stay in bed a little bit longer, I can think of a few ways we can pass the time."

She laughed. "I'm sure you can, but Cruz will be here soon to take us to the old outbuilding he found last night. He wasn't too keen on letting me see it, so I don't want to give him any reason to change his mind. Catching us in bed might be just the excuse he needs."

Lincoln planted his fists on the mattress, one arm on each of her sides, and pressed his lips to hers. He pulled back, sighing. "Fine. I figured you'd say that, so I grabbed a change of clothes from my cabin while Wyatt did his business. Mind if I take a quick shower?"

The warmth of his body so close to hers—along with the thought of him naked in her shower—made her core burst into flames, but she had to keep a level head. "Go for it. I'll make that coffee." She kissed his forehead then ducked under his arm to scurry off the bed.

She padded her bare feet across the cool wood floor, keeping her back to Lincoln so she didn't change her mind and offer to join him in the shower. When the bathroom door closed and the water turned on, she got a cup of coffee started then rummaged through her dresser for a change of clothes. By the time Lincoln reemerged with water dripping from his long strands of hair, she'd thrown on a pair of yoga pants and a tank top and had her feet stuffed into a pair of tennis shoes.

"Do you always get ready so fast?" He quirked up an eyebrow, but there was no denying his admiration for her speediness.

"Only when I need to. And since I'll always pick sleep over more time to get ready, most mornings involve rolling out of bed and into the first thing I pull out of my drawer." She grabbed the mug of coffee and handed it to him as she doctored a cup for herself.

"Thanks." He took a long sip before setting the mug down on the table. "Have you heard from Cruz?"

As if on cue, a knock sounded at the door.

Wyatt lifted his head from his food dish and let out a deep bark before bounding for the door.

Brooke tilted her head toward the sound. "Is that some kind of weird twin thing? Like you felt his presence drawing near or something?"

Laughing, he circled her wrist with his hand and pulled her close. "Nah, that's just knowing my brother is uptight and always on time." He crushed his mouth with hers then swatted her ass. "Better let him in before he loses his shit."

Setting down her untouched morning fuel, she turned for the door and couldn't stop her grin. The easy back and forth between them was so natural. So fun. An effortlessness she'd never experienced with a man before. "You're horrible." She brushed Wyatt aside with her foot and opened the door to a stern-faced Cruz.

Cruz nodded and a frown pulled down his lips. "Morning."

Lincoln came up behind her and rested a hand on her shoulder. "Morning. Anything new to report?"

Cruz pet Wyatt and shook his head. "Nothing we didn't already know. Fingerprints were confirmed. The place is Shay's, but still no sign of him. You two ready? I want to get to the outbuilding and check it out."

"We're ready." She crouched and squeezed Wyatt's face between her hands. "We'll be right back, boy." She kissed his forehead then followed Lincoln and Cruz out the door, making sure to lock up before jogging down the stairs and falling into step beside Lincoln.

Cruz glanced over his shoulder. "We'll need to hike about a mile into the woods."

"Only a mile?" She couldn't help the bite of fear at the idea of Shay being so close.

Lincoln grabbed her hand and squeezed. "He won't get near you. I promise."

She offered him a weak smile but didn't respond. Shay had proven more than capable of catching her unaware. The only way to make sure he didn't get close to her again was by finding him and throwing him back in jail. She kept all her worries and concerns to herself as she brushed aside low-hanging branches and focused on her footing through the dense underbrush. Sweat beaded on her hairline and coated the back of her neck.

"Almost there," Cruz said. "Just on the other side of this huge oak."

Staying close behind Cruz, she pivoted and a young officer came into view.

The young woman dipped her chin. "Morning."

"Anything to report?" Cruz removed his hat and rubbed an arm across his brow before returning it.

"Been quiet since I got here."

Brooke peered around the woman and shock rooted her to the grassy ground. A square structure stood in a small clearing. Ropes attached to the nearby trees hoisted a camouflaged tarp overhead. The sides of the tarp flowed down to cover the old structure. "How in the world did you spot this?"

"Luck," Cruz said on a snort. "When we came back here searching for Shay after he showed up at your place."

Lincoln darted around his gaze as if waiting for someone to jump out from behind a tree. "Can we head in? Do we need gloves?"

"Already dusted the whole place for prints, so we're fine. Just let me know if anything stands out to you, Brooke. Anything that could help point us in a direction he could be hiding." Cruz took the lead and peeled back a section of the tarp, revealing a narrow door.

Lincoln placed his fingertips to the small of her back, urging her forward.

She didn't want to admit it, but she needed the encouragement. She moved forward, licking her chapped lips, and entered the outbuilding. Her stomach dropped, and her feet turned to led. Dozens of pictures stared back at her—most shots of her taken around the retreat. All driven into the walls with thumbtacks. Bile sloshed in her gut.

Shay had stalked her for weeks. He'd waited and watched and when the time was right, he'd attacked. And while he'd stood so close, taking pictures and plotting his revenge, she'd gone on with her days with no idea how close the monster lurked. He could have grabbed her and caught her unaware so many different times. In the one place she'd finally felt safe, she'd been nothing more than a sitting duck who couldn't even sense the danger around her.

LINCOLN'S BLOOD pressure spiked in his ears, and anger rushed through his veins. Almost every inch of wall space was covered in pictures of Brooke.

Brooke outside her cabin. Brooke shooting an arrow in the clearing. Brooke leaving the Chill N' Grill.

He wanted to make a slow circle and take in every inch of the area, but Brooke leaned against him as if she'd topple over if he left her side. "Are you all right?"

She nodded, although her wide eyes and pale face told a different story.

"If this is too hard, we can step outside." He squeezed her hand, letting her know he was here no matter what she decided.

She glanced at him through tear-rimmed lashes. "I'm fine. Really. This is just...disturbing." Slipping her hand from his, she approached the closest wall and skimmed a finger over a glossy picture of her and Julia laughing on the back deck of the lodge. "Sonofabitch. He lied. Said he didn't even know who Julia was. A tiny part of me wished he'd been telling the truth. That he hadn't murdered an innocent girl because of some vendetta against me." Her voice cracked and she crossed her arms over her chest.

Lincoln cringed, understanding not wanting to believe the worst, even when the truth was right in his face. He swept his gaze around the room. The space was bigger than he'd imagined. Probably close to ten-by-ten feet. A cot was tucked to one side, an army-green sleeping bag rumpled on top. A couple of flashlights sat beside a blue cooler and a bow with a few arrows leaned against the wall beside the cot.

He took a couple steps to cross the space and pointed at the weapon. "Grace will be happy to get her bow back. She was pretty pissed that Shay broke her lock and stole property from the retreat."

Cruz came up beside him and dropped into a crouch in front of the bow. "This doesn't look like one of yours, Brooke."

Sighing, Brooke joined them. "Can I touch it?'

"Go for it," Cruz said, and took a step back to give her space.

Brooke grabbed the bow and studied the rounded handle of the weapon. "This is Shay's. He's had it since he was a boy."

Cruz frowned. "I thought you said Shay was more of a city boy, even when he lived in a small town."

"True, but his grandad was a big hunter. They'd take a trip every summer into the mountains. They stayed in luxury cabins but brought down whatever wildlife they could." She waved a hand through the air as if pushing back a curtain. "The fact he can live like this might surprise me, but him hunting doesn't."

Lincoln picked up one of the arrows that had fallen to the ground after Brooke moved the bow. He ran his finger over the red feathers at the tip. "Are these the same arrows you found yesterday?"

Cruz shrugged. "Look similar, but the arrows aren't as distinguishable as the bow. The retreat's bows all have their logo branded into the wood. The arrows are harder to tell apart. Do you know, Brooke?"

She screwed her lips to the side. "I don't have the slightest idea, but Grace might. After you compare these with what you found, I'd take one to her to look at."

"Good idea." He took the arrow from Lincoln and let it dangle to his side.

Lincoln moved around the perimeter of the room, wanting to get a better sense of the things Shay had thought important enough to pin up. His tennis shoes made the loose and decaying floorboards squeak with each step. "He really did his homework. Maps of the town, a layout of the retreat property, pictures of you and most of your friends." Faces of people he'd met the last couple days dotted the walls, increasing his fury.

Ring, Ring.

Brooke raised her brows and glanced at Cruz as he dug his phone from his front pocket. "I'm surprised you get service out here. I left my phone at home because reception this deep in the woods always sucks."

He offered a quick smile then answered the phone. His smile fell and the lines of his face tightened. "Okay. I'll be right there." He disconnected and returned his phone before turning toward the door with the arrow in his hand. "The white plumbing van's been spotted just outside of town. We gotta go."

Lincoln's pulse kicked into high gear as he followed his brother from the outbuilding and retraced his steps back to Brooke's cabin. Shay must be either too injured to keep torturing Brooke or too spooked to continue his stakeout, so got out of dodge. He'd stay with Brooke at her place until the bastard was caught, and Cruz slapped a pair of cuffs on him.

He emerged from the dense woods and the sun beat down. First thing he'd do inside the cabin was drink a gallon of water. Second thing was strip off Brooke's clothes and keep her mind occupied as they waited for word of Shay and the van.

Cruz offered a quick wave then jumped into a golf cart and took off toward the lodge.

Brooke blew out a long, shaky breath and climbed the porch steps. "I know I needed to see all that, but damn, I wasn't prepared. It was like walking into a real-life nightmare." She unlocked and opened the door, then slid to the side to let Wyatt charge out.

"I'm sorry you had to see it. I'm disturbed, and I wasn't the one whose face was plastered all over the place." He led the way inside. "Can I get you some water?"

"Yes, please." She called Wyatt inside then closed the door and dropped onto the couch. She lifted her phone from the end table and groaned.

He glanced over his shoulder. "Everything okay?"

She sighed. "My mom called. I haven't told you much about her, but she's exhausting. I don't have the energy to deal with her right now."

A punch of pity slammed into him. He'd been dealt his fair share of shitty cards in life, but his family had always been by his side. He couldn't imagine not having his mom or brother to lean on when times were tough. "Then don't. You can call her later. After all this is behind us and you don't have to worry anymore."

"Good idea. I'll listen to her voicemail—which I'm sure is just full of whiny requests for money."

He filled two tall glasses with ice cubes from trays in the freezer then water from the faucet and carried them to where she sat on the couch with her phone pressed to her ear.

Her gaze shot to his, and her mouth dropped open. Tears dotted the corners of her eyes. She lowered the phone. "Shay has my mom."

21

B rooke didn't pause for Lincoln's response. She pressed her mother's number and waited for her voice to fill the line. Nervous energy zipped through her veins, and she tapped her sneakered foot against the floor. Wyatt sat at attention in front of the sofa and stared at her with rounded eyes.

"Brookie? Is that you?" A shiver sliced the words into too many syllables.

Pushing to her feet, Brooke tightened her grip on the phone and kept her gaze locked on Lincoln. "It's me, Mama. Are you okay?"

A sob ripped through the speaker and tore Brooke's heart in two. "Shay's here. He shot Rick. He said he's going to kill me unless I called you. Honey, I didn't know what else to do. I'm so sorry."

Brooke blew out a breath, willing her vocal cords to stay calm. "You did the right thing, Mama. Is Shay still there?"

"Yes. He's mad, Brookie. I don't know what he plans to do. But Rick...oh God. There's blood everywhere. He needs help, but Shay won't let me—"

"Hello, Sweetheart." Shay's deep baritone filled the line. "So glad you called. I wondered if you'd even bother. I mean, I know all about your shitty relationship with Glenda. But everything's gone to hell, and this is my last shot to finally get what's mine."

Fury assaulted her senses, red coloring the frame of her vision.

Lincoln stepped in front of her. "Put it on speaker." He mouthed the words.

His presence calmed her enough to get the shaking in her hand to stop and push the button. She held the phone out between them. "Mama doesn't have anything to do with this. Let her go."

"Your mama is the only way to get to you. You've got too many people around you all the time up at that fancy retreat of yours. I waited too long, and that asshole with the long hair and beard is always hovering nearby. Never leaving me enough time to talk some sense into you. I never thought using your mama would be the best way to get you alone."

Brooke locked her gaze with Lincoln, wanting him to tell her what to say. How to act. What the best way to play this out was. She couldn't trust her instincts when her stomach was tied in a million knots. But only one fact stood out clear as day in her mind. Her mama might not have been the best mother, but she had loved Brooke the best way she could. Brooke couldn't let Shay hurt her. She'd do whatever was asked, then figure a way out. But first, she had to get Mama away from Shay, and get Rick medical care. "What do you want me to do?"

Lincoln tightened his jaw, and fire lit behind his ice-blue eyes.

"Come save your mama, Brookie. I'll let her get help for her pathetic boy toy, and you and I will go get married and live our lives the way we were always supposed to. And don't even think about calling the police. If I see anyone with you, or even hear a siren, I'll kill them both."

The line went dead. Brooke stared at the phone resting in her hand, mentally preparing for what she had to do. Circling the cabin, she searched for her things while her mind spun. She needed her keys and purse and to take Wyatt to the kennel. Tucker would keep him until she got back. "Dammit, where are my keys? I always leave them on the counter."

"Brooke, just take a minute. Let's think this through."

She huffed out an irritated breath and pinched the bridge of her nose. "Shit. I don't have a car. I'll have to take one of the retreat's trucks."

Wyatt stayed in step beside her as she moved through the home. He could sense her anxiety and wanted to remain by her side to calm her down. But it was too long of a trip and too big of a risk to bring him.

The heat of Lincoln's gaze followed her as she scooped her purse off the back of the kitchen chair and rummaged through the junk draw for spare keys to the maintenance truck parked at the lodge.

"Brooke!"

She fisted the keys in her palm and slammed the drawer closed. "What?"

"Wait a second. Let's talk about this."

"There's no time to talk. Mama lives an hour away. I need to get on the road." Action was required right now, not discussing a plan that included her, and her alone. She knew what had to be done, no matter how hard it would be to put herself within Shay's reach again. There was no other option.

"We need to call Cruz," Lincoln said.

A well of emotion threatened to erupt from the pit of her stomach. She couldn't let it. Couldn't let the fear and anger and guilt cloud her judgement. She faced off with Lincoln, knowing he wouldn't like what she had to say. "No."

He arched his brow so high a river of wrinkles rippled across his forehead. "Excuse me?"

Anchoring her feet to the floor, she stood her ground. "You heard what he said. No police. Only me. Or he'll kill my mama and her boyfriend. I can't do that, and it's not fair of you to ask."

A gun, she would take a gun with her. And a pocketknife. If Shay spotted the gun, she'd still have something she could defend herself with. She jogged to her nightstand and grazed her hand under the stand for the Glock she always kept tucked away. Retrieving it, she checked to make sure the safety was on and put it in her purse.

"What the hell are you doing?" Lincoln asked, irritation making his voice raise.

"Preparing myself. Now where the hell did I put my pocketknife?" She returned to the junk drawer that somehow managed to collect the most random shit and pushed aside scraps of paper, pens, and little candles.

A hand on her shoulder halted her motion. She tensed, then turned to face Lincoln.

"You need to take a breath and absorb everything you just heard." Concern lined the corners of his mouth, and he kept her pinned in place.

"She's scared." Her voice wobbled at the thought of her helpless mom facing off with Shay. "She might be my mama, but I've always been the one who's taken care of *her*. She's got her faults, but she's also got a good heart. Sitting there with Shay, frightened and worried, must be eating her alive. I have to get to her now."

"I agree."

She blinked, trying to make sense of his words. "You do? You said we should call Cruz and we needed to think this through. That doesn't sound like accepting I need to hurry up and get the hell out of here."

"I'm not accepting you need to go."

Annoyance had her biting down on the inside of her mouth. "Stop playing games. Now isn't the time."

He tucked his thumb under her chin, lifting it slightly until their eyes met. "*You* are not doing anything. *We* are driving to your mama's, and *we* will figure out a plan on the way."

She shook her head. As much as she wanted to accept his offer and head out with him beside her, it was too risky. "Shay said no one but me."

Lincoln grinned. "What Shay doesn't know won't hurt him. It's me and you, Brooke. Together. Or I'll call Cruz myself."

She sighed, liking the way *together* sounded way too much. "Fine. You and me together. Now let's get going. We need to figure out how to nail Shay's ass to the wall."

LINCOLN TAPPED his palm against the thigh of his jeans. A sea of solider-like pine trees flew by in a haze as they barreled down the highway. Being in control was something he always strived for but driving a truck he wasn't used to on roads he'd never been on didn't make any sense.

Especially when there was no way in hell he'd take the hairpin turns down the mountain at the same speed as Brooke. Memories of crashing over the side of the cliff might turn his stomach, but he trusted Brooke and her ability to get them to her hometown in one piece.

And the fact that Shay wouldn't be slamming his van into them made his tense muscles loosen just a fraction.

The thought sparked a question. "If Shay is at your mom's house, then who is Cruz chasing down? The call he got said the van was just outside of town. That can't be Shay. He would have been close to your mom at that point, hours in the opposite direction."

Brooke tightened her grip at ten and two on the steering wheel and shot him a questioning look. "Maybe someone spotted a different van, and Cruz is searching for the wrong guy? Or maybe Shay ditched the van and had another vehicle on standby to leave the area?"

"Don't you think he should have a heads-up just in case they have an entire police force after the wrong van?"

This time the scathing look she gave him had his balls jumping back up inside his body. "It's not worth the risk. No way Cruz won't call this into the station back home."

She was probably right, but it didn't stop the drum of anxiety beating against his skull at charging into a dangerous situation without backup. "They won't fly in with guns blazing. They'll want to help you—protect you. Not to mention it's not fair to let Cruz waste his time."

Her shoulders dropped, and she traced her tongue around her mouth. "I don't want to be the reason my mama is hurt."

"No matter what happens, you won't be the reason anyone is hurt. That's all on Shay. But we have to be smart." He held his breath. If she didn't agree with him, he'd still have to make the call to his brother.

She drew in a quivering breath. "You're right. Cruz should know what's going on."

Before she could change her mind, he dug his phone from his pocket and dialed Cruz's number.

"Hey, man. What's up?" Cruz asked, clearly distracted.

"Shay has Brooke's mom and her boyfriend hostage at her home outside of Gatlinburg. The boyfriend's been shot. Brooke and I are on our way there now. He told her not to call the police, or he would kill her mother and the man."

"Shit."

"Did you locate the van?" He doubted it, since he hadn't heard from Cruz, but he needed to know for sure.

"No. Not like it matters now."

"You have the captain's number from Brooke's hometown. I'll let you coordinate with them while Brooke and I make a plan for once we get to the house. Remember, discretion is crucial. I'll be in touch." He disconnected, a sense of relief washing over him now that his brother was clued into the situation. "Okay, Cruz will handle the police. What's your plan?"

She shrugged, taking the exit that led off the highway and onto a country road tucked between colossal evergreens. "Knock on the door, see my mom and her boyfriend safely out, then deal with Shay."

He snorted. "We've been in the car for close to an hour and that's all you've come up with?"

"Simple is always better." She pressed her lips together and gave him some serious side-eye. "No need to overcomplicate things."

He scratched his chin and ran over every possible way her plan could blow up in their faces. A hundred scenarios sprang to mind, but he needed her to understand he wasn't questioning her decisions or trying to take charge. He just wanted to make sure she wasn't on the receiving end of a bullet when stepping into the lion's den.

Opening the glove box, he searched for something to write on. "Is there paper or a pen or anything in here?"

She lifted the top of the black leather center console that separated them. "Probably in here. I don't drive this thing very often so I'm not sure what you'll find."

Peeking inside, he grabbed a pen but came up empty on the paper. He glanced over his shoulder at the second row of seating. "This truck is way too clean for a work truck. Not so much as an old fast-food bag to write on."

Flipping his palm toward the ceiling, he drew a square in the center of his hand. "Does your mom have a door in the back and the front of her house?"

"Yes. The back door feeds into the kitchen." She glanced down at his hand and furrowed her brow. "What are you doing?"

"Mapping out your mom's house. I want to know the layout. All the ways I can sneak in, and all the ways Shay can try to get you out."

She set her mouth in a firm line. "He won't catch me off guard this time. I'm not going anywhere with him."

Reaching over the center console, he rested a hand on her arm. "Do you really think he's going to make this easy on you? After everything he's done the last few days—all the trouble he's caused—he's not going to let you walk away and he won't leave that house without you. That means there are limited options on how to get you and your mom out safely."

She tapped her index finger against the wheel, yielding to oncoming traffic before making another turn. "If I think too hard about that, I might not have the courage to walk through the door."

His gut twisted. She'd shot into action so quickly that he hadn't considered she would have a hard time facing Shay.

"We've got this. You just tell me how to get inside. I'll make sure he never hurts you again."

Nodding, she brushed aside a stray tear. "Like I said, a door opens into the kitchen, but Shay will probably have that covered. If we're going to get you inside without him knowing, the best way is through the basement."

Something in the way Brooke said the word basement made a shiver dance down his spine. He doubted she meant a finished basement with all life's comforts. "Is there an exterior door?"

She scrunched up her face. "Kind of."

"What does that mean?" He was afraid to hear the answer but had to know what he was getting into.

"She has a root cellar. There's a door from the outside that's flush with the ground. You can get inside there and make it through the cellar to the basement. Stairs lead up to a small hallway between the dining room and kitchen."

He tensed. Root cellars weren't something he was too familiar with, but he knew the space was small and tight. Especially for a man his size. But if he had to squeeze through the confining space to ensure Brooke made it out alive, he'd do it in a heartbeat. She'd faced too many hard times alone in her life. He wasn't about to let that happen again. "Okay. We've got a little time. Let's go over exactly how we want this to go down."

22

Sitting in the idling truck and watching Lincoln lope around the far edge of her mama's property made Brooke's anxiety skyrocket. Even if she agreed with his plan and understood he'd make his way back to her while she was inside the house, an ache at his absence threatened to ruin her resolve.

Squinting against the glare of the afternoon sun, she swept her gaze along the deserted street. If the police were near, she'd never know. Bile crept up the back of her throat as she shifted into drive and inched down the gravel driveway that led to the house she'd grown up in. The ranch-style home was tucked away in a patch of woods, far enough that their closest neighbor had never heard her mama's cries of pain when suffering at the hands of whichever new man she called her baby.

Either they didn't hear, or they never really cared.

None of that mattered now as Brooke drove down the familiar lane. Patches of dead grass spoiled the lawn Glenda never bothered to maintain. Gnarled oak trees she once climbed as a girl welcomed her with a gentle dip of their ancient branches.

A flash of motion caught her peripheral vision. She squinted, making out Lincoln's silhouette tucked behind a shed that stood at the corner of the backyard. He'd agreed to stay there until she was inside. Then he could make his way to the root cellar while Shay was distracted.

She continued up the driveway and sweat coated her palms. Her heart hammered against her chest, and panic squeezed her throat. Parking behind her mama's VW Bug, she closed her eyes and concentrated on slowing her breathing. Once she felt more in control, she swiped her gun from her purse and shoved it in the waistband of her jeans, then threaded her arms through a long cardigan before hopping out of the truck and heading for the door.

Cracks slithered along the concrete sidewalk, but a new black railing bordered the front stoop and a fresh coat of red paint covered the door. The white siding was weathered, but flowers lined the narrow bed. Tearing her gaze from the yellow daisies, she fisted her hand and knocked.

The door swung open. Glenda, eyes wide and terrified, stood on the other side of the storm door that separated them. "Brookie." Her name came out on a rush of relief.

Shay lurked in the shadows behind her, out of direct view of anyone who didn't know to look for him.

He nudged Glenda aside with the barrel of a gun. "Let your beautiful daughter in. We've waited long enough for her to get here."

Glenda took a step back but lifted her chin a fraction of an inch. Something fierce flashed in her hazel eyes that Brooke had never witnessed before, but she didn't have time to dwell on it.

"I got here as fast as I could," Brooke said, opening the

storm door and stepping across the threshold onto a tiny patch of linoleum. The green carpet of the living room met the cream-colored flooring. The lights were off, casting the room in dark shadows, but the thin strips of flowers lining the wallpaper were still visible. As much as she hated this house, she welcomed the nostalgic touches of her former life in such an unsettling situation.

Shay slammed the door closed, making her jump. He pointed to the kitchen. "Let's go have a chat."

She rooted her feet to the spot. "Not until you let Mama go. You got me here. No need for her and Rick to stay."

Shay cackled. "Rick isn't going anywhere."

A spike of fear pierced her spine. "We had a deal."

Glenda laid a trembling hand on her arm. "He's unconscious. I tried to stop the bleeding, but he lost so much. I don't know if he'll make it."

"Then at least let Mama go." Hopefully Rick would still be alive by the time help arrived, but she couldn't worry about that right now.

"Why are you wearing a sweater? It's hot as hell outside." Shay narrowed his eyes, studying her.

Her skin crawled under his scrutiny. "I had the air conditioning on in the truck."

He pulled back his arm and slammed the back of his hand across her face. "Don't lie to me, dammit." Spit spewed from his mouth as he yelled the words in the quiet space.

Pain vibrated her skull, and the metallic taste of blood filled her mouth. She tensed her jaw, fighting not to react. Not now. Not when her mama was in harm's way.

"Take off the sweater."

"Shay, really. Now you're telling my baby what to wear. Haven't you done enough?" Glenda kept her grip clasped on Brooke's arm and squeezed.

Shay turned a hard glare her way. "I've had enough of your lip to last a lifetime. Count your lucky stars I haven't put a bullet in you yet."

Lifting her hand from Brooke's arm, she pressed it to her chest. "I...I'm sorry. I didn't mean—"

Shay lifted the gun and aimed it at Glenda.

Brooke's heart dropped. She hadn't come all this way and put herself in danger to see her mother gunned down in front of her. "Shay, please. Don't. Let's go to the kitchen and talk."

He didn't spare her a glance. "I've sat here for hours listening to you complain and whine and bitch. I don't need you anymore. Not since Brooke came running."

Glenda held up her hands and shook her head. "Don't kill me. I'll be quiet. I promise."

Tilting the gun so the barrel faced the ceiling, he brought the butt down hard on Glenda's temple.

Glenda dropped to the ground, blood seeping from the wound.

Brooke gasped and covered her mouth with her hands. She fell to her knees beside her mom and checked her pulse at the side of her neck. "Mama. Wake up. Oh my God." A fear like she'd never known burrowed into her gut. Her mama might not be perfect, but she'd tried her best. Brooke couldn't lose her.

Shay gripped her bicep with biting fingers and jerked her to her feet. Fire burned like black embers in his eyes. "Take off the sweater. Now."

Swallowing past the lump in her throat, she peeled off the cardigan and tossed it to the floor.

"Turn around." Smirking, he circled his finger in the air.

Tears stung her eyes, but she did as he said.

"Tsk-tsk. Did you really think I wouldn't look for a gun?"

He yanked the weapon from its spot. "Now, I will tell you one more time. Go to the kitchen, or I will put a hole in your dear old mama's forehead."

Not wanting to provoke him further, she stepped over her mama's still form and crossed the living room. An archway separated the space from the kitchen. Entering the 50's-style room, she took a quick survey of the space. The dining room was on the other side of the far wall. A tiny hallway separated the two rooms. That was where Lincoln would enter the house. She had to make sure Shay couldn't see the door to the basement, which would be nearly impossible if they stayed in the kitchen.

Unless she could get him to sit at the table with his back to the dining room. With that in mind, she sank onto the retro chair at the square table that positioned her back to the archway, facing the back door. If Shay wanted to be near her, it would place him in the one spot that gave Lincoln the best chance to sneak in undetected.

If Shay remained anywhere else in the kitchen, Lincoln would be screwed. Which would leave them all in the hands of a madman.

A GENTLE BREEZE stirred the humid air. Lincoln stayed low to the ground, his back pressed against the decaying shed. He sent off a quick text to Cruz, letting him know he was about to enter the house, then silenced his phone and slid it in his front pocket. Brooke had been out of his sight long enough. He needed to get inside.

Dashing from behind the crumbling structure, he used whatever barrier he could to shield himself from the windows at the back of the house—an overgrown shrub, a billowing tablecloth drying on a drooping line, the gas tank close to the shabby deck. He slid around the rusted tank, glancing at a moving shadow behind white plastic blinds.

He studied the flat patch of land nestled between two rolling slopes about six feet from the house. Squinting, he could make out the wooden planks that made up the door to the root cellar. Blowing out a steadying breath, he ran toward it. He darted his gaze between the silhouette in the window and the door, making sure no one spotted him.

Reaching the door, he flung it open, and his stomach fell to the ground. A rickety ladder led down into a dark pit. Dirt walls pressed around the ladder, leaving barely enough space for his large frame to shimmy through.

He grabbed his phone, turned on the flashlight, and got his ass in gear. He couldn't waste time wrestling his stupid phobia. He had to get inside fast, before Shay could put his hands on Brooke. Turning his back to the cellar, he checked to make sure his gun was secure in his waistband then dropped one foot into the pit until it connected with a rung of the ladder. He kept his phone tucked in the palm of his hand, light facing out, as he lowered himself into the hole.

A chill swept over him and the jagged earth on either side scraped against him causing dirt to break free and crumble into the dank hole. Cobwebs brushed against his skin. He concentrated on evening his breathing and keeping a tight grip on the ladder. Only a few steps down, he reached the hard ground. He swept the light of his phone around and cringed. The space where he stood narrowed into more of a tunnel than a cellar. The wall he just slid down jutted to the side, morphing into a ceiling that came up to his chest. Broken glass and overturned jars littered the floor and the wooden shelf built into the earth.

Feeling like he'd stepped into a warped version of *Alice in*

Wonderland, he scrunched down and charged through the crypt-like room as fast as he could. When he got to the dust-covered door keeping him from the basement, he tugged on the rusted handle. The hinges jumped, but the barrier didn't budge.

Panic swelled in his chest. Sweat coated his forehead despite the chill. He closed his eyes and visualized gripping an axe in his hand and hurling it through the air, remembering the release of tension when he screamed in the woods. His heartrate slowed, he tightened his grip on the handle, and pulled. The door gave way and he stumbled backward, then charged from the oppressive room into a dust-strewn and dingy basement.

Using his phone's light, he found the staircase and crept up the steps. He pocketed his phone, not wanting any light to wash under the closed door at the top of the stairs. He circled his palm around the knob and pressed his ear to the thin door. Mumbled voices sounded close—too close. He visualized the layout of the house Brooke had described. He fought every instinct to charge inside. If Shay saw him coming, they'd all be in trouble.

A sharp scream split the air, and his pulse skyrocketed. *Brooke*. He couldn't wait any longer. He had to get to her. Slowly turning the handle, he pushed open the door a slit and scanned the narrow area. He couldn't see a damn thing but the hallway, so he swung the door open further.

"Come on in and join the party." A deep voice boomed from inside the house.

Lincoln's blood turned cold. Schooling his features to remain passive, he grabbed his gun, emerged from the basement and faced Shay—who stood by the table with his lips twisted in a snarl. The weight of the weapon sat heavy in his hand. He itched to pull the trigger, but doubt gnawed at him —would his hand cooperate?

Brooke sat at a red and silver diner-style table. Worry shone bright in her brown eyes and blood pooled at the corner of her lip—a fresh bruise circled one eye. Tears poured over her cheekbones.

Shay grinned and lifted a gun to aim it at Brooke's head. "Don't be shy. Take a seat next to Brooke. Make sure to drop the gun first, unless you want me to shoot Brooke right now."

Damnit. If he kept the gun, he'd jeopardize Brooke's life. He had no choice but to do what Shay said. Keeping his gaze locked on Shay, Lincoln dropped his gun and strolled to the table. He sat with his back to the wall. He needed to keep his eyes on this lunatic holding them hostage. "Why don't you tell us what you want?" He asked, keeping his voice low and steady. "I've got some decent connections. Money? A car? Hell, what about a flight to some fancy island in the Bahamas?" He splayed his hands open wide, forearms on the table. "Name anything."

Pulling out the chair beside Brooke, opposite Lincoln, Shay plopped down and hooked an arm around Brooke's neck. "I've already got what I want."

Brooke winced, her body coiled as tight as a spring ready to snap.

Lincoln weighed his options. Shay was already pissed Brooke had brought him along. He probably planned to kill Lincoln and take Brooke, assuming no one would know what he'd done. He only had one ace left to play, even if it meant making Shay even more angry. "And how do you plan to keep her? Shoot me?"

Shay shrugged. "Why not? It'd be pretty easy to make it look like you shot her mama and that jackass. Brooke and I would be well on our way to start our new life before anyone realized what happened."

Leaning back in his chair, Lincoln tried to appear at ease. He couldn't let panic cloud his thinking. One wrong move could mean not only the end of his life, but Brooke's. "That might have worked if we hadn't called the police."

Brooke's eyes widened for a second, then she dropped her chin to her chest and folded her hands across her lap.

A flash of disappointment pulsed through him. He couldn't exactly blame her for not trusting him, but he had to follow his instincts. And right now, his gut said letting Shay know other people were aware of his scheme was the only option.

Shay slammed his fist on the table and shot to his feet. "Dammit, Brooke. You can never just follow a simple instruction, can you?" Threading his hands in her hair, he fisted her long strands and jerked her head back.

Lincoln tensed, needing to act but not wanting to jeopardize Brooke. Anger pushed against his veins as he helplessly watched Brooke struggle not to show her pain—her fear. Shay could put a bullet in her head a lot faster than Lincoln could catapult over the table. He rose slowly with his hands in the air. "Let her go, man. I mean, did you really think she'd just walk in here with no help? After everything you've done?"

Shay aimed the gun at Lincoln's chest. "You don't know what the hell you're talking about. All I've done is try to get my woman back. *My* woman. Not yours or anyone else's." He pulled harder on Brooke's hair, lifting her chin at an awkward angle.

Brooke stared hard into Lincoln's eyes and dipped her chin.

He held his breath, sweat dampening the collar of his shirt.

"Let go of me!" Brooke growled then swiped up her hand, a pocketknife nestled in her palm, and slashed the blade across Shay's arm.

Shay released her hair and stumbled backward a couple steps. Blood poured from the gash.

Lincoln lowered his shoulder and charged around the table, wrapping his arms around Shay's waist. He drove him to the ground with a snarl and circled his hand around Shay's wrist that held the gun.

Shay grunted and connected a knee to Lincoln's groin.

Lincoln loosened his grip and doubled over, breaths wheezing through his clenched jaw.

Still on his back, Shay whipped the gun toward Brooke, his gaze darting between her and Lincoln. "I'll shoot her, you asshole. Get the hell off me. I swear to God I'll kill you both right now."

Adrenaline pumped through his veins, but Lincoln hurried to his feet. Dammit. Where the hell was Cruz or the police? They needed help. Now.

Shay staggered to his feet, and his injured arm hung loosely at his side. "All I wanted was to talk some sense into my woman, and now I'm backed into a freaking corner."

Tangled strands of hair hung in front of Brooke's face. "I'm not your woman." She spat out the words through clenched teeth.

Shay cocked his head to the side and smiled. "No one here can save you, Brooke. I'll finish off this dipshit then we're gone."

A flash of movement caught Lincoln's eye, but he kept his palms in front of him and his gaze locked on Shay. In his peripheral vision, a woman with the same build as Brooke with blood pouring down the side of her face gripped a candlestick and snuck up behind Shay. She lifted a wiry arm and slammed the makeshift weapon with a satisfying thunk into the back of Shay's head.

Shay's eyes fluttered, and he fell to the ground, the gun dropping to the floor.

Brooke gasped and ran forward, catching who he assumed was her mother before she collapsed beside Shay.

Lincoln hurried and kicked Shay's gun to the other side of the room then searched for something to secure Shay. It didn't matter if the sonofabitch was unconscious or not, he wasn't taking any chances. Using the long electrical cord from a kitchen appliance, he wrapped Shay's hands together behind his back and propped him in the corner before turning to Brooke.

Brooke sat on the floor with the woman's head in her lap. "Mama. You did it. You saved us." Tears streamed down her face as she stroked her mother's head like a child. She glanced up at Lincoln. "We need to get help."

He nodded and retrieved his phone, placing a call to Cruz. "Shay's unconscious, Brooke and I are all right, but we need an ambulance here. Now." He disconnected and lowered himself to his knees beside Brooke. With his focus locked on Shay's unmoving form, he rested a reassuring hand on Brooke's shoulder. "It's going to be okay. Help's on the way."

The wail of a siren sounded in the distance as he watched the woman he loved cry over her wounded mother. He could only hope her mom received medical attention in time. If something happened to her mother because of Shay —because of Lincoln's inability to get them safely out—she might never forgive him.

23

L ifting the cup of weak coffee to his mouth, Lincoln inhaled the subtle aroma of the sludge the hospital vending machine had spit out an hour before and took a sip. The liquid had long turned cold, but the lingering scent kept away the sharp edge of disinfectant and hand sanitizer. Although, the last couple of hours spent in the waiting room may have permanently etched the pungent smells into his nostrils.

Brooke leaned against him, her body vibrating with the constant motion of her foot tapping the stained carpet. She'd barely said a word since they'd arrived, deep in her thoughts as they waited on news of her mother and Rick.

Setting the paper cup on the little stand beside him, Lincoln stretched an arm over Brooke's slender shoulders and pulled her close. He pressed a kiss to the side of her head and skimmed the tips of his fingers against her arm. "Can I get you anything?"

She shook her head. "I don't think I could eat or drink right now." She jumped to her feet and peered around the corner of the waiting room into the wide, brightly lit hallway. "Why is this taking so long? We've been here forever. A doctor should have told us something by now."

"I'm sure your mom will be okay. She seems like a strong woman." He scrubbed his palms down his cheeks, hoping his words were true.

Brooke leaned further into the hallway then spun toward him with wide eyes. "Here comes Cruz."

Lincoln stood. After the police and a couple ambulances arrived at the house, transporting Glenda and Rick to the hospital had taken precedence. By the time another ambulance arrived to transfer Shay for medical attention, Cruz had shown up and jumped into action. Lincoln hadn't heard from his brother since he'd hopped into the back with the EMT and the still unconscious Shay.

Heavy eyes and a deep frown dominated Cruz's clean-shaven face. He lifted a hand in greeting and surveyed the empty waiting room. He offered Brooke a weak smile then hurried over the worn carpet to give Lincoln a quick hug and hearty pat on the back. "Glad you two are okay, man."

Brooke took what had become her place of comfort, at Lincoln's side. "What's going on with Shay? Did he wake up?"

Lincoln fisted his hands at his sides. If the bastard was awake somewhere in the small county hospital, he'd have a hard time not finding him and making the asshole pay for everything he'd put Brooke and her mother through.

Cruz blew out a long breath. "He's awake. Has one hell of a headache, and a nasty concussion, but he'll be fine. The doctor wants to observe him for a while longer, then he'll be carted off to jail. He won't hurt you again, Brooke."

Brooke nestled her hand inside Lincoln's. "He confessed?"

Shaking his head, Cruz rubbed the back of his neck.

"Not to everything. He admitted to stalking you, breaking into your cabin, attempted kidnapping when he grabbed you at Mel's Diner, and the whole mess that happened with your mom."

A sharp pain burrowed behind Lincoln's eyes. "What about killing Julia and nearly killing Brooke and I twice?" Shay's confession wasn't needed to lock him up for years, but if he insisted he was innocent of the rest of the crimes, he wouldn't get as much time as he would for murder if Cruz and the rest of the police couldn't prove his guilt.

And Chet wouldn't get the closure he needed knowing Julia's killer was not only behind bars but had taken responsibility for what he'd done.

"Shay claimed he didn't know what I was talking about when I questioned him regarding those things." Cruz screwed his lips to the side and jammed his hands in his pockets.

"He told me he had Julia when he grabbed me at Mel's. Why would he just say that?" Brooke's voice shook and echoed off the cream-colored walls. "I just want to scream and tell him to stop lying. Nothing will get him out of the mess he made."

Leading her back to the waiting room chairs, Lincoln coaxed her down then sat in the hard chair beside her. He kept his hand in hers and rested them both on her knee. "Cruz will get to the bottom of this. I promise. You don't need to worry about Shay. Not anymore." He glanced up at Cruz and tightened his jaw. "Thanks for the update. Keep me posted on anything else you find out. But right now, Brooke needs to focus on her mom."

Cruz nodded. "Understood. Brooke, I don't know your mother, but I can tell she's a fighter. She'll be okay."

Brooke sniffed back tears and rested her head on Lincoln's shoulder.

Lincoln watched Cruz leave and a knot of tension loosened in his gut. Shay might try to wiggle his way out of some of the shit he'd pulled, but they had him over a barrel on too much to let him walk away. He'd be back in jail where he belonged soon enough, and Brooke could live the rest of her life knowing Shay would never show up to hurt her or her family again.

And if he slipped through the cracks of justice and wormed his way back into Brooke's life, Lincoln planned on being by her side for as long as she'd let him.

Lifting his free hand, he brushed a tear from Brooke's cheek. "Cruz is right. Your mama's one hell of a woman. She saved our asses. I owe her my life. No way she'll let some scumbag like Shay get the best of her."

"She lost so much blood. And the gash on her temple..." A small sob escaped her, stealing the rest of her words.

"She took a nasty hit, but she woke up and did what she had to do to take Shay down."

"I've been distant lately. We've had so much animosity between us. I don't even know if she understands how much she means to me. How much I love her. What if I don't ever get a chance to tell her?" Tears rolled faster down her face, soaking through his T-shirt.

He wanted to tell her she'd get the chance to tell her mama everything—have time to build a new and better relationship with her—but he could only spew so many empty promises. Promises he prayed came true.

The sound of footsteps approached the waiting room, and Lincoln held his breath. A nurse in green scrubs with a low ponytail of dark hair pushed a wheelchair around the corner.

Glenda Mather slouched against the chair, her matted hair pulled away from her pale face and stitches lined along the side of her head. "Hi, Brookie."

He rose, keeping Brooke steady as she sprang to her feet and rushed to her mother.

Brooke dropped to her knees and wrapped her arms around her mom's waist.

The nurse smiled. "She insisted I bring her to see you before heading back to her room."

Glenda folded herself over Brooke and moved a hand up and down her back.

Lincoln stayed on the perimeter, not wanting to be a third-wheel in a moment that was solely theirs. His heart swelled, watching Brooke lean back and brush away happy tears from her face. Shay had done a lot of horrible shit the last few days, but at least Brooke now had a second chance to make things right with her mom.

Brooke kissed her mama's forehead then stood, keeping a hand latched on Glenda's. "I've been so scared, Mama. I didn't know if you'd wake up. Didn't know if I'd get a chance to tell you I love you. To thank you for saving me." She turned toward Lincoln and smiled. "For saving us."

A twinge of guilt and insecurity threatened to steal Lincoln's happiness, but he pushed it aside. It didn't matter who the hero was as long as they were all alive.

Glenda's chin trembled. "I got you into this mess to begin with. I shouldn't have called. I tried to resist, but when Shay shot Rick, I panicked. I'm sorry, baby. I should have protected you from monsters like Shay your whole life. I've never given you what you needed. I've never been there for you like a mama should. I want to start doing that now."

Tears spilled over Brooke's cheeks. "I'd like that."

Lincoln stepped forward. "You did what you had to, Ms. Mather. Shay won't be bothering you anymore."

Glenda winced. "Did I kill him?'

"No," Lincoln said. "He's awake, and he'll pay for what he's done."

The nurse cleared her throat and offered an apologetic smile. "I need to take her back to her room now. You both can follow. The doctor will be in shortly to talk with you about her CT results."

"Wait." Brooke turned wide eyes to the nurse then down to Glenda. "What about Rick?"

Tears dotted the corners of Glenda's eyes, but she lifted her lips a fraction. "He made it out of surgery. He's not out of the woods, but they're optimistic he'll make a full recovery."

Brooke brushed aside a strand of her mom's strawberry blonde hair. "Good. I'd really like to meet him."

Crying, Glenda nodded and held on tight to Brooke's hand. "I'd like that, too, baby."

Lincoln followed along behind the nurse as she pushed the wheelchair down the white-tiled hallway, Brooke attached to her mom's side. Brooke's mom was fine, Rick was alive, and Shay's reign of terror was over. Excitement swelled in his chest and a new-found sense of joy warmed his soul. Joy that had everything to do with finding the woman of his dreams.

THE FULL MOON sat high in a sky filled with stars by the time Brooke unlocked the door to her cabin and followed Lincoln inside. Exhaustion pulled her down onto the couch, and she tilted her chin to the ceiling, her head resting on the plush backing.

The cushion dipped, and Lincoln's familiar form settled in beside her. He clapped a hand on her thigh. "How you holding up?"

Turning her head, she faced him and smiled. The day had been as close to hell as she ever wanted to get, but through it all, Lincoln had stayed by her side. Supporting and encouraging her. Keeping her calm and sticking around the hospital until she was ready to leave her mama's side. "I'm okay. Just tired and overwhelmed by everything."

He raised his brows. "Everything?"

The trepidation that danced in his baby blues brought a smile to her lips. "Not you. You've been great. But I've been so wrapped up in this nightmare and it ended so..." She shrugged, trying to conjure the right words. "I can't wrap my mind around it all. I'm just tired."

"Do you want me to head back to my cabin for the night?" He frowned, pulling away from her side. "No need to stick around to keep you safe. If you want some space, I can grab Wyatt while you relax. Then we can meet up in the morning, or whenever you want. Today's been a lot. You need to rest."

She fisted the neck of his shirt in her hand and yanked him forward. "I want you."

He grinned. "Yeah?"

"Yeah." She planted a firm kiss on his lips then pulled away, keeping him close to her. "But I do have to get Wyatt. Then a shower. I want to wash this whole nightmare off me. Then maybe we can scrounge up some dinner before getting that rest?" She wiggled her eyebrows on the final word. Her body might be tired, but no way she wanted to just fall into bed and sleep when she had limited time with Lincoln.

Sadness clenched her heart. She'd gone through the

ringer the last few days, but the idea of Lincoln leaving weighed down on her in a way she'd never experienced.

"Food sounds good. How about I grab Wyatt from Tucker's place while you get a shower? I can even pick up some food from the Chill N' Grill if you want."

Her stomach rumbled at the thought of one of Wade's burgers. "Sounds perfect. I'll write down Tucker's address, then give him a call to let him know you're on your way." Leaning to the side, she rummaged through the drawer on her end table and found a pen and scrap of paper. She wrote the information and handed the slip of paper to Lincoln. "He lives down the road. I'll call Wade and put in an order that you can just pop in and pick up."

"Perfect." He stood then leaned down to give her a quick kiss. He pulled out his phone. "I'll put the address in the GPS to be safe."

She clapped her hands under her chin. "A man who's not afraid to ask for directions. I love it."

He threw a grin over his shoulder as he made his way to the door. "You sure you'll be fine by yourself?"

She smirked and widened her eyes. "I'm a big girl. I can handle myself."

"I have no doubt. I'll be back soon."

She watched after him for a minute before pushing to her feet and stretching her arms over her head. Finding her phone, she typed out a message to Tucker then placed an order at the Chill N' Grill. She slid her phone on the coffee table and made a beeline for the bathroom. If the night progressed the way she planned, she didn't need Lincoln smelling the fear that clung to her skin from earlier. Or the sweat. Or the pungent stench of the hospital.

Turning on the shower, she disrobed then stepped under the steaming spray. Beads of hot water beat down on her skin. She lifted her face and relished the feel of the liquid cleansing all she'd carried for so long. Not just the grime of the day, but the weight of Shay and her bad relationship with Mama, and her unwillingness to trust another man, all floated away and circled the drain along with her favorite strawberry scented shampoo and body wash. Everything might not be perfect, but it was a start. A moment in time when everything in her life was finally on the right path.

She stepped out of the shower feeling lighter than she had in years. Life would be different from here on out—no matter what her future held with Lincoln. She was done closing off parts of herself to her family and friends. She'd repair her relationship with Mama and let down her walls. All of them.

She dotted the soft towel against her skin then hung it back on the hook attached to the door before she wrapped herself in her red robe. Maybe she should stay naked under the robe until Lincoln got here. The idea had her smiling as she stepped out of the bathroom and into the open space that connected the rest of her home.

A man stood with his hips against the back of the couch, his skinny arms crossed over his chest, and a gun in one hand. Brooke staggered backward, clawing at the door jamb of the bathroom to stay upright. He charged across the room before she could verbalize any of the questions piling on her tongue, like who he was or why he was there. She opened her mouth to scream.

Whack!

The gun connected with her skull. Her consciousness flickered and she slunk to the floor, darkness swallowing her cry for help.

24

A gentle breeze flowed through the open sides of the golf cart, and Lincoln sucked in a deep breath of fresh mountain air. The smell of burgers and fries seeping through the white paper bag with the Chill N' Grill's logo made his stomach growl. The food he'd managed to find at the hospital earlier hadn't stayed with him for long, and he couldn't wait to tear into the grease-filled goodness Brooke had been thoughtful enough to order.

Wyatt brushed his black nose against the bag and sniffed.

Lincoln laughed and lifted his and Brooke's dinner from the bench of the golf cart and placed it on his lap. "Sorry, buddy. Nothing in there for you."

Wyatt whined then jumped off the vinyl seat as Lincoln slowed the cart and parked beside Brooke's cabin.

Chuckling, he grabbed the key and the food and hurried up the porch steps. The reflection of stars twinkled against the smooth lake and the world just seemed bigger here—more open and filled with possibilities. He'd never imagined a life outside the city, but he'd also never dreamed of meeting a woman like Brooke.

He shifted his view and spotted Wyatt with his nose shoved in the overgrown grass, tail straight and rigid. He gave the dog another minute, and when Wyatt continued snooping, Lincoln whistled to gain his attention before opening the door.

Wyatt rushed past Lincoln to get into the cabin, the thick fur around his neck pointed straight up.

Lincoln shook his head at the dog's weird behavior and pushed the door closed. "Dinner's here."

Silence greeted him. Walking further into the cabin, he set the take-out bag on the table and strained his ears for signs of Brooke.

Nothing.

"Brooke?" He rounded the corner of the kitchen to the small bathroom tucked in the back of the cabin. She'd mentioned taking a shower, but maybe she'd opted for a bath in that fancy clawfoot tub of hers instead. If she was waiting for him in a tub of hot water, the food would be cold by the time they got to it.

The bathroom door stood wide open. No one inside. Strange. Why would Brooke leave if she knew he would be back soon with food? Maybe something needed her attention at the lodge, and she had to leave. Fishing his phone from his pocket, he called her.

Ring, ring, ring.

He swung his gaze to her chirping phone on the coffee table. Anxiety pitched high in his chest. The odds Brooke would leave her phone behind while running an errand or seeing to issues were pretty low, but he couldn't panic. Shay was in the hospital, after which he would rot behind bars.

Brooke probably just ran out of the house and forgot to grab it.

Crossing the room, he swept up the phone and pressed the home button, hoping a new message or missed call would pop up and clue him into where she'd gone. Nothing but a picture of Wyatt and a request for her password showed. He tightened his grip on the hard plastic. Something was wrong, and he wasn't the only one who sensed it. Wyatt's nose was all but glued to the wooden planks of the floor as he sniffed through the living room and kitchen.

He placed the device back on the table and shoved his hand through his hair, sweeping his eyes on every visible corner of the room. Calling Wyatt back to his side, he raced out the door and placed a call to the lodge. Maybe someone there could tell him where Brooke had taken off to.

"Hello, Crossroads Mountain Retreat. How can I help you?" An unfamiliar voice was way too perky for the growing unease brewing in Lincoln's gut.

"I need to speak to Brooke Mather." He snapped out the request as he rounded the back of the cabin.

"I'm sorry, but she's not here at the moment. Is there anything I can help you with?"

"This is Lincoln Sawyer. I'm staying at one of the cabins —the one beside Brooke. Can you tell me if she was called up to the lodge for any reason?" He walked slowly over crushed blades of grass behind the cabin and crouched low to study the tread marks.

"I'm sorry, Sir. I haven't seen her."

Wyatt whined and turned a tight circle at Lincoln's side. Lincoln sidestepped to see what had gotten the dog so worked up. Crimson stains dotted the grass, and his heart dropped to the ground. Blood. "I need you to ask if anyone has seen her then call the police if they have." He disconnected and called Cruz as he ran back into the house. Wyatt was glued to his side.

"What's up?" Cruz answered on the first ring, urgency clear in his question.

Lincoln couldn't help but wonder if, even with miles between them, Cruz understood the panic rising in Lincoln's throat by the second. "Did Shay have a gunshot wound on his leg?"

"No gunshot wounds, just a bad cut down the front thigh on the left leg. He said he fell in the woods. Why?"

Lincoln pinched the bridge of his nose. "Brooke swore she shot whoever hunted us down in the woods. The blood was proof. Shay was limping when he showed up on Brooke's porch and she said he had blood on his leg. If Shay didn't have a recent bullet hole in him, he wasn't the person who was after us."

"I don't understand. How is that possible?"

A loud whine followed by fierce barking turned Lincoln's head toward Wyatt. The dog pawed at the floor. Trepidation danced across Lincoln's nerve endings, and he crossed the room to the dog's side right outside the bathroom. He pushed Wyatt out of the way, and horror stole the air from his lungs. Drips of blood dotted the wooden floor and a tiny square object lay between the baseboard and bottom of the partially opened door. A matchbook? He'd never seen matches at Brooke's place before, and if she wanted to light a fire or candles, she wouldn't have much luck with the matches meant to light a cigarette or cigar.

Crouching, he studied the front of the paper, careful not to touch the loud pattern on the booklet that had caught his attention. The name of a bar—Shilling's Place—was sprawled across the top, its location listed directly below the thick black font.

Nashville, Tennessee.

His pulse picked up and he stood. Shilling's Place was located in East Nashville, the same area Ian Samuels lived.

The same bar where Lincoln had tracked him down and attempted to put the bastard under arrest.

A hundred little inconsistencies of Shay's case slammed against his brain. The recent track marks on Julia's arm and Chet's insistence that his cousin would never use drugs. The autopsy hadn't come back yet, but Lincoln was pretty sure she had died by drug overdose. Then there was the tampering of the locks on his cabin door, his gut response a guy like Shay with a history of domestic abuse wouldn't escalate to kidnapping and murdering Julia, even the bow in Shay's hideout not being the one missing from the storage shed.

Now, Brooke was missing from her cabin and a matchbook was left from the same neighborhood as a twisted criminal. A criminal who'd evaded the Nashville Police Department since he'd fled the scene of Lincoln's car accident a month before.

"Cruz, you need to get to Brooke's now. She's missing, and I think I know who took her."

A GRADUAL AWARENESS washed over Brooke, like lazy waves lapping ashore—pushing higher and higher up the beach with the incoming tide. A tingling sensation in her toes, an achiness in her muscles, a tug of discomfort in her shoulders. She struggled to lift her heavy eyelids, the movement causing spikes of pain to erupt against her temple.

Wincing, she forced her eyes open. Darkness surrounded her, and the gentle vibration of speeding tires shook the cold floor she lay on. Loud music blared from the speakers, making the pain in her head pulse with each forceful beat. The scent of oil and dirt stung her nostrils. She tried to push herself to a seated position, but her wrists refused to come apart, her arms pinned behind her back. Something dripped down the side of her face, thick and wet.

Blood.

Her breath hitched in her throat, terror and confusion threatening to wrap her tight in their unwavering clutches. She couldn't let them. She had to think and push past the panic growing inside her as she took in the shadowed space. Had to figure how she'd ended up with bound hands in the back of a van.

A van.

Shay had stolen a van and used it to ram her and Lincoln off the side of the mountain. But how could he be driving her in a van if he was in the hospital, under police supervision?

A flash of a memory came back to her, and her back stiffened. A man. In her cabin. He'd charged her and slammed a gun against her head.

It hadn't been Shay. But who was it? Who would want to kidnap her?

An icy blast of wind rattled her bones. A thin strap kept her robe closed over her naked body, but the flimsy material didn't do much to fight off the cool night air. She couldn't worry about that now. Now, she needed to figure out how to get the hell away from whoever was driving.

Licking her lips, she flexed her fingers to get the blood moving in her extremities. Once the stabs of sleepiness left, she roamed her fingertips over the slick material keeping her wrists together.

Duct tape.

The first pulse of hope since waking swept through her. She'd learned a lot of useful skills while on the force, one being different ways to get herself out of this exact kind of situation.

Summoning all her strength, she scrambled onto her knees and ignored the pitch of nausea that rose high in her stomach. She hooked her arms under her feet, bringing her hands in front of her. Pressing her palms together, she raised her arms above her head and chanced a quick peek at the crop of brown hair above the driver's seat before swiftly swinging her arms toward the ground, spreading her hands apart like she'd been taught to do when she'd worked on the police force. The tape gave way and relief almost knocked her over.

She held her breath and moved only her eyes to scan the dirty back of the plumbing van for anything she could use to defend herself. Naked except a robe, and probably battling a concussion, the element of surprise was the only thing she had working in her favor.

A small shelf took up an entire side of the space, but nothing was on it. Whoever grabbed her must have tossed out whatever had been in the van. An appliance dolly was propped against the shelving unit, and a stack of orange traffic cones was next to Brooke. Neither would be useful. She chanced another glance at the driver then inched forward to scan the opposite side of the shelves, closest to the door.

No whirling streetlights or signs of passing cars flickered through the glass. A shimmer of a reflection from under the lowest shelf caught her attention. With her gaze trained on the stranger's head, she stayed as low to the floor as possible and slipped her hand under the shelf until her skin connected with something hard. She whacked the object with the side of her hand until a tool of some kind slid free.

Tears of relief dotted her eyes. A wrench. She fisted it in her hand and pressed her back against the side of the van, out of the sightline of the rearview mirror. The van bounced along, moving slowly as if the path it traveled wasn't well paved. A country road or dirt lane. Hopefully somewhere that she could escape into the cover of the woods once she got herself out of this mess.

The van slowed, and she inched her way forward. Now was the time to strike—when the vehicle wasn't moving fast enough to kill her once she attacked the driver. A ball of fear sat heavy in her stomach, making her movements slow and jerky. But she couldn't let it stop her. She refused to finally be free of Shay's clutches just to fall victim to some other asshole.

She crawled forward, ignoring the cold that swept up her body as she moved. She swung her arm back and the van stopped, the sudden lack of motion throwing her forward.

The man whirled around and grabbed her wrist, not allowing her a chance to smash the wrench against his head. "Don't even think about it, sweetheart."

Defeat crushed down on her. She'd lost her chance. Now her only option was to run. She pulled her wrist back as far as she could and threw the wrench at his face.

He released his hold on her. "You bitch." He lunged over the center console toward her.

Not wanting him to jump out the driver's side door and block her escape out the back, she waited until he was halfway over the seat before she turned and ran toward the back door. Throwing it open, she leapt down, and the soft pads of her feet connected with sharp rocks. She winced but didn't bother to inspect the damage. She pushed all the pain and fear and curiosity about who the hell the goateed man with the fire-spitting eyes was and sprinted off the mountain road into the dense forest.

She didn't know how long she'd been knocked out, or how far they'd driven, but no signs of civilization spoiled the creaking pines. Getting lost in the Smoky Mountains could mean a whole host of dangerous outcomes but staying anywhere near a kidnapper with a gun meant a lot worse. Running was her only option.

Twigs snapped under hurried footsteps, and she weaved between moss-covered tree trunks and thickets of brush. Adrenaline coursed through her veins and beat back the growing queasiness in her stomach. Pain throbbed against her knee, but she had to keep moving. The traitorous moon shone bright overhead, highlighting her pale skin like a deer caught in headlights.

Leaves rustled impossibly close behind her, and her heart leapt with tiny explosions as she turned to look back briefly. The subtle vibration of the earth as her kidnapper came after her made her core tremble. She licked her lips, trying to decide which way to go, afraid that whichever way she turned would bring her closer to her captor.

Her only option was forward. She charged ahead, wrapping her robe tighter around her middle, as a bright beam of light exposed the patch of ground six feet to her left.

He was close, and now he could see her with just a smooth sweep of a flashlight. She sidestepped to the right and pressed her back against the rough bark of an evergreen. The smell of sap mixed with the scent of fear, and she melted between the pine needles surrounding her. Sweat coated the back of her neck, and her pulse beat a steady drum in her ears.

The beam from the flashlight brushed in front of her, and she sucked in her stomach as if she could disappear inside the tree.

But she wasn't stupid. Any second the light would touch her and the branches scratching against her skin wouldn't conceal her. With nowhere else to go, she grabbed a handful of pokey pine needles and twigs and climbed. She'd rather fall to her death than have this sonofabitch get his hands on her.

A few feet off the ground, the glare of a flashlight landed on her face. She winced, and her heart dropped. He might have found her, but she'd never give up. Placing her foot on another branch, she scooted up the tree and prayed for a miracle.

25

Twenty minutes later, not even the buzz of mosquitoes around Lincoln's head broke his concentration from the path Grace carefully walked, pointing out drips of blood and flattened patches of land. Helplessness had him clenching his jaw as he listened to her explain why she made a sharp turn or was confident Brooke was hauled through the thick woods behind her cabin.

Brooke was nothing more than an innocent bystander caught in a game of revenge she hadn't realized she'd been playing. Guilt threatened to break through the haze of panic and fear surrounding him, but he refused to let it gnaw at his gut. Not now. Not when she needed him most.

"Searching for Brooke out here is like looking for a damn needle in a haystack." He threw the words out of the side of his mouth toward Cruz, quiet enough that Grace couldn't hear. He didn't doubt her ability to figure out which way Ian had taken Brooke, but they'd been down this road before, and it had led to a dead end. Too much wilderness and too few clues to point them in the right direction.

"She can't be too far." Cruz pushed aside an outstretched limb that poked out by his head. "How long were you gone?"

Lincoln released a frustrated breath. He'd already been over all of this, but he understood what his brother was doing. Cruz wanted to keep his mind far away from all the horrible possibilities of what could be happening to Brooke. "No longer than forty minutes."

"The damp towel in the bathroom means in that time she took a shower as well. Whoever took her probably has about a thirty-minute head start. Grace and I know these mountains. We can catch up. And every available officer is searching for her on the highways." Cruz twisted toward the sound of an owl, the light from his flashlight exposing a shallow ravine to their left.

"I know who took her. It had to be Ian. He was right under my nose this whole time, sneaking around, waiting for the right time to attack. He was in that damn van when you called off the search because Shay had taken Brooke's mom hostage. I should have trusted my gut and dug deeper." Guilt wound around his throat. If his theory was right, Ian already tried to kill Brooke twice. The only thing that would stop him from succeeding this time was catching him before it was too late.

"You really think this guy would follow you here and take Brooke to get revenge?" Doubt dripped into Cruz's words.

Lincoln tripped on an upturned root and swore as pain shot up his leg. "Not only did I connect his drugs to the death of a child, but that connection caused a raid of his supplier which messed with multiple dealers on the east side of Nashville. The cops were after him, but so was half the scum of the city—wanting payback for messing with their cash flow."

Grace whipped around with a scowl on her full lips. "Would you two be quiet? It doesn't matter who took Brooke if we can't find her."

Lincoln ground his teeth together. She was right, but damnit, he needed Cruz to believe him. The evidence might be murky, but his instincts screamed he was right.

A narrow clearing appeared and the canopy of interwoven greenery above him opened up. A dirt lane with deep ruts of tire tracks crossed their paths. The sight had him staggering backward. "Is this a road?"

Grace aimed her flashlight on the ground and swung it back and forth, glancing up and down the trail. "Kind of. There are a lot of crudely built roads like this around the mountains. Hunters and homesteaders utilize them to get better access to more remote parts of the woods."

"Where does this one spill out?" Lincoln asked, afraid to hear the answer. If Brooke was already on a highway, finding her in time would be nearly impossible.

Cruz grabbed his radio that connected him to dispatch. "I need officers at the crossing of the Pine Valley Express and the access road just south of Crossroads Mountain Retreat."

Lincoln walked a wide circle, studying the tracks. "The tracks start over here. Then dip over into the grass on the opposite side of the road, indicating he had to back up and turn around to leave."

"Makes sense," Cruz said. "He's heading back toward the highway."

Not needing more information, Lincoln took off at a sprint down the road.

Cruz fell into step beside him, leaving Grace behind to call in her exact location to the station.

Having his brother beside him made his heart jump up

his throat. He'd missed working with Cruz, spilling over the pieces of an investigation and bouncing ideas off each other. He didn't trust anyone on this earth to have his back like he did Cruz and being beside him now gave him the boost he needed to keep moving.

Beams of light bounced along with every step, illuminating his path and catching flashes of wildlife skirting around the underbrush beside them. A large object sat on the side of the makeshift road up ahead, and Lincoln pushed his muscles harder—pumped his legs faster. His lungs burned. His heart beat faster with each heavy fall of his foot as he barreled toward a large white van.

He skidded to a stop at the back of the vehicle. The back door was flung open wide. He grabbed his gun and swept the inside of the van.

Empty.

"She's not in there. Dammit!"

Gun drawn, Cruz rounded the front of the van. "Nothing up here, either."

Lincoln gasped for breath and lifted his arms above his head. Where the hell did they go? Grace wasn't here to work her magic and point him in the right direction.

Bang!

Lincoln stilled and locked eyes with Cruz as panic ripped him in two. "Gunshot." He turned in a circle, trying to pinpoint which direction the noise came from. The reverberation from the tree trunks threw off his senses.

"Came from this way." Cruz nodded his head in the direction of the noise. "Let's go."

He took off after his brother, ducking and weaving through the trees and hopping over muddy logs. A bright light shone ahead. Slowing, he shut off the flashlight and motioned for Cruz to do the same. If Ian had a gun, it'd be better not to announce their arrival.

The crack of a branch had him shooting his gaze skyward, and a flash of red fabric wove between the shadowed branches of an evergreen. Dread grabbed him by the throat. Brooke's robe. She was up in a damn tree.

Tiptoeing to Cruz, he nodded toward Brooke. "I think that's her," he whispered and pointed toward the tree a few feet away.

"The light's coming from the front of that tree. He must be shooting at her from the ground on the other side. I'll circle around behind him and catch him off guard. You stay here." Cruz didn't wait for a response before disappearing into the darkness.

Lincoln stalked closer to the tree Brooke had scurried into with his gun in his hand. He couldn't get to her while she scaled through the limbs and pine needles, but he couldn't just stand there and do nothing. He stayed low to the ground, gaze fixed on the orb of brightness from Ian's flashlight trained on the vibrant fabric of Brooke's robe.

The crack of a limb made him freeze. Brooke's panicked shriek made his blood pressure skyrocket. If she fell from where she'd manage to climb, it could do more damage than a bullet.

Bang!

Brooke's soul-piercing scream and the sound of splintered wood had him to the base of the tree in three long strides. To hell with being spotted. If Ian wanted him, he'd give the bastard what he came for. Then he'd be distracted enough for Cruz to grab the sonofabitch. He rounded the side of the tree until Ian's thin frame appeared, his pistol pointed toward where he'd heard Brooke yell out.

"You finally showed up." The low, gravelly voice of the

man who'd left him broken and trapped inside a totaled car raised the hairs on Lincoln's arms.

Lincoln kept his gun aimed at Ian, his finger aching to pull the trigger. He seemed thinner than the last time Lincoln had seen him, and scraggly tufts of hair clung to his chin. The nerve endings in his hand screamed as he tightened his grip on the handle of his gun. Doubt at his ability to shoot the weapon crept into his psyche, but he couldn't focus on that now. "What do you want?"

Even through the shadows, Ian's hatred was evident in his weaselly eyes. "I want to take everything away from you like you did me."

"That's not going to happen." Lincoln fought to keep his gaze on Ian and not search through the mangled branches for Brooke. Her earlier screams echoed through his mind. She needed to hold on for a little longer. "Lower your gun and put your hands up."

Ian chuckled. "No way in hell."

A twig snapped behind Ian, and he widened his eyes.

"Hands in the air, asshole." Cruz yelled the command.

Ian swung around, his gun aimed at Cruz.

Fear constricted his throat. The tendons in his hand tingled and saliva pooled in his mouth. He couldn't choke. Not this time. Not when Cruz's and Brooke's lives depended on him. Lincoln summoned all of his pent-up anger. He squeezed the trigger and pain encased his hand, shooting up his arm. The blast rang in his ears.

Ian crumbled to the ground and screamed out in pain, grabbing his thigh where the bullet had pierced his flesh.

Cruz rushed forward with cuffs in his hand.

"Brooke!" Lincoln burrowed through the sappy greenery of the tree, searching for a foothold.

Another limb snapped from above. "Lincoln! I took a bullet in the arm." Pain threaded through her voice.

He catapulted himself up the tree, the rough bark biting into his palms. Brooke's silky red robe whipped in the wind, the sash tied tightly around her waist. He grabbed the branch over his head, and his hand screamed from the effort it took to keep a firm grip on the wood. Fighting through the pain, he pulled himself up.

Brooke sat huddled on the joint of a bending branch. One bare foot nestled on top of the other, her legs trembling either from the cold or shock. She had one arm wrapped around the thick trunk, the other hung limply at her side— blood soaked through the fabric, making the bold red darker.

The talons of fear around his heart loosened at the sight of her but didn't fade away. Not when she was still at least two feet above him. "I can't get up there. The limb is bending too much. My weight will snap it right off. Can you get down to me?"

"I...I can't." Shivering made her words tremble. "I'm sh-shh-shot."

"You're going to be okay. I'll get you." He hiked up his knee and found another limb wide enough for his foot. He held his breath and pulled himself up, inching closer to Brooke. "I'm right here, baby. But I need you to help me. Just a little. Can you give me your hand?"

Brooke glanced at the arm hugging the tree and winced. "I'll f-fall."

Bracing one hand on the bark, he extended his other one to Brooke. "I won't let that happen. Trust me. Just look at me, honey. Look at my face, let go of the tree, and give me your hand."

She nodded and leaned forward, offering him her palm.

He reached up and grabbed hold of her. "Good. Now take a step down to me. You got this. I promise."

Squeezing his hand, she lowered herself next to him.

"Good job, baby. You're doing great."

A gust of wind ravaged the pine needles around him. The tree swayed with the breeze, and he tightened his grip on Brooke.

Brooke's foot slipped and she fell forward. "Lincoln!"

He hooked an arm around her waist and yanked her to his chest. "I've got you." His heart pounded, but he tightened his grip and secured Brooke in his arms. "I won't let you go."

She swallowed hard and pressed her face against his neck.

"Can you take another step down?"

She lifted her face and locked her gaze with his. "Yes. If you stay by my side."

He grinned, and little by little, he worked his way down the tree with Brooke beside him. When their feet hit the ground, he wrapped his arms around her and held her tightly against him. He inhaled the scent of her—strawberry shampoo mixed with the sap from the tree—and roamed his fingers up and down her back. Now that he had her in his arms, there was no way in hell he'd ever let her go.

BROOKE SHIFTED the sling around her shoulder, wincing when the motion caused jabs of pain to spike against her tender muscles. Getting shot had always been a possibility when she'd been an officer. She'd never imagined she'd face more danger as the owner of a rehabilitation retreat than on the streets, but hopefully that didn't become a habit.

She rolled her chair closer to the conference table in the lodge and tried to use her non-dominant hand to finish the list of topics that needed discussed at today's staff meeting. Messy loops and scribbles dominated the lined paper, and frustration combined with her aching shoulder to increase her bad mood.

Or her grouchiness might have more to do with Lincoln's last day at the retreat drawing near.

After he'd saved her, they'd spent most of the night in the hospital then dropped into bed to sleep when they'd dragged themselves home at daybreak. The next few days were filled with police reports and Lincoln being immersed in Ian Samuels' case.

Not that she blamed him for wanting to be hands-on with wrapping Ian up as tightly as possible for the prosecutor. He'd shouldered the blame of Ian blasting into their lives and causing so much trouble. And even though she'd tried to convince him none of what happened was his fault, she understood his feelings.

Hell, she still held on to guilt for the mess Shay had created for her mother and Rick.

She glanced at the clock before straightening the stack of papers in front of her. Lincoln should be done at the station by now, which would leave only two more days before he returned to Nashville. The idea of him not being close by sat like a boulder in her stomach.

A soft rap on the open door drew her attention. "Anyone ever tell you that you work too much?" Lincoln entered the room with Chet at his heels.

She shrugged, then winced. "Duty calls."

Lincoln kissed her cheek then took a seat beside her.

Chet stood at the head of the table, the mountains a stunning backdrop through the windows behind him.

"How'd it go at the station?" She asked. Lincoln had invited her to watch Ian being interviewed a second time—this time with a lawyer present—but she'd refused. She'd spoken her peace and didn't want to give the man any more of her time.

Chet frowned. "He finally broke about Julia. Turns out he'd met her in Nashville. She'd been to his neighborhood one night with friends. After I got the name of the bar where they met, I called her old roommate. She said they'd venture to this place when they felt like being rebellious. They'd show up at a sketchy bar then giggle about the risk they'd taken. Just kids being stupid, really. Julia just never realized doing what seemed like such a little act of danger would put her in the path of someone who'd take her life." He dropped his gaze and sniffed back tears.

Lincoln rested a hand on hers. "Julia saw Ian at the bar the night I got into town, and she approached him. He didn't want her to tell anyone he was here, but I got in the way of him taking her from the parking lot. He grabbed her when he got the chance. Then shot her up with drugs. The autopsy will show a drug overdose as cause of death."

Sadness weighed her down. Julia had done nothing wrong. Simply being in the wrong place at the wrong time was enough to get her killed. "I'm so sorry, Chet."

He wiped his eyes. "Is it okay if I head home? I can't sit here for the meeting. I need some time."

"Please. Take as long as you need. We're all here for you." She watched him go, wishing there was more she could do to take away his pain.

"He held it together today. Shocked the hell out of me. I don't know if I could have been so strong if someone I loved had been ripped away from me." He squeezed her hand then brought it to his lips. "If you'd been ripped away from me."

She stared into the depthless blue of his cobalt eyes. Was he saying that he loved her? Her brain tried to form sentences, but she didn't want to confess her feelings to him if she misunderstood what he was telling her. She might have vowed to tear down her walls but being the first one to take that leap of faith was scary as hell. Especially after such a short time.

Especially when he'd be leaving soon. Now that it was obvious his hand would heal, he had no reason to stick around. His job and life back in Nashville waited.

"In the short span of two weeks, two men have almost taken you away from me. I won't let it happen again." He drew in a shuddering breath. "I talked to Cruz today."

She blinked at the sudden change of topic. Disappointment pinched her chest. "I assumed you'd speak with him down at the station. How is he?" Not like she cared at the moment, but she wasn't sure how else to respond.

Lincoln worked his jaw back and forth. "Turns out he has an extra room in his house."

She raised her brows, trying to keep up. "Okay..."

Laughing, he shook his head. "For me. If I want to stay. If *you* want me to stay."

She gasped, not believing what she'd heard. "But Nashville. Your job. You love your life there."

"Not as much as I love you." A hint of red stained the visible skin around his beard.

A slow smile spread her lips. "You love me?"

"I know it's crazy, but I can't deny how I feel. I love you, Brooke Mather. And if you don't feel the same yet, I understand. But I want nothing more than to stick around and wait for you to get there."

She hurled herself into his arms and kissed him hard. "I love you, too. I just never thought you'd want to be here, in this little town in the mountains."

"Honey, I want to be anywhere you are." He pressed his lips to her cheek. "Besides, what's better than a cozy cabin in the Smokies with the woman I love by my side?"

"Absolutely nothing." She beamed, her heart fuller than it'd ever been.

EPILOGUE

Keeping his back leg straight and lunging forward with his front leg bent at a ninety-degree angle, Lincoln lifted his arms above his head and gritted his teeth. His muscles shook as he fought to keep the position. A bead of sweat dripped down his face and splattered on the blue yoga mat between his feet and the green grass.

He swiveled his head to glance at Brooke. She was the only reason he'd attempted yoga in the first place. After her physical therapist recommended trying certain poses to strengthen her injured shoulder, he'd promised to stick by her side while she fought her way through the exercises.

Four months later, and he was still suffering through pose after pose. At least when Zoe held class outside, he could distract himself from his screaming muscles with the majestic mountains and crystal-clear lake he'd grown to call home.

Zoe's soothing voice dictated he lower his arms into Warrior Pose before bringing his feet together and folding forward.

Following her instructions, he bent at the waist and hung his head toward the ground. He locked his hands on his elbows and felt the stretch along his spine.

Brooke faced him and grinned.

He couldn't hold back his own smile as he straightened and brought his hands to prayer. All the while, his eyes locked on her petite body. A body wrapped in tight yoga pants and a strappy tank top that left little to the imagination. A sight that made every ache and pain he earned in the stupid class well worth his time.

Brooke circled her shoulder. "That wasn't too bad, was it?"

He gave an exaggerated cringe.

Zoe appeared and swatted him with a towel. "That better not be about my class. Bad for business."

He swept a palm through the cool air. "Good thing it was a private class."

Cruz rolled up his mat and joined the group. "Not private enough. Next time I need to remember to set up in front of you. Watching you bend over isn't how I want to start my day."

Brooke chuckled. "Really? It's the best way to start *my* day."

His heart did a silly pitter-patter he thought only happened in those sappy books his mom liked to read. The past four months had proven the best part of any time of his days were spent with Brooke.

"I have to get going," Cruz said. "See ya at home, later?"

Lincoln pressed his lips together and widened his eyes, hoping his brother understood his meaning. Cruz knew what he had planned and replying to his question would ruin the surprise.

Cruz might not have noticed his mistake, but Zoe did. She swung the end of her towel in Cruz's direction. "I thought we could grab some dinner tonight. What do you think?"

A weird coloring crept up from Cruz's neck. "Sure. Sounds good. See you guys later." He jogged up the hill toward the lodge with his mat tucked under his arm.

"I'm heading out, too," Zoe said. "Thanks for being my guinea pigs this morning with some new routines."

Lincoln watched them go and hooked an arm around Brooke's waist. "How long before those two realize how they feel about each other?"

Brooke smirked and tilted her head to the side. "You see it, too?"

"I guess when you're in love, it's easier to see it in other people." He wiggled his eyebrows, then grabbed her hand and towed her toward her cabin. The best part about yoga class with Brooke was the shower they shared after.

"What time do you need to get to the station today?" Brooke asked.

"I took the day off. Wanted to spend the whole day with you." Relocating to Pine Valley and taking a position on the local police force meant Cruz would pick up an extra shift if Lincoln needed him to.

And today, he needed time off more than ever. Either to celebrate with Brooke or nurse a bruised ego. He'd know for sure in a few minutes.

When they reached Brooke's cabin, he bounded up the porch steps and opened the door. His pulse jumped in his ears as he waited for her to enter her home.

She quirked her brows and her lips tipped at one corner as she passed him.

A sharp gasp reached his ears and lifted his lips.

"What is this?" Brooke asked, astonishment clear in her voice.

Flickering candles covered the room, and Wyatt sat by the door with a thick ribbon tied around his neck—a diamond ring dangling from it.

Lincoln sucked in a deep breath and spun Brooke to face him.

Her brown eyes were wide and filled with questions. "How did you do all this?"

"Chet. He's a giant of a man, but the guy's a big softie."

"But why?" She swept her gaze around the room before landing it on him once more.

He clicked his tongue and Wyatt hurried to his side. He slipped the ribbon necklace off the dog and secured the ring between his fingers. "Because I love you. I love you more and more each day. I love the man I am when I'm around you and the home I've found by your side. You bring out the best in me, Brooke Mather. You soften my edges and, hell, even get me to do yoga in between therapy sessions."

Tears dotted her lashes, and she pressed her fingers to her mouth.

He dropped down to one knee. "You see me for who I am and make me the happiest I've ever been in my whole damn life. If you let me, I want to spend all of my days trying my hardest to make you as happy as you make me—to show you every day how much I love you. Brooke, will you marry me?"

A soft giggle bubbled through Brooke's trembling hands still hovering over her mouth. Her giggle transformed to the belly-deep laugh he loved so much. "Yes!" She wrapped her fingers around his hand. "I can't believe this is real. That I finally have a man in my life who loves and respects me.

Who treats me with kindness and compassion. Who I love with my entire heart. Of course, I'll marry you."

Standing, his smile spread so wide his cheeks ached. Pulling her close, he crushed his mouth down on hers, savoring the taste—the feel—of her. His best friend. His love. His soon-to-be-wife. Joy exploded like fireworks inside him as he pulled away and slipped the ring on her finger. Never would he have imagined that being forced to come to Crossroads Mountain Retreat to heal would be the best decision he ever made and bring him face-to-face with the woman of his dreams.

A woman he would cherish for the rest of his days.

~

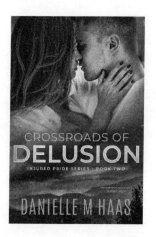

Don't miss Cruz and Zoe's story in Crossroads of Delusion. After Zoe's attacked, Cruz stays close to her side. They make their way closer to the truth, but when delusion is involved, the enemy can be nearly impossible to see.

ACKNOWLEDGMENTS

I'd like to throw a huge shout out to everyone who has encouraged me to take this risk. Choosing to write a series I would publish on my own was terrifying, but I had so much support and love behind me, I knew I couldn't fail. To my husband, Scott, thank you for being my biggest cheerleader and best sounding board. Your unwavering faith in me has been humbling. I hope I do you proud! To my parents, thanks for listening to endless conversations centered around plot and characters, fears and concerns. Your constant support continues to push me forward.

To my two critique partners, Samantha Wilde and Julie Anne Lindsey, this book wouldn't be what it is without your amazing notes and cherished friendship on the days I want to pull out my hair. To Kate Scholl, my editor, your notes are always spot on and I'm so glad our paths crossed. And Melinda Crown, thank you for your eagle eyes to help make my pages shine.

To my Haas' Hustlers! You guys are AMAZING!! You've given me so much love and confidence leading up to this release and made this experience so much more fun! I'm blessed you all chose to help me on this incredible journey!

And finally, to my readers. Thank you for picking up this book and giving it a chance. I hope you fell in love with the characters the way I did, and I hope to see you back at Crossroads Mountain Retreat soon.

Much love to you all,
    Danielle M Haas

ABOUT THE AUTHOR

Danielle grew up with a love of reading, partly due to her namesake—Danielle Steele. It seemed as though she was born to write out the same love stories she devoured while growing up.

She attended Bowling Green State University with a dream of studying creative writing, but the thought of sharing her work in front of a group of strangers was enough to make her change her major to Political Science.

After college she moved across the state of Ohio with her soon-to-be husband. Once they married and had babies, she decided to stay home and raise her children. Some days her sanity slipped further across the line to crazy town so she decided to brush off her rusty writing chops and see what happened.

Danielle now spends her days running kids around, playing with her beloved dog, and typing as fast as she can to get the stories in her head written down. She loves to write contemporary romance with relatable characters that make her readers' hearts happy, as well as fast-paced romantic suspense that leaves them on the edge of their seats. Her story ideas are as varied and unpredictable as her everyday life.

ALSO BY DANIELLE M. HAAS

Bound by Danger

Girl Long Gone

Murder of Convenience Series

Matched with Murder

Booked to Kill

THE SHEFFIELDS

Second Time Around

A Place In This World

Coming Home

Made in the USA
Middletown, DE
25 September 2022